IRON CITY

Also available from Titan Books

Alita: Battle Angel – The Official Movie Novelization

ALITA
BATTLE ANGEL

IRON CITY

THE OFFICIAL MOVIE PREQUEL

BY PAT CADIGAN

BASED UPON THE GRAPHIC NOVEL ("MANGA") SERIES "GUNNM" BY YUKITO KISHIRO
SCREENPLAY BY JAMES CAMERON AND LAETA KALOGRIDIS

Alita: Battle Angel – Iron City
Hardback edition ISBN: 9781785658358
E-book edition ISBN: 9781785658365

Published by Titan Books
A division of Titan Publishing Group Ltd
144 Southwark Street, London SE1 0UP

First edition: November 2018
1 3 5 7 9 10 8 6 4 2

Did you enjoy this book?

We love to hear from our readers. Please email us at readerfeedback@titanemail.com
or write to us at Reader Feedback at the above address.
To receive advance information, news, competitions, and exclusive offers online,
please sign up for the Titan newsletter on our website
www.titanbooks.com

This one is for:

Yvonne Navarro
Who provided the road-map
Couldn't have done it without you

And

Amanda Hemingway aka Jan Siegel
Don't know where to begin
To list all the things
I couldn't have done without you

And always for The Original Chris Fowler,
My one true love in all the universe

PROLOGUE

As General William Tecumseh Sheridan pointed out in the late 1870s, *war is hell.* In the hundreds of years that have passed since Sheridan and his army burned the city of Atlanta, Georgia, to the ground, many people have expressed their agreement with this statement.

What no one has ever pointed out, however, is, war is temporary. Some wars have been short, some unbearably long. But all wars, without exception, come to an end.

The same is not true of Hell.

Hell does not finish. Hell is not temporary. Hell is eternal, and it is populated by the lost souls caught in the temporary insanity of war, those left behind with nowhere to go when it was over.

Time moves on as it always does and recollections of war grow increasingly dim until they pass from living memory. Events become stories, which morph and mutate in a generations-long game of Chinese Whispers. Winston Churchill noted that history is written by the victors. But without reliable methods to create and preserve a record of events as they happen, history passes away with the people who made it and is replaced by whatever stories people remember. And when the major portion of daily life is taken up with matters of survival, people don't remember much. Only those with full bellies and a strong sense of security indulge in the luxury of looking backward. For those not so blessed, history is merely what happened before they arrived.

In this way, human history on Earth came to an end.

Most people had always thought of the end of human history as the end of time itself, when the universe finally ran down or blew up or went out like a light, an event that might or might not involve the appearance of a deity who would sit in judgment of humanity. But there was no bang, just a whimper so faint no one heard it. History came to an end for a very simple reason: after the War no one wrote any.

Before the War there had been a multitude of cultures that shared their advances in science and technology to accomplish extraordinary things. Chief among these were the sky cities, twelve shining metropolises that floated above various locations around the world. People had considered them proof that humanity had truly reached a high level of development, even enlightenment. At no other period in human history had there ever been cities that flew. People up there lived with privilege and comfort, and people down below looked up at them with pride and hope.

Then the Great War broke out, harsh and violent and deadly as wars always are. It killed billions of people, laid waste to the world and everything good about it, and sent what mankind thought were their last, best creations crashing to the ground—all, that is, save one. Devastated and traumatised, humanity didn't pause in its fight for survival to write history. There had been a war; an enemy had attacked and people had fought them with everything they had. Lives were lost, property destroyed, hope obliterated. What else was there to know?

The survivors at ground level gathered in the shadow of Zalem, the only city still flying, and they cobbled together a semblance of civilisation—structures to live in made from scraps of metal and rubble, in a society made from scraps of ideals and order. A hierarchy developed, with those who could thrive and prosper at the top, and everyone else jockeying for the next most desirable position below them.

Welcome to Hell.

In order for Hell to be truly hellish, however, it needs an audience, someone to watch and appreciate it, to be enlightened by what transpires or, at the very least, entertained. But not passively—pre-War technology had made many of the entertainments of the day interactive. There was no reason that shouldn't continue.

It was a small audience. But then, Zalem's population wasn't very large, to save wear and tear on the environment. This also allowed them to enjoy a more comfortable standard of living. There had been a lot of changes in the flying city—nothing could ever be the same after the War—and most of those changes were philosophical.

Once the actual hostilities ceased, Zalem's residents saw the virtue of a more structured society, with stronger leadership. Everyone hoped war would not come again for a very long time, but when it did, having a distinct and strong authority in place would prevent them from becoming hostages to misfortune.

In fact, unambiguous leadership was crucial to their survival now. The carefree days of plenty, when there were a dozen sky cities and travellers came and went at will, were gone forever. What hadn't changed—and never would—was Zalem's complete dependence on ground-level support.

The ground-level world would gladly, willingly, continue to support the last remaining flying city. Zalem symbolised the peak of human accomplishments and showed that, someday, humanity might reach that peak again.

Until then, however, there could be no travel between Zalem and the ground. Aeronautics was a lost technology, and besides, it was the best way to maintain stability in both places. Everyone had to agree to this— they had to be united under a single authority. The best single authority to oversee both Zalem and the ground-level society that came to be known as Iron City was someone who could literally oversee them. Zalem's leader took charge, appointing a chosen few to be his representatives on the ground.

The leader had lived a very long time, longer than most people knew, and far longer than any of them would have imagined. He was far too old to be excited merely by the prospect of having power over heaven and earth. Power was boring unless it was gratifying. His long lifespan made him an expert in gratification, and he knew there was none in simply being an overseer. He had to be a Watcher *in situ*, but without having to leave the comfort of the flying city.

Thus Hell became interactive entertainment, and the Watcher's feet never touched the ground.

As for history, it was irrelevant. What happened yesterday or the day before or last week was important. History was gone. So there was a Great War against an Enemy—so what? Nobody remembered who fought or why. It was three hundred years ago. Get over it, why dontcha.

CHAPTER 1

"Okay, Sarita, I want you to relax for a minute," said the pale thin man to the patient on the treatment table. She was a middle-aged woman with a round, good-natured face, a halo of salt-and-pepper curls and, below her collarbone, nothing else—nothing she'd been born with anyway. She was one of the Total Replacement cyborgs the pale man regularly treated at the clinic. She'd gone TR early in life; no doubt someone at the Factory had told her it was the best way to get ahead. As if anyone ever really got ahead at the Factory.

At the moment he was stretching her arm out on a support that put it perpendicular to her body, with her hand resting on a tray. The body she had swapped for her own had given her some years of reliable service, but probably not as many as she had been led to expect. For the last couple of months, she'd been showing up at the clinic at least once a week, needing this or that part replaced. She wasn't the only cyborg in Iron City suffering the effects of shoddy workmanship. The pale man had been helping people like her since the day he had arrived.

Back then the clinic had been a mom-and-pop operation. Now he wasn't even pop any more, which made it harder to keep the sad reality of life in Iron City from getting to him, not just day-to-day in the clinic, but in his other, late-night job as well.

"Okay, are you comfortable?" he asked. "Good. Now I want you to think about your right hand."

"Which one?" she asked.

Across the room the kid sitting in one of the refurbished dentists' chairs burst out laughing. The man had actually forgotten he was there; he turned and made an impatient shushing motion at the kid even though he couldn't help chuckling a little himself.

"As far as I know, Sarita, you only have one."

"Well, yeah, but—" The woman grimaced. "The first thing I thought of was my old flesh-and-blood hand. Not the real one."

"Both hands are real," the man told her, trying to sound comforting as well as firm. "Remember how I told you your mind has a sort of reproduction of your body inside in it? Well, to your mind, your hand is your hand is your hand is your hand. In fact, it's better if you imagine your organic hand. That's what we want your brain to think, that this is the one you were born with."

"But if the nerves are all connected, shouldn't it do that anyway?" the woman asked.

"It would take me quite a while to explain. Even when everything should be working perfectly, we sometimes have to play little tricks on the mind to help it along," the man replied. "I don't think you can take that much time off work."

"Yeah, I suppose not." The woman's fingers wiggled, then began tapping on the tray. She heard the noise and raised her head. Her fingers kept moving. "Well, will ya look at that!"

The man helped her sit up. "And that's what it's all about," he said cheerfully. "How does it feel?"

"Natural as anything," she said, still tapping her fingers on the tray. "No drop-out sensation at all." Her smile faded slightly. "I hope it lasts."

"If you have any trouble, just come back." The pale man hesitated, wanting to tell her that he was working on something, and if it turned out the way he wanted, no cyborg would ever have any delayed motor function between older and newer parts again. It would make her happy and she deserved something to be happy about, to look forward to. But he didn't know how long it would take him to get the chip working properly—another two weeks, or a month, or six months. Or the whole thing might blow up in his face and he'd have to start over from scratch.

Meanwhile, she'd be waiting, patiently at first but eventually she'd get anxious, and so would all the people she told about it. And there he'd be, unable to produce an instant miracle and unable to explain why, at least in layman's terms. So there they'd all be, with one more thing to be unhappy about.

The cruellest thing he could do to these people was to give them too much hope too soon. If he wanted to be a nice guy he could give them lollipops. Lollipops were real, now, and all his patients loved them. He took one from the jar on his desk and handed it to her. "If you get caught short," he said, "I can show you a trick with a box and a mirror that—"

"You showed me already, remember?" the cyborg said, tucking the lollipop in the breast pocket of her overalls. "It was back when lefty here"—she flexed her hand—"fell apart, and the replacement was late, and it felt like someone was twisting my fingers, even though I didn't have any."

"It can help with coordination too," the man said.

"Really?" said the kid in the reclining chair. "A mirror and a box?"

The cyborg gave him a look. "What's it to you, meat-boy?" She turned back to the man suddenly, looking apologetic. "No offence, Doc."

The pale man laughed. "None taken, Sarita." He showed her out and went to call the next patient in. But the row of chairs in the hallway outside the treatment room was empty.

The doctor frowned, trying to remember who had been waiting there earlier. Perhaps he should have sent the kid out with a clipboard to take names; it was important to acknowledge people who were waiting.

And then again, maybe not, he thought as he heard a thump behind him. The kid had set the chair at an extreme angle without belting himself in and he'd slipped out onto the floor on his head.

"Put it back the way it was, Hugo," the man said. "Or at least fix it so people won't have to sit upside down."

The kid's face was pink with embarrassment as he readjusted the chair and then moved to the far less elaborate one beside the desk that had once belonged to the man's former partner, who also happened to be his former spouse. The chair had not been easy to come by—his ex had insisted on good lumbar support. When he'd finally found this one for her, she had complained it wasn't good enough. Not that anything ever was, not compared to what they'd had before they'd come to Iron City.

Hugo was now rolling himself back and forth across the width of the office. The wheels rattled. The pale man might have thought it said something significant about Iron City that a seventeen-year-old amused himself with the chairs in a cyber surgeon's office rather than doing almost anything else. But he knew Hugo well enough to know the kid wasn't merely bored. Hugo dropped by regularly, and no matter how busy he was he couldn't bring himself to chase the kid out. Too many people had turned their backs on Hugo already.

"You're not fooling me," Hugo said suddenly.

"About what?" the man said with some alarm.

"I know how you got that mark," Hugo said. He touched a spot in the middle of his own forehead. "It's not from acne or chicken pox, or getting hit with a ball bearing at a Motorball game. And it's not a birthmark either."

"Well, congratulations." The man sat down at his workbench on the far side of the room and removed a sheet covering a partially disassembled shoulder joint attached to an arm. "Since there aren't any other patients right now, I'm going to work on a project for a while, and I'd like a little peace and quiet so I can hear myself think."

"What is it?" Hugo asked.

"A chip for better performance."

The kid laughed. "Are there any chips for lousier performance?"

"In this town, too many," the man said, angling a magnifying lamp over the ball joint.

"I bet you could get all the peace and quiet you want in Zalem," Hugo said. "They've probably got soundproof rooms and an army of security guards to keep punks like me from bothering you. Why would you ever leave?"

The man turned on a monitor and studied a scrolling display of read-outs.

"See, you being from there—that explains a lot," Hugo went on after a few moments. "But, like, there are some pretty smart people in Iron City—I'm no dummy myself. You gotta have *some* smarts to survive here. But even the smartest people in town don't know what you do. They aren't—" The kid paused, searching for the right word. "*Educated.*"

The pale man paused in the act of adjusting some very thin wires just below the shoulder joint to look at the kid from under his eyebrows. Hugo's assessment of his own intellect was correct as far as it went—i.e., he was no dummy. But in truth, Hugo had no idea how smart he actually was, which made him too smart for his own good. Which might well get him killed.

"We don't get much education in Iron City," the kid was saying. "The only reason they make anyone go to school is so they can work for the Factory when they grow up, worker bees that can read and write and count past ten without taking their shoes off. They—"

"Hugo, do you ever stop talking?" the man said and was instantly sorry when he saw the stricken expression on the kid's face. "Sorry, I didn't mean to—" He hesitated. "I just keep losing my train of thought and this is really important. It could make a big difference to how well cyborgs function, especially TRs."

"Oh, yeah? Too bad you didn't get here before my old man dropped dead. He mighta had another twenty years to *perform better* in the Factory." He rolled himself across the floor to the workbench. "What's so great about this chip?"

"It'll improve integration between newer parts and older ones. This will reduce rejection and speed up the healing process. That means less medication. It has other potential—no more drop-out, hesitation or scrambled signals to nerves."

The man felt himself warming to his subject. He was really just thinking out loud. But thinking out loud felt so much better with another person in the room, even if the other person was a street kid who didn't understand more than two words in every five. "See, what happens sometimes is, in high- or extended-performance situations a cyborg will intend some movement—maybe something small with the fingers, or something large, like walking up steps—and suddenly nothing happens. It only lasts a second or half a second, but it's startling, disturbing, especially when you're in the middle of some complex task.

"And if you're lucky enough to have achieved a state of flow, it's like having the floor pulled out from under you. If I can do something to preserve flow for cyborgs, I'll die happy." The man frowned. "No, actually, I'll die happy if I can also eliminate hesitation and stutter. That's really just drop-out on a much tinier scale—you make a movement, nothing happens, and you make the movement again. Which is different from echo, where the same intentional movement repeats two or more times.

"The problem—I mean, the *overall* problem—is the speed of brain impulses. Even the most advanced cyborg body isn't quite as fast as organic nerves. *Almost*, but not quite. I've been trying to speed up cyborg bodies, and I don't just mean accelerated movement. However, accelerated movement is mostly what I get." He was about to go on but decided to have mercy on the kid just for staying awake.

Hugo was silent for a long moment. Then: "See, that's what I'm talking about—there's no place to go in Iron City if you want to learn stuff like that."

"I could teach you if you wanted to learn," the man said.

"Oh, yeah, right—can you see me as Doc Hugo? Is that why you came here, to teach kids like me how to be doctors? I wouldn't buy that for a second. I can hardly believe you're here fixing up cyborgs. Why didn't you stay in Zalem, where you could have everything you need? Why would you come to a place like this?"

The pale man was saved from having to think of a way to dodge the question by the sound of the clinic door opening and closing. "My next patient is here," he said. "Do me a favour and bring them through, will you?"

"Sure thing, Doc," Hugo said. "But just as a favour. I don't want a job as your receptionist."

"You could do worse," the man said.

Hugo laughed. "I already do a lot better."

Business picked up later in the day, as it always did. By the time the last patient left, the pale man was too tired to see him out. He collapsed in the refurbished dentist's chair Hugo had been playing around with earlier and put his feet up. When Hugo asked him if there was anything else he wanted him to do before he left, the man waved him off.

"Okay, Doc," Hugo said. "See you tomorrow!"

Not if I see you first, the pale man replied silently.

Dr Dyson Ido, educated cyber-surgeon to Iron City's cyborgs, Good Samaritan and befriender of street kids too smart for their own good, told himself he had to get serious about hiring some staff. A nurse at the very least; the income from his other job was enough that he could afford someone good, even if it wasn't enough to send Hugo to med school. No amount of money would be enough for that; the Factory chose very few people for further education. The rest, like Hugo, were left to the social Darwinist crucible that was Iron City.

Yet Ido still kept hoping that he could awaken something like intellectual curiosity in a street kid who mainly saw him as a customer for various bits of tech… when he wasn't pumping him for information about Zalem.

It was just that Hugo seemed more thoughtful than most of the kids running around Iron City. He had a gang of friends, a crew that he hung out with, played Motorball with, raced gyro-bikes with. Occasionally there was a girlfriend but none of them held Hugo's interest for long. Hugo had something different on his mind. He talked about Zalem so much that sometimes Ido thought he had a fixation. That was never good.

Zalem fever was a phase most young people went through. Young people loved the idea of beating the system to make their way to the last and greatest flying city of them all, the one the Enemy could not crash. Youth was all about believing that if you wanted something badly enough, if you were willing to do whatever it took, all that effort, all that motivation would become a magic beanstalk you could climb all the way to Zalem. And, once there, all that determination and resolve would earn you a hero's welcome.

Most people grew out of Zalem fever sooner or later; later was more difficult. But Ido could understand the reluctance to let go of the Zalem dream. It must have felt like giving up on the whole idea that there could be something better than plain old everyday life; like turning your back on Heaven.

Ido couldn't help thinking that Iron City's existence was proof that there was a very big difference between giving up your dreams and waking up to a reality where a force beyond your control had given your dreams up for you.

And that wasn't true only in Iron City. It was true in Zalem too. Most people in Zalem had no idea. They had everything they could possibly want, so there was no need to dream.

Unless you weren't perfect.

His daughter had been destined to be perfect. Her lineage, like that of everyone else in Zalem, was impeccable. He and Chiren had lived properly, without giving in to weakness or decadence.

And as far as he was concerned, his daughter *had* been perfect, the most beautiful creature in their beautiful floating world. Her illness had not been a flaw. Zalem's geneticists had missed something, failed to correct it; Ido didn't care. Nothing could spoil her perfection for him.

The flaw was in Zalem's notion of perfection.

Or more precisely, the flaw was in the vision of Nova, the man in charge. The chrome optics he had over his eyes supposedly gave him enhanced perception, beyond the spectrum normally visible to humans. But Ido didn't think it was enhanced at all if Nova couldn't see his daughter was perfect.

It was Nova who evicted them from Zalem. He sent glorified errand boys to their home to tell him and Chiren they had to leave. A very hard decision, the errand boys said, neat and apologetic in their immaculate errand-boy suits, but there was no other way, nothing to be done. Ido and Chiren had produced something so flawed, normal life would be impossible for her. The girl had to be enhanced simply to do what normal people did unassisted. This was not how things were meant to be in Zalem. A flying city had to be inhabited by people *better* than those at ground level. Otherwise there was no difference between the two places, and they might as well let the grimy unwashed come up and track dirt all over the place. No one wanted that. Surely Ido and Chiren could see how important it was to preserve Zalem as it was supposed to be—especially since it was the only flying city left.

In his mortification and anger, Ido had finally understood why there were no physical defects, no disabilities or atypical mentalities—in fact, no marked differences in perspective among the privileged population of Zalem—and then he was only too glad to leave. But first he demanded that Nova come to their home in person to say all those things to his face, to Chiren's face, to his daughter's face. To see they were not merely names crossed off a list but living people condemned to exile.

Chiren had been utterly devastated, but her heart had not yet frozen over; there had still been enough humanity in her to persuade Ido that having an autocrat tell their daughter she wasn't good enough for Zalem would be even more destructive. In the end, Nova's refusal to see them was his one and only small mercy.

The manner of their leaving was one more humiliation. Heavier-than-air flight was forbidden, punishable by death, a sentence carried out by ground-level robot enforcers called Centurians. Mostly Centurians existed to make sure people born on the ground didn't try to get above their station—literally. But neither would it do to have the residents of Zalem lowering themselves—also literally. If they did, the people on the ground would demand to visit Zalem, resulting in a complete breakdown of the social order. For the last three hundred years the world had been stable and at peace—no wars, no internal unrest, no problems. It would be insane to risk doing anything to spoil it.

The supply tubes that ran from dispatch centres on the ground up to Zalem receiving stations were only for cargo—food, manufactured goods—and they were set for one direction. Nothing ever came *down* through a supply tube. Zalem didn't exist to supply anything to the world below.

The only way anything went down was via the ragged disposal chute on the underside of Zalem's disk. At one time the chute had been longer, but it had been too much of a temptation for daredevil ground-dwellers and had to be shortened. That was what most people had been told; any other story had passed from living memory. Only people with the extensive education available on Zalem knew more.

Not that it mattered. The long and the short of it was, the chute had always been used for waste disposal, and it was the only way Ido, Chiren and their daughter could travel to the ground.

Nova allowed them to have a pod constructed so they could survive the landing without serious injury. The pod would be good only for that one landing and would accommodate only themselves and very little else. They were forbidden to take with them anything that could reveal detailed information about Zalem—what the city looked like, how many people lived there, what they had. People on the ground were better off just imagining how much better Zalem was; if they actually knew, they might get so dissatisfied, they'd do something foolish.

Yes, it *was* too bad they had to leave the girl's wheelchair behind, but Ido and Chiren could make another for her out of the materials available to them. The place wasn't called Iron City for nothing—there was plenty of salvage to be repurposed. The people there had become very good at finding new uses for Zalem's discards.

The landing hadn't been the mild bump the bureaucrats had claimed it would be, but Ido had added a lot of extra padding, especially for their daughter. She came through the landing without physical injury or trauma.

The final humiliation was where they had landed. Ido and Chiren had known in advance, but that did nothing to lessen the effect of what they saw when they opened the pod's escape hatch. Zalem had thrown them out with the trash—had thrown them out *as* trash.

And then, as if to drive the point home in the most obvious way possible, more refuse poured down on top of them, some of it bouncing into the pod through the open hatch. Chiren stared in horror at the fragments of plastic, dented pieces of metal, shredded bits of cloth, wires and machine parts. A moment later she tore herself and their daughter out of the safety cushions and rushed out with the girl in her arms, her face wild with panic.

Ido followed, intending to tell her she should have waited; if something had fallen on them, they might have been killed. But as he made his way over the absurd and treacherous landscape formed from generations of junk and discards, he spotted a small bowl, scratched but intact. Some impulse made him pick it up—first thing for their new home, he thought. Then suddenly he understood why Chiren had bolted. She had been terrified of seeing something she recognised. He tossed the bowl away.

Their daughter had been young enough that Ido had hoped adjusting to their new life wouldn't be too hard. Obviously, they were living in reduced circumstances, but children were always just children, even when they were disabled—they didn't know if they were rich or poor. Occasionally the girl asked why they were doing without something they'd had in Zalem. She accepted Ido's explanation that there were some things Iron City just didn't have cheerfully, without complaint. Which was a relief—Chiren complained enough for all of them.

Ido did his best to keep his own spirits up for her sake, trying to make himself believe his daughter's condition wasn't getting worse before his eyes. It had taken Chiren throwing a soft, near-rotting tomato at him for him to realise how far they had really fallen; all the best food went up to Zalem. Iron City ate only what the flying city rejected.

The patients at the clinic introduced them to the black market. Ido was shocked at how quickly it became as normal to him as the open-air food market. Even so, they might have ended up having to close the clinic and find squat space under the causeway if they hadn't discovered Motorball. Or maybe Motorball had discovered them. Word had got around from their patients that there were a couple of cyber-surgeons in town that could work miracles with a little masking tape, copper wire and spit.

The work paid well—not enough to restore them to anything near their previous standard of living, but they wanted for nothing. Ido began working on a project that might change their daughter's life for the better.

Their daughter, A—

Ido was about to speak her name when he opened his eyes. The clinic was dark and silent; he'd fallen asleep in the chair. He should get up, eat something, and then go out. He needed the income that only his night-time business could provide.

Except there was someone banging on the clinic door and ringing the bell, over and over and over. That was what had awakened him, Ido realised. Somebody had an emergency and they weren't going to go away. He struggled out of the chair, stretched and half-stumbled to the door.

It was an emergency, all right, but not the kind he usually took care of.

"What the hell happened to you, Hugo?" he asked, easing the kid into the wheelchair he kept near the entrance.

Hugo made a noise that might have been, *Don't ask.* Or possibly, *Kicked my ass.* Ido didn't pursue it.

CHAPTER 2

Some hours earlier, about the time Dyson Ido was dozing off in his dental chair, Hugo was thinking about breaking a rule that, in his personal code, was supposed to be unbreakable.

Prior to that, he'd been thinking about Ido. Nobody worked as hard as the Doc, and cyborgs all over Iron City sang his praises. There was no one else with his cyber-medical knowhow in Iron City who was willing to treat cyborgs even if they couldn't pay right away. Or at all.

Well, there was his wife—his ex-wife, rather. When the clinic had first opened, they'd split their time between it and taking care of Paladins at the stadium. The Motorball income must have let them keep the clinic open. Hugo had no idea how Ido kept the clinic going since he'd quit Motorball. His wife was still working at the track but no longer at the clinic, having left Ido. Hugo doubted she was donating anything. There weren't a whole lot of ways to make good money that didn't involve something dangerous and/or illegal, and the doc didn't seem like the type for either. Oh, he'd done a little trading on the black market, but everybody did. Obeying the law all the time in Iron City was a good way to starve. The Factory made the rules and the game was rigged.

If you wanted to do better than just survive you had to make your own rules. Sooner or later this would put you on the wrong side of the law. It was more important to stick to your personal code. Your word had to be your bond. Anyone you dealt with had to know without a doubt there were lines you wouldn't cross, no matter what.

Hugo had been scrupulous about not violating his own code. But then he wasn't much like other guys his age and he knew it, albeit in an oblique, mostly unconscious way. Early in his life circumstance had caused his focus to shift from material things to intangibles like trust and honesty, will and intention, even inspiration and love. Not that he understood himself in those terms. Hugo didn't spend a lot of time contemplating abstractions.

For most of the day he'd been at Ido's clinic, partly to find out what Ido was in the market for—besides servos, that is; Ido always needed more servos—but also to pump him for information about Zalem. Ido seemed to think he was curious about scientific and medical stuff, like he wanted to be a doctor or something. He didn't, and he'd have been shit out of luck if he did; people like that came from the Factory. Nobody knew where the Factory got them, but Hugo knew it wasn't Zalem. They didn't have the mark.

Which raised all those questions about how Ido had ended up on the ground, why he wasn't trying to go back, why Zalem had let him and his wife go in the first place, and so on and so forth, around and around and around. The doc was trying to play it close to the vest but Hugo felt like he was wearing him down. Ido had started to let things slip now and then. Hugo hoped if he let the doc keep talking about things like his famous chip that would integrate new this with old that, Ido would get talkative enough to confide in him. The doc *wanted* someone to confide in—he was obviously lonely as hell. He probably would have preferred another doctor like his ex-wife, but he'd settle for someone who'd listen to his scientific blah-blah-blah.

Right now, however, Hugo was wishing he hadn't given in to his hunger pangs, or that he'd gone instead for a pineapple-coconut shake he could have tied onto his gyro-bike handlebars and sipped as he rode home. But no, he'd felt like falatel, and he'd parked near the coffee shop while he ate it, in a spot that had given him an unobstructed view of the woman sitting alone at one of the sidewalk tables.

It was just chance that she was there having an extra-large cappuccino at the same time. It was also just chance she'd decided to wear a bracelet today. And it was just chance that he saw her wearing it. She was a slightly plump woman with dark-brown skin, short corkscrew curls and large dark eyes, dressed in a t-shirt with a bunch of black cats on it and jeans faded almost to white. She was anybody; Hugo couldn't have said whether he'd seen her before or not.

But the last time he'd seen the bracelet she was wearing, it had been on his mother's arm. It had been a gift from his father, and his mother had worn it constantly, waking and sleeping, until the day she died.

꧁꧂

Gifts had been few and far between at Hugo's house. His father had done his best, but being a drone on a Factory assembly line didn't pay a fortune, and money had to stretch even further when Hugo had suddenly come along. He'd been a surprise to his middle-aged parents, who had thought any diapers in their future would be on their grandchildren.

Hugo had never doubted his parents loved him. His father called him "an unexpected pleasure", and his big brother was overjoyed to have a little brother to look out for. It was a happy home, and like all kids from happy homes, Hugo hadn't known they were poor. Only later on had he realised that sometimes his parents and even his brother had skipped dinner to make sure he never had to go to bed hungry.

His mother had talked about getting a job when Hugo started school but his father begged her not to. *Then you'll get enhancements too. One of us has to stay completely human for our boys, querida.*

His mother told him he was the most human person she knew, no matter how much of his body got replaced, but she honoured his wishes. She'd tried to pick up extra money by taking in laundry or doing housework, but most people gave their business to those who were enhanced with special devices and attachments rather than someone who only had two natural hands. Once in a while, though, those cyborgs got all booked up and they'd throw some work her way.

The infrequent gifts were most often useful, necessary things, not some extravagant nonessential like jewellery. Jewellery's only purpose was to use up money better spent on groceries. But one night Hugo's father had come home and put a small drawstring bag made of dark-green velvet on the kitchen table in front of his mother. Hugo and his brother had been jumping up and down, yelling *Open it! Open it!* while she stared at it like she thought it might bite her.

The expression on her face when she saw the bracelet was one Hugo had rarely seen. Big Bro told him later she was like a line in a poem he had read once: "surprised by joy". The bracelet was the last thing she'd expected to get, something she hadn't even known she'd wanted until that moment.

She held the two-inch band of hammered copper in her hands and examined it closely. There was a dark-green gem set into the middle of the band—the same dark green as the little velvet bag, which Hugo thought was a very cool thing. He asked if it were an emerald and everyone burst out laughing.

Hugo waited for his mother to say his father had to take it back because they couldn't squander money on useless things. But she hadn't. Instead, she put it on and never took it off.

Big Bro told her she shouldn't do that, because someone might mug her for it; she should put it away in a safe place. She had refused. *Jewellery is meant to be worn, not hidden*, she said. Hugo had worried—he hadn't been too young to know Iron City was a dangerous place. But nothing bad ever happened. His mother called it her lucky charm, and Hugo wondered if maybe that little bit of copper with the pretty piece of glass really had some kind of power to ward off evil.

If so, it hadn't extended to his father. It didn't stop him from replacing more and more of his body until there was hardly any organic flesh and blood left.

The first time his father had come home with a cyber-limb, Hugo had run away from him crying. His father had been baffled at Hugo's reaction—he'd thought Hugo would find his machine arm fascinating, especially when he saw how it could unfold, extend and rotate, and how the telescoping fingers could bend in every direction.

His mother and brother had told him he'd hurt his father's feelings. Big Bro spent a lot of time trying to talk him around. *People lose their arms and legs in accidents, or they get cancer in their bones and have to have something amputated. You* really *think they shouldn't be allowed to replace them?*

Hugo hadn't known how to explain that his father hadn't *lost* his arm, he'd traded it for something that didn't even *look* human. He did apologise to his father—but from under his bed, where he couldn't see the metal *thing* attached to his father's body.

His father had not taken offence or been angry. He said he'd keep the arm covered up at home to give Hugo time to get used to it. Later on, Hugo overheard him telling his mother and Big Bro that you never knew what might scare a little kid or why; the world looked a lot different at that angle. It wouldn't do any good to say he *shouldn't* be afraid of something; instead, they had to show him they still loved him and not everything that looked scary was something to be afraid of. Hugo had loved his father so much for that. This was the father he knew and loved and trusted; he just didn't understand how that same father could want a machine arm. It wasn't only that it looked scary; it ruined hugs too.

In any case, his father did cover the arm at home and Hugo tried hard to act like he was okay about it. In truth, the thing was scarier when he *couldn't* see it. What was it doing when his father put a blanket or a sweater over it? He had nightmares about it detaching itself from his father after everyone was asleep, crawling into his room and trapping Hugo in his bed so it could saw off his arm and replace it with a machine exactly like itself.

After a while the nightmares tapered off—though not as soon as Hugo let everyone believe. He was no longer afraid of the machine sticking out of his father's shoulder, but he didn't like it. The best he could do was tolerate its presence.

No one told Hugo when his father had replaced his legs; he wouldn't have known at all except one morning his father had forgotten to lock the bathroom door. Hugo was too old by then to run away and hide under the bed. The legs were more humanlike, but Hugo couldn't help thinking about his nightmare. Now he imagined the machine arm had replaced his father's legs while he slept, although he was too old to believe things like that could really happen.

But he was not too old for nightmares. In the new ones, his father was telling him to get up; they were going to be late for work at the Factory. Hugo rolled over to find his father was all metal, with four machine arms and two heads. Then he threw back the covers and saw his own body was also all metal. Sometimes he had eight legs like a spider, other times a single wheel like a gyro. Occasionally his father would start falling apart, and when Hugo tried to get out of bed to help him, he did too.

In retrospect Hugo realised his father had already replaced his legs when he'd given his mother the bracelet; it was around the time he'd noticed his father was walking differently. The Factory must have given him a bonus for becoming more of a machine. That was what they had in the Factory after all—lots of metal machines.

Only machines weren't supposed to die.

Wasn't that why his father replaced his entire body, so he could go on working at the Factory forever with the rest of the machines? When a Factory drone keeled over on the job, shouldn't they have just called tech support or maintenance and had them fix whatever was wrong? When a machine malfunctioned, you just replaced the faulty part or whatever, and it went back to work. Factory reps didn't come to the house and tell the machine's family he was dead.

His brother had had to barricade him in his room so his mother could talk with the reps without Hugo's calling them liars and trying to punch them. After the reps left Hugo sat out on the front step stubbornly waiting for his father to come home so he could tell him about the lying Factory scumbags who had come to the house claiming he was dead.

Hugo didn't remember much about the weeks after that. Big Bro and his girlfriend Nana got married; Nana spent a lot of time with Hugo and his mother while Big Bro was at work—at the Factory, of course, but his job was better than their dad's. Hugo begged him not to swap any parts of his body for machines. His brother had promised he wouldn't and didn't mind when Hugo insisted on checking.

Two and a half months later their mother died in her sleep. When Hugo found her, she'd still been wearing the bracelet. Some good luck charm—it had failed his mother when she'd really needed it. He'd never expected to see it again, hadn't even thought about it in years.

And now here it was, on the arm of some stranger who had no idea what she was wearing.

Hugo finished his falafel, tossed the bunched-up napkin in a nearby trashcan and got ready to start the gyro. Without thinking about what he was doing, he walked the gyro forward, through the no-parking area in front of the café, until he was parallel with the woman just as she ordered another cappuccino. He waited until the waitress went inside before he started the engine. Then he reached over, swiped the bracelet off the woman's forearm and took off.

Sorry, lady, he thought without looking back. *But frankly, it didn't go with your outfit.*

Hugo knew no one would chase him. The woman wasn't hurt and a cheap metal bracelet wasn't worth the effort. But just to be sure, he took a lot of back alleys and side streets, even walking the gyro along a few passages that were too narrow to ride through.

Half an hour later, he fetched up on the southeast edge of the trash pile. It wasn't an area he'd spent much time in; apparently no one else did either. Normally that would have been reason enough to head for someplace more populated, where a person was less likely to get mugged. Although that hadn't helped the lady at the café—she was out one bracelet.

Well, tough stuff. At least she hadn't been roughed up. The bracelet was just some piece of costume jewellery to her; she'd forget all about it as soon as she got another. And maybe if he told himself that enough times, Hugo thought, he'd forget that he'd sworn he'd never steal from all-natural people or those with only a few cyborg parts. Only Total Replacement cyborgs were fair game.

TRs were just talking heads riding around in metal bodies. Jacking TRs was okay; they could take it. All you had to do was give them a few shocks with a paralyser to take them down, then disconnect the cyber-core. After that, you tipped off the Factory Prefects anonymously; they'd pick the core up wherever you left it and put it on life-support. Meanwhile, you chopped the body and shopped the parts, unless someone wanted the whole thing, no assembly required.

Losing a body was nothing for a TR because they'd *already* lost their body—they'd traded it for hardware. They could always get another and, with any luck, they wouldn't get jacked again too soon. But so what if they did? It was still all just hardware. It wasn't a *real* body.

Hugo put his feet up on the gyro's handlebars and leaned back a little, turning the copper band over and over in his hands.

After his mother died he'd assumed his brother had given the bracelet to Nana and she'd just put it away and never worn it. She and Big Bro took him in and became his mother and father, which was sort of weird. But only a little—they were his family after all, and they were all he had left.

He kept waiting for Big Bro and Nana to have kids so he could be like their big brother. But it never happened. He wondered if they were going to do what his parents did: wait till he was all grown up and then have an "unexpected pleasure".

Not even close as it turned out.

Big Bro kept his promise and never got even one enhancement; he never needed to. The Factory had trained him as an all-purpose engineer. Which meant any time they wanted to do something, Big Bro said, they asked him to show them how to do it. It certainly paid better than their father's old job, and Big Bro didn't have to work as hard. Sometimes the Factory called him in when there was a problem with something, but they always paid him extra for it. That didn't happen a lot though. Big Bro got to spend more time with him than their father ever had.

Nana called them "her guys". She never minded when they went off for hours on long walks. Sometimes they went trash-picking together, looking for really weird things Zalem had thrown away and making up crazy stories about what they were and why they'd been thrown out. Other times, they'd find a good spot where they could get a glimpse of the buildings on the edge of Zalem's five-mile-wide disk and try to imagine what the people in them were doing, whether they were looking down and wondering what people on the ground did every day.

Those had been happy times. Hugo hadn't even known how happy; children seldom do. He hadn't imagined things would ever be any different, even after he grew up and got a job. Sometimes he thought maybe he could be an engineer like Big Bro and tell everyone how to do things. But he seldom looked that far ahead. Mostly he was just glad his brother shared his fascination for Zalem; Big Bro was so smart, so imaginative, so much fun.

The thing was, though, Big Bro was an engineer. Just dreaming and making up stories wasn't enough, he told Hugo one day. He didn't just want to imagine what Zalem was like, he wanted to find out for real, so he'd been thinking very hard about how to do that. He took Hugo up to his workshop in the attic and showed him what he had come up with. That was the beginning of the end.

In truth, the end had begun earlier when Big Bro had decided to build the flying machine, before he let Hugo in on it. Hugo knew it was seriously illegal. Heavier-than-air flight was a challenge to Zalem—just being caught with one of those machines was a capital offence. Even if the thing couldn't actually fly, a Hunter-Warrior could take your head without there even being a marker out on you and collect a sizeable bounty.

If by some crazy turn of events, you *did* get the machine off the ground, Centurians would shoot it out of the sky. And if there were friends or family or anybody else with you or even just standing nearby—well, too bad for them, better luck next lifetime.

No one had tried anything so foolish in years. Even birds gave Iron City a wide berth, as Zalem defences didn't differentiate between living creatures and machines. As a result, the only place people could see uncaged birds was way out in the Badlands—*way*, way out—which meant plenty of Iron City residents lived and died without ever seeing an actual bird in flight.

In any case, Big Bro wasn't just some Iron City fool. He was capable of building a machine with a video camera to transmit whatever it saw. Big Bro's only problem was noise. Once he fixed that, he told Hugo, he'd fly it on a night when there was no moon in the sky. The video camera was built into the thing's actual framework, which was mostly cardboard. What little metal there was wouldn't show up on any sensors. It would fly all the way up to Zalem and then they'd finally see what was really going on up there. In the meantime, Big Bro told him, they had to keep this between the two of them. No one else could know, not even Nana. Not yet, anyway. They could tell Nana later, when they were ready to launch.

That made Hugo feel a little funny. How could Big Bro keep a secret from his wife? He was pretty sure the only secret his father had ever kept from his mother was saving up for the bracelet, and that wasn't the same thing at all. The time that Big Bro and his parents hadn't told him his father had replaced his legs—that was closer. Except it hadn't been illegal.

Well, Big Bro wasn't his real father, and Nana wasn't even a blood relative. But she was as much family to him as anyone could be. It felt wrong to keep something so big from her.

But he respected Big Bro's wishes and didn't say anything, although he thought sometimes he was going to burst. His brother kept working and he got the motor a little bit quieter, but it was still louder than he wanted. The materials available in Iron City just weren't good enough.

And then one rainy night, his brother came up with the answer: he'd waterproof the flyer and send it out in the rain, which would mask the motor noise. The machine would fly up to Zalem with a night-vision camera and they could pick up the transmission by tuning into the right wavelength.

When the batteries started to get low, the flyer would go straight up, as high as possible; the higher-altitude winds would blow it far away from Iron City, getting rid of the evidence. They'd be the only people who knew anything about Zalem. Maybe someday they'd be able to use what they knew to their advantage, or maybe they'd never be able to tell anyone else till the day they died. Either way, they'd still know the biggest secret in the world.

Hugo thought the big night would never come, but finally Big Bro said conditions would be right. The weather forecast said it was going to rain all night, and it just happened to be the new moon so the overcast sky would be nice and dark. And, to Hugo's enormous relief, Big Bro said they could finally let Nana in on their secret.

But when his brother told Nana about the flyer she wasn't happy at all. She thought it was the worst idea anyone had ever had. She said she didn't want to know things about Zalem that no one else in the world—or at least Iron City—knew, and she didn't understand why anyone would when it was against the law.

Her reaction made Hugo feel weird, even kind of scared, like maybe they *shouldn't* do this. But when he talked to Big Bro about it, his brother told him it was just because Nana wasn't an engineer. She was artistic— she wove beaded jewellery a friend sold for her in the market, and she wrote poetry and fairy tales about talking animals and robot elves. Nana's head was full of impossible things she could only *wish* were real, Big Bro said. She couldn't get her mind around the fact that not all forbidden things were impossible. Hugo thought Big Bro was seriously underestimating Nana's intelligence, but he could talk to him about that later, after they saw the video of Zalem.

The day seemed to last forever. Finally, late in the afternoon, when the clouds were starting to build up, Nana suddenly handed Hugo a shopping list full of things he could only get at one of the markets on the other side of town. He tried to talk her into waiting until tomorrow but she pleaded with him, saying she'd been putting off getting these things for too long and it would mean so much if he'd do it for her. She'd do something really nice to reward him for helping her out.

That late in the day, traffic was slow and the queues at the market were long. Sometimes Hugo would get to the front of one only to find the vendor was out of what he wanted and he had to stand in a different queue and hope for better luck. It was raining by the time he was done and the traffic was worse. Hugo managed to squeeze onto a bus that took twenty minutes to travel a block and a half before it broke down. He waited a while for another, then gave up and walked; even if he'd had money for a cab, he wouldn't have found one. Taxis in Iron City always disappeared when it rained.

After a while Hugo realised he kept looking up at Zalem's shadow in the rain clouds and told himself not to. If someone at the Factory saw him on a surveillance camera, they might wonder what he was looking for up there and get suspicious. They might decide to send a Centurian to his house to ask questions, or even search the place. Then the Centurian would find the flyer and it would be all over, case closed, thank you and good night.

When he finally did get home, Nana was waiting outside in the rain. The look on her face made him drop the bags and run for the front door, but Nana was too quick for him. She swept him into her arms and held him tight, saying, *You can't go inside, Hugo, I'm sorry, I'm so sorry. There was no other way. He'd have taken us down with him.*

Hugo tried not to believe it. But then two men came out the front door carrying a stretcher with a body on it, all covered up. They were joined by a lumbering and hulking Centurian and a Hunter-Warrior with a bounty bag. Hugo tried to tell himself it couldn't be his brother's head in the bounty hunter's bag.

Even after he and Nana were finally allowed back in the house, Hugo kept calling for his brother. He went up to the attic room and pounded on the locked door, demanding Big Bro let him in. Nana didn't tell him to stop or be quiet. She waited for him to wear himself out and carried him to bed. While he slept, she scrubbed the room from top to bottom, so there was no trace of his brother left.

The next day, Nana told Hugo it was just the two of them now. They'd be all right for a while. She wouldn't have to get a job right away. That was when he realised she'd collected a hefty bounty for Big Bro. Well, the Factory didn't pay death benefits to the family of a criminal. The fact that Big Bro hadn't been just some disgruntled slob but a Factory engineer made the offence even worse, although Hugo suspected they'd given Nana something for the emotional pain and suffering of having to turn in her own husband.

Or maybe not. *He'd have taken us down with him,* she'd said, holding him while they both cried in the rain. She had been so sure Big Bro would get caught that she decided she might as well go for the money.

Hugo wasn't surprised she wanted them to go on being family—he just didn't understand how she thought it was possible. Originally he planned to give it a month before he left but he found he couldn't stick it out even for a week. He took some of his brother's old clothes and some food, and let her keep her blood money.

His note had been brief: *Don't try to find me.* He thought she might anyway, but maybe she'd known better, because he never saw her again. Some years later he sneaked back to the old neighbourhood to see what had become of her and found a different family living in the house. He considered asking the neighbours, but he didn't recognise them either and decided he really didn't need to know if she were happy or miserable or dead.

Case closed, you know the rest. Thank you and good night.

"You think maybe he's deaf as well as dumb?"

Hugo looked up from the bracelet to see that he was surrounded by six guys, while a seventh moved in to lean casually on the gyro's handlebars. They were all a few years older than he was, several inches taller and a good deal heavier. The guy leaning on the gyro wasn't the biggest but his arms were all hard muscle, the kind that promised to hurt you real bad if you weren't careful; if he noticed you were alive, you hadn't been careful.

Hugo most definitely hadn't been careful, in a way that was downright embarrassing. Every part of Iron City was somebody's turf. You could get away with just passing through but Hugo was trespassing, an offence compounded by his being so wrapped up in his own thoughts, he hadn't even noticed when the crew had come up around him to tell him to get lost.

"We can tell you're not from around here," the guy leaning on the handlebars said. "Otherwise you'd know it belongs to us. This exact spot where you are right now? It's a no-parking zone, especially for a piece-of-shit gyro like yours. It's ruining the scenic beauty of our trash pile."

The guy straightened up and swiped the bracelet out of Hugo's fingers. "This ought to cover part of the fine. My guys'll collect the rest." He stepped back and someone kicked the gyro over.

Hugo had never been much of a fighter, surviving more by his wits than his fists. He'd learned how to talk his way out of trouble and if that didn't work, he went to plan B—i.e., running away real fast. Being in a fight *hurt*, even when you were winning. You might get the upper hand, but you might also break it. A broken hand was a serious disadvantage when your opponent and/or their friends came looking for payback.

Unfortunately, sometimes you couldn't talk, run or punch; the fourth and least desirable alternative was curling up on the ground and trying to protect your softer parts while hoping your attackers didn't get so caught up in what they were doing that they forgot to stop.

The beat-down seemed to go on for hours before the leader finally called them off. But of course, someone had to give Hugo a parting shot, one last kick in the kidneys. He was going to pee blood for a day or two.

"I think this punk's learned his lesson about no-parking zones and going where he ain't wanted," the leader said. "Prob'ly won't take him but five minutes to pull himself together and ride this piece-of-shit home to Mommy. And I'm sure he knows we'll come back in five minutes just to make sure." The guy laughed. "Hey, you have a nice night, loser, okay? And thanks for the bracelet. It doesn't go with your outfit."

They were all laughing as they walked off.

Hugo waited till he couldn't hear them any more before he pushed himself to a sitting position. An intense sharp pain on both sides of his ribcage made him catch his breath. He felt around gingerly, careful not to press too hard. Doc Ido had told him once that bruised ribs hurt worse than broken ones. Unless you had a broken one poking your liver or spleen. Which side were those on? Was the pain different when you speared an organ?

He took a slow, deep breath, which also hurt, then managed to get the gyro upright. That hurt a lot too, and so did pulling himself to his feet. There was a cut on his head bleeding copiously; the doc said cuts above the neck bled a lot because of all the capillaries, but unless you were a haemophiliac, you weren't in danger of bleeding to death.

It was painful to swing one leg over the gyro, and painful to sit on the seat. But the good news was, everything would hurt a lot worse tomorrow. Hugo caught sight of himself in the gyro's side mirror and flinched—one eye was swelling shut and his split lower lip was the size of a hot dog. He felt a sudden, intense surge of anger. What he really wanted to do instead of limping off home was find those guys and run them all down, put a tyre track across all their faces.

Oh, yeah—you and what army of Centurians? he asked his reflection silently.

He started the gyro; the bastards hadn't done something to it that would end up killing him. No, they just wanted to show how tough they were, not commit murder. Besides, it wasn't like he'd actually *done* anything. He hadn't stolen from them—

No, you stole from someone else, some poor innocent lady who had nothing to do with your family. Stealing from someone with no cyborg parts was crossing the line. You only got what was coming to you.

Hugo sighed heavily, ignoring the pain it caused. As if life was all educational moments and learning lessons. This was just another day in Iron City, where the strong preyed on the weak and you did whatever you had to do to survive. Like Nana had. Big Bro would never have got away with sending a flyer up to Zalem, and she'd been the only person in the house smart enough to know it. When she couldn't talk him out of it, she'd done the only thing she could to save herself and Hugo. Just because you loved someone didn't mean you had to let them get you killed.

He rode slowly down a side street, wincing at every bump until he found the main road. The ride would be smoother, if much slower—the traffic was as heavy now as it had been that day when he'd come back from the market to find Nana outside in the rain—and he wasn't up to his usual swerving between cars and trucks.

So today had been a bad day—actually, a pretty terrible one, worse than most. He had to remember never to let anyone get close enough to hurt him. Also, to pay more attention to what was going on around him.

CHAPTER 3

"Stop right there," said the elegantly dressed, dark-skinned man in the back seat of the limo. His name was Vector and it was his limo. Admission was strictly limited to those people he considered worthy enough to breathe his climate-controlled air.

An observer might have wondered about the man sitting next to him. Gamot didn't look like he belonged in a limo. He was, however, one of Vector's most valued employees, although his employment was informal, which was to say, off the books. It was one of the reasons Vector chose to meet with him in the limo. With his lank, greying hair, his puffy face rough with old acne scars, his ragged clothes and dirty feet in flip flops, Gamot belonged in Vector's office even less.

"What is it, boss?" asked Gamot, politely puzzled. For all that he looked like a beggar, his manners (with his boss at least) were impeccable.

"I thought I just heard you say the word 'late'," Vector said, with the kind of serious expression he knew none of his employees wanted to see on his face. "As in, 'Hugo and his crew are going to be late delivering'. *Is* that what I heard?"

"Yeah, sorry," Gamot replied, looking apologetic. "The kid took a bad beating."

"Hugo, you mean?"

Gamot's apologetic expression intensified. "Yeah. See, a few nights back, he was out in south-town—"

"What the hell *for*?" Vector said, annoyed. "I never sent him there. There's nothing in southie except white punks on dope."

"Dunno, boss, I guess he was just there," Gamot said. "He was near the trash pile so he coulda been pickin' around and took a wrong turn. Anyway, he got beat up pretty bad. Cracked ribs, a concussion, one eye swole shut—it was seven against one, and he didn't have a chance. That's how they do in south-town. I saw him the day after. Kid's lucky he didn't end up in a coma."

"Was he in the hospital?" Vector asked stiffly.

"Well, no. He just went to Doc Ido. The doc fixed him up, even though he isn't a—"

Vector made a short impatient gesture with one hand. "If he wasn't in the hospital, then he wasn't hurt *that* badly."

"The doc told him he *shoulda* gone to the hospital—"

"But he didn't and he's still alive anyway, isn't he?" Vector paused and Gamot nodded. "Well, then, there's no good reason for him to be late. That's no way to do business."

"Sorry, boss," Gamot said, looking glum. "I dunno what to tell you."

"You're not the one that owes me an apology." Vector took a breath. He had a tremendous urge to backhand Gamot, then have the driver pull away and when they got up over thirty miles an hour, open the door and push him out. But Gamot would probably take it the wrong way, not understanding he wasn't who Vector wanted to punish. It was better if the street staff didn't know Vector considered them interchangeable; they all knew too much, even if most of them had no idea they knew anything.

Also, Gamot was good at what he did. It was bad form to kill the messenger unless he was incompetent.

Still, this was really disturbing. Hugo had never failed him before, never turned up late, or short or with a load of crap that he tried to pass off as the good stuff.

"When was this famous beat-down?" Vector asked Gamot after a bit.

"Four, five days ago, something like that."

"Then he's over the worst," Vector said briskly. "Kids heal fast. They have to. Find him and bring him here. He and I need to have a conversation."

"You got it, boss." Gamot made to open the car door.

"Not so fast," Vector said. "There's something else I want you to do."

"Anything," Gamot promised. His sincerity was all but palpable.

"Before you pick up Hugo, swing by the market and look for a vendor called Mario. Tell him I sent you to get a pair of shoes for yourself. I don't care what they look like, what colour or style, as long as they're closed. Make it fast and be wearing them when you get back with Hugo, and from now on." Vector shifted a little and sat forward. "Got it?"

"Got it, boss." Gamot was obviously trying not to look at his own feet. He looked at Vector's instead.

"They don't have to be like mine," Vector told him. That would have been impossible, anyway. Vector had swapped them out of a shipment for Zalem, sending a pair of lop-sided Iron City brogues in their place. Zalem hadn't queried the substitution. Maybe they thought it was some kind of street chic; people up there were probably as stupid as anyone else.

"I'm on it, boss," Gamot said. "Shoes, then Hugo, and shoes from now on."

"I want you well-shod, not shoddy," Vector said.

To his surprise, Gamot got the joke. "Good one, boss," he said. "You want anything else? Late lunch? Churros?"

"Just make sure you leave at least one runner in shouting distance of the limo. But *not* leaning on it or sitting on the bumper."

"I'm on the case," Gamot assured him. "I mean, cases."

He got out of the car and a blast of hot, damp air hit Vector squarely in the face. He told the driver to turn up the a/c and the dehumidifier before he drowned. The driver obeyed without so much as a *Yes, boss*, which was how Vector liked his drivers—alert, obedient and silent.

There was no telling how long he would have to wait for Gamot to come back with Hugo but that was all right. He could use the time to think about the number one item on his to-do list: his brilliant, hot and now single Tuner.

Vector took out his tablet and looked at some video taken in the pits during the last game. This woman was going to build him champions bigger and better than Grewishka had been even at his peak—in fact, people would forget they'd ever heard of that burn-out. And now that she'd split from Dyson Ido, the genius lady was all his. She was kind of a cold fish though, which had nothing to do with the end of her marriage. She had always been chilly, an iceberg sailing through the world, never melting, offering only bright, shining brilliance... and frostbite. The blue in her eyes was the arctic, not the sky; Vector had seen her freeze Paladins where they stood just by glaring at them.

Truth to tell, Vector had wanted both her and Ido on a full-time, exclusive contract, but Ido wouldn't go for it. When Chiren left him, Ido quit Motorball altogether—a damned shame for the players who'd come to depend on his superior skills. Anyone who wanted to see him now had to go to his shabby little clinic and wait with the saddest of the sad and the most wretched of the refuse.

Vector thought it was actually a shitty thing to do, especially for a sanctimonious *pendejo* who wanted everyone to think he was on the side of the angels. But there was no forcing someone to work in the Motorball pits. As with most things, bribery worked best—but not with the virtuous Dyson Ido. Someday Vector wanted to ask His Holiness what was so noble about turning his back on people after letting them believe he would always be there for them. How did *that* work?

But he'd probably never have the chance. Dr Self-Righteous wouldn't have anything to do with him, which was fine with Vector. If he could only have one, he'd take Chiren. The Ice Queen was a lot better-looking than Ido, with her long dark hair and perfect skin and slender, lithe body, and that pretty little purple gem in the middle of her forehead. Vector only wished she were a bit shorter—it was easier to dominate someone when you had at least four inches on them, and genius lady was almost as tall as he was. But it was her height that made her look so good in designer clothes. It was like she had been made to wear them… and then drop them on his bedroom floor. After that, she'd be looking up at him.

All told, it was better to have her inside the tent pissing out, rather than outside the tent pissing in with Ido. Without Chiren it didn't matter where Ido stood when he pissed. He probably didn't even have as much water pressure as his ex.

Vector permitted himself a chuckle at that one and poured himself two fingers of excellent Zalem-only whisky from the bar, just to do something other than watch the losers of Iron City walk past the limo and whisper to each other about it. Most of them would know who it belonged to, and they showed their respect by giving a little ground as they went by so they didn't stumble and scratch it by accident.

They also looked properly respectful, even awed, which Vector definitely approved of even if it didn't make him like them any better, or at all. It was only right that they understood he was at the top of the food chain and they were below him. While it wouldn't get them invited to his penthouse for drinks or dinner, it wouldn't shorten their lives either.

He had finished the whisky and was about to pour another when Gamot rapped on the window. Vector pressed a button in the console to open the door. Hugo tumbled in and landed on the floor at Vector's feet, looking very much the worse for wear.

"Thank you, Gamot," Vector said. "How are the shoes?"

Gamot lifted one foot; grey hiking boots. Heavy-duty. Mario must have had the same reaction to Gamot's feet. "They feel kinda strange," he told Vector.

"Get yourself a supply of socks on the way home. Mario can help you with that too."

"I didn't see he had any," Gamot said.

"Not everything is readily visible," Vector told him and made a dismissive gesture.

"You're the boss, boss," said Gamot. "Have a nice night."

Vector had already stopped caring; he was focused on Hugo, still sitting on the floor. Wisely, the kid didn't move to the seat without permission; he remembered that, at least, even if he'd forgotten how to deliver on time. Maybe the beat-down had given him partial amnesia.

"What. The. *Hell.* Happened to you?" Vector demanded. "You fall into the blender at the Kansas Bar?" The kid opened his mouth and Vector put up his hand. "If the next thing out of your mouth is an excuse, I will add some new colours to your face."

"I cracked my ribs too," the kid said in a small voice.

"What the *hell* did you do *that* for?" Vector snapped. "Didn't your mother ever tell you not to get your ass kicked?"

Something flashed in the kid's eyes, a fraction of a second of pure fury. Then he dropped his gaze. "Sorry," he mumbled. "I shoulda been more careful."

"You're goddam right you shoulda!" Vector barked. "This is gonna screw me up. I got Paladins who were counting on those parts and upgrades for the next game. That's not gonna happen now. They're gonna have to play without what they need, if they can even play at all. What do you suppose would happen if I told them it's because *you* dropped the ball?"

"I might be able to get some of the parts—"

"Oh, swell. I can tell the guys we can fix *some* of them. Which ones? Shut up," he added. "You *really* didn't have anyone who could step up while you were getting your ribs taped? Even *I* got people who can cover for me in an emergency, and I run this whole goddam town!" Vector sat forward a little. "Get your shit together right now, Hugo, or you're gonna be off my go-to list. And then I'll make sure you're off everybody else's too. You won't be able to *give* yourself away as a punching bag."

Vector saw the kid take a deep breath. Oh, God, was the kid gonna *cry*? If he did, Vector really would have to give him some new contusions. There was no crying in the black market.

"Well," the kid said finally, and his voice was steady. "I think I might be able to make it up to you—a little," he added quickly, looking up at Vector. His eyes were dry. "Just a little."

"Oh, really." Vector looked down on him as if from a great height. "What are you gonna do, pull my delayed order out of your ass?"

"I've got a line on something nobody else knows about," Hugo said.

Vector sat forward a little more. "This had better be good."

The kid hesitated, looking unhappy. Vector moved forward again so he was looming over him. If Hugo didn't understand that he'd better come across with something good right now, then he was a lot stupider than he looked. Or he was too ethical to sell someone out when he needed to, and Vector was pretty sure that neither characteristic applied to the kid.

Finally, Hugo took a breath and said, "Dyson Ido's working on this chip for cyborgs he says can cancel out any conflicts between old hardware and new equipment—no more hesitation or drop-outs. And it speeds them up, makes them do everything faster."

"Is that so." Vector took a sip from his glass so the kid wouldn't see how interested and impressed he was. Who knew the kid could be so useful when he was in deep shit? "When you say 'working on', do you mean he's trying to do it, he's done it, or he's going into production tomorrow?"

Hugo hesitated again. "He did it. I don't think he's going into production right now, but when he does, he'll give them away like always. Most cyborgs have really old parts that—"

"Don't talk when I'm thinking," Vector said quietly. "Dyson Ido made a chip that fixes compatibility issues between older equipment and new stuff, and instead of selling it to people who can pay what it's worth, who really deserve it, he's going to just give it away. Is that what you're telling me?"

Hugo opened his mouth, then just nodded.

Vector gazed at him in silence for so long he saw the kid start to squirm. Let him, Vector thought. While the information did make up—a little—for Hugo's failure, it also made Vector furious to think that, had Hugo delivered on time, he'd have never known and the chip would have been all over the place before Vector could do anything about it. And a bunch of walking junk piles who were just treading air until they died would get to function better than they had any right to.

"What really happened to you?" Vector asked Hugo. "Gimme the whole story. Nobody gets a beat-down without a reason, even if it's a stupid reason."

Hugo told him a fast story about stealing a bracelet that had belonged to his mother and then having it taken away from him by a southie gang who beat him up for parking near the trash pile.

"Well, I gotta tell you," Vector said when he'd finished, "that's the lamest, most pathetic thing I've heard in years."

Again, Vector saw a flash of anger in Hugo's eyes, which quickly gave way to a neutral, obedient look.

"Hugo, when I put you on my payroll, I didn't put an asterisk next to your name and a note that said 'Only if he's not too busy with his mommy issues'. If you work for me, *that's your job*. You don't do stupid shit somewhere that's got nothing to do with *your job*. And there's nothing in south-town—*nothing*—that has any connection to *your job*. Got that?"

Hugo nodded again.

"You want a bracelet, buy one. I pay you enough. You want to stare at it and stroll down memory lane? Do it on your own time. Which is not when you're doing *your job*. Is that clear?"

Another nod.

"Great. Now take your ass outta my sight and bring me the stuff I asked you for. And if you're ever late again, all the fancy, advanced cyber-chips in the world won't save you. Go on—*go!*"

The kid scrambled out of the car as though Vector had given him a little kiss with a cattle prod. Vector didn't turn around to watch him run. Maybe he should have knocked Hugo around a little, he thought as he told the driver to head for home. But he'd only wanted to put the fear of God into the kid, not hurt him any more than he already was. And it wasn't because he was soft. Kids like Hugo didn't react well to corporal punishment. They didn't fight, so they didn't respect physical power; they were more likely to run away from it.

Besides, it was the kid's first offence. Vector was pretty sure they'd need snow ploughs in hell before the kid screwed up again. Plus, the information Hugo had given him really was damned good. He could reward the kid for it later to remind him what a good idea it was to tell his employer whatever he found out.

Vector was still a little mad at the kid for not telling him about the chip until he'd screwed up, but he could feel himself getting over it already. He needed to devote his mental energy to figuring out a plan for this wonder of a chip. He could hold a grudge later, if it was useful.

Hugo didn't stop running until he'd put at least six blocks between himself and the limo, going down to the lower level streets below the abandoned causeway just to be sure. It was virtually impossible to get a limo down there. Then he hid in the shadows by a set of stone steps leading back up to the upper level to catch his breath.

He had done a terrible thing, betraying the doc like that. Vector would find a way to steal the chip and use it for his own purposes—Motorball for sure and who knew what else—and shut Ido out completely. After all, Ido's ex-wife was working on his Paladins at the track. She could probably figure the chip out, maybe even build a better one. Then the only people who would ever see the benefit from it would be those who could pay Vector's going rate, which would be as far beyond the reach of the Factory cyborgs as Zalem.

No matter what happened, though, Hugo had to make sure the doc never found out who screwed him over. He could talk to Vector about that later—much later, when Vector was feeling so rich that he no longer cared about the late delivery.

Oh, sure. And then maybe Vector would even invite him up to his fancy office for drinks. Vector would talk business with him while they were admiring the view, maybe even ask him if he knew about any hot Motorball prospects.

It would never occur to Vector to tell Ido or anyone else how he found out about the chip. Hugo's little secret would be safe to gnaw away at him. No one would ever have to know about it, or that the art of the ass-saving betrayal was actually a family trait, not limited to blood relatives.

CHAPTER 4

Ido had worked himself ragged, then gone out to pick through the trash pile with a flashlight. After bringing home his meagre findings, he'd sorted them into *usable*, *possible* and *probably not*. Then he sorted the third category into *questionable* and *hopeless*. And now here he was at stupid o'clock in the morning, breathing in the aroma of a mug of camomile tea, his wide-open eyes like a couple of dried-out boiled eggs.

He'd never slept much. It had bothered Chiren when they were first together. Waking up to find she was alone in bed made her anxious. She told him as much when she came to find him. He would apologise and go back to bed with her. Sometimes he stayed and watched her sleep until the sky started to lighten and he finally dropped off himself.

But other times he would get up as soon as he was sure she was asleep again. He'd read or work on one of his enhancement projects. The beautiful people in Zalem, they loved their enhancements. They had to petition Nova for them and he didn't always say yes. Nova said the exalted population had to be superior by their very nature in the first place to deserve further enhancement. They should not need machine parts to be more than the sad, sorry creatures dwelling at ground level.

He had been in charge during the War. All the other sky cities had fallen but Zalem was still aloft; that alone seemed reason enough to leave him in charge.

Three hundred years later, give or take a few decades, he gave the order for Ido and Chiren to remove themselves and their defective daughter from his perfect vision of Zalem and decamp to ground level with all the other abnormalities, inferior goods and broken machines. Chiren had gone to beg him to reconsider.

Looking back on it later, Ido wondered if she had been hoping Nova would relent enough to give her a choice between staying in Zalem alone, or going with Ido and their daughter to the surface. Ido knew Nova would never have done that. But he knew what Chiren would have chosen.

He'd known it back then too, although he'd have denied it. He would have told himself he was absolutely certain that the woman who came to find him when she woke up alone in the middle of the night would never have chosen to stay in Zalem alone.

Nova would have told Chiren that, as the mother of the identified imperfect child, she simply didn't belong there any more. Except Nova refused to see her.

If it hadn't been for their daughter, Chiren might have spent the first year on the ground in a catatonic state. But she'd still had enough mother in her to think of their child, and enough compassion to set up the clinic with him. They'd found an old house with what had been a dental practice on the ground floor. The building was old and it had stood unoccupied for a long time. But the structure was sound; with a little TLC it became a home with a clinic downstairs.

Ido and Chiren built their daughter a wheelchair, and she scooted around happily in it. Chiren home-schooled her, although as she got older, the girl talked about going to school with other kids. Chiren told her it was out of the question; the school building had accessibility problems. Ido wasn't sure if this were true or not, but doing it Chiren's way meant she had that much less to be miserable about.

Their little girl wasn't miserable. What was exile for them was an adventure to her. She liked helping out in the clinic, and she liked the patients—they were so much friendlier to her than people in Zalem had been. Ido didn't tell her it was because down here, they didn't see her as defective.

He thought—hoped—Chiren would come to understand how much better this was for the girl in the long run, to be accepted as normal, or at least not abnormal. But Chiren was mortified by her daughter's new, more outgoing behaviour and her willingness to mix with people who had never known anything but the ground they walked on.

Once in a while, however, Chiren got busy enough that she'd forget to be miserable. Patients were intensely grateful to have a clinic that would treat them for whatever they could afford to pay, or even if they couldn't pay at all. They were appreciative in a way that Chiren wasn't used to, and Ido could tell that sometimes she was touched by their gratitude. Although she was still baffled as to how people could be happy without all the material things and creature comforts she missed so much.

Then they found Motorball. Or rather, Motorball found them after one of their patients, a Paladin turned Hunter-Warrior, spread the word about the new cyber-surgeons with the extreme skills that had to be seen to be believed. Overnight, Ido and Chiren went from barely scraping by to more than comfortable. Team owners paid them well in credits, benefits and favours, giving them all the best materials and equipment to work with. Motorball financed the clinic, with enough left over for Ido's new pet project: a new body for their daughter.

The girl was happy but not healthy, and becoming less healthy every day. Iron City's polluted environment and poor air quality made it hard for her to breathe. The climate was heavily humid; the joke went that you had to keep moving in Iron City or the mould that grew on everything would get you too. Frequent scans and inhalation therapies were necessary to make sure the girl's lungs weren't hosting microorganisms.

Ido managed to sell Chiren on the idea of replacing their daughter's body altogether. Chiren hadn't liked the idea of making her into a Total Replacement cyborg, but she eventually agreed it was the girl's best chance for—well—if not a *normal* life, then a longer one.

The two of them worked on it together, and Ido knew Chiren was putting her heart into it. One of the very few times he had seen her smile with genuine enthusiasm was when he had begun etching floral designs on the cyborg arms and legs.

Ido had actually thought that between Motorball and the clinic and constructing a new body for their daughter, Chiren was finally too busy living her life to hate it.

Chiren did seem to like Motorball as much as he did, if not more. She loved the excitement, the challenge of working under pressure to fix a player's equipment on the fly, and seeing one of her Paladins score the winning point. But it was all in spite of herself, not because she was embracing any part of this life. She used Motorball the way someone might use alcohol or drugs: to relieve the pain of her existence. And as with alcohol or drugs, the escape was only temporary. The pain was still there, ready to resume when the games were over and the cheering crowds had gone home.

Ido thought—hoped—that finishing their daughter's body would do his wife some good. Seeing their little girl strong and healthy rather than wheelchair-bound might be just the thing to show Chiren there was more to life on the ground than things she hated. Maybe she would even remember that this was something they'd never have been allowed to do for her in Zalem. Maybe it might break down the wall of misery she'd built up around herself and let in a tiny bit of light.

And who knew, it might have gone just like that. Their little girl continued to deteriorate in the lousy damp air and polluted environment. By the time they'd finished her new body, she was too weak for surgery; the general anaesthetic alone might have killed her. They had to build her up so she could withstand the physical shock and heal. Ido turned to the black market for more nutritious food and ingredients he could use to make vitamins and supplements.

Chiren told him it was no use, it would never work, their daughter would never be strong enough. But Ido persisted and, miracle of miracles, the girl began to improve. It went more slowly than Ido would have liked but it was happening. Their daughter even said she felt stronger. Ido knew it wasn't just the power of suggestion—her colour really was better and she was starting to put on weight.

And then they ran out of time.

Break-ins didn't happen often at the clinic; when they did, it was usually someone looking for drugs. Ido kept anything worth stealing in a safe in the cellar floor, so there had been nothing for the desperate cyborg addict to steal. That hadn't stopped him from tearing the place up, of course.

Ido had been horrified to discover he knew the man. He'd been one of the Paladins he and Chiren had worked on, young and strong, a good candidate for upgrades, who healed fast and adapted to new hardware even faster. But only for a while—his performance began to fall off. Talent and ambition hadn't been enough to overcome the conflicts between new hardware and older equipment; neither had the performance-enhancing drugs. Eventually the day came when the team owner, a sleazy bastard named Vector who wore bespoke suits, stolen shoes and an evil smile, cut him from the roster.

By then Ido and Chiren were doing a lot of work for Vector. He paid better than anyone else and he could provide equipment and parts Ido hadn't thought were available at ground level. Nonetheless Ido had refused to sign an exclusive contract with him. The man wasn't simply a predator; he was greedy. Vector had a way of looking at things as if he were wondering how good they might taste, Chiren included. When both Ido and Chiren were in the pit, Vector kept his distance, but Ido knew it wasn't out of respect for their marriage. The man didn't want to do anything that might jeopardise his relationship with the best Motorball techs in town.

Vector was less considerate of his players. They were winners or they were out. Once they were out, they no longer got the first-class treatment Paladins were entitled to. This included the performance-enhancing drugs, the ones that were supposed to keep a cyborg body and organic brain aligned. The drugs boosted neural cells so they fired more quickly and intensely. One of the side effects of the drugs was a feeling of invincibility. Another, less salutary, side effect was addiction, both physical and psychological.

The cyborg who had broken into the clinic had already sold off some of his parts to finance his habit. His left arm was a mess of cheap replacements for the components he'd had the last time Ido had seen him; only half of his right arm remained. He'd run out of things to sell.

Ido had tried to talk him down enough to hit him with a sedative, but the cyborg had already understood he was getting nothing. He threw Ido into some shelves and stormed off to look elsewhere for what he needed. Except Ido's daughter was between him and the exit.

She hadn't made much of an obstacle.

In the days that followed, the world around Ido had seemed thick, blurry and colourless, as if he were mired in underwater mud. Hunter-Warriors he had been treating came to the clinic promising they'd bring the bastard who'd murdered his little girl to justice. Ido could even have the guy's head on a pike if he wanted. Ido told them quite truthfully: It was tempting. Chiren locked herself in their daughter's bedroom and refused to see anyone, including—especially—Ido.

The bounty hunters told Ido to give her some time. No parent should ever bury a child, they said, it was always worse for the mothers, always, because the child had come out of her body. Didn't matter how long ago that had been, the physical connection was always there.

It was the most comfort Ido received, then or ever.

Chiren stayed in their daughter's bedroom for five days and nights. On the sixth day she was gone. Ido was only surprised that he hadn't heard her—he'd been sure he hadn't slept at all the night before, but apparently he had dozed off just long enough to miss her leaving.

Would he have tried to stop her? He didn't know. He couldn't even find it in himself to be sorry she was gone. When the numbness wore off he would miss her desperately. But if he had caught Chiren at the door with her suitcase, Ido didn't know what might have come out of his mouth. The thought of no longer bearing the weight of her unrelenting misery was a profound relief.

Chiren blamed him for their daughter's death. She never said as much—she didn't speak to him for a very long time after that night—but he knew she did. Even though they had both worked on the ex-Paladin, she had to blame him. Blaming herself even partially was unthinkable. It had to be *his* fault that they'd worked at the Motorball track; *his* fault that they'd set up the clinic together; *his* fault because he'd been unable to stop Nova from exiling them. If he'd been strong enough, intelligent enough, skilled enough, Zalem would have wanted to keep them, and their daughter would still be alive. And Chiren would not have had to spend the last years of her daughter's life hating her own existence.

Ido did miss Chiren. Life in this place, where corruption was the order of the day and trustworthy people were few and far between, was harder on those who were alone. Yet, somehow, he persisted. Maybe because Iron City was built on scraps, discards and broken things; he fitted right in.

Missing Chiren didn't lessen Ido's relief that she was gone. He blamed himself for his daughter's death and always would; he didn't need Chiren's help to do that.

Chiren hated her apartment.

She'd hated it on sight, but it was just a couple of blocks away from the Motorball stadium and, now that she had to travel to and from the place alone, that mattered. The only other good thing she could say for it was she didn't have to live there with Ido. It wasn't home, but then nothing in Iron City could be. Iron City was an ugly, dirty place with bad-smelling air, bad-tasting water and bad days that only got worse. All bad shit, all the time, as the kids said, and they were bad too. Little delinquents, most of them, who grew up too fast and turned into thieves, con-artists and black-market wheeler-dealers, doing anything to make a little money. Which they spent on God only knew what.

Their dirty faces even turned up at the Motorball track. The first time she'd found herself looking down at a little knave named Hugo, she'd thought he must have sneaked in. Hadn't even started shaving, but there he was with a box of servos and half a dozen circuit boards. She'd called Vector to ask him if he was running a daycare centre.

Vector had come down from his fancy box to introduce Hugo to her formally, then apologised for not having done it sooner.

I asked Hugo to take the new inventory straight to you, he smarmed. *Figured you'd need it. Hugo's becoming my number one go-to guy for hard-to-find items, or for things we're always running out of. The one thing I've never heard anyone in the pits say is, "We have enough servos." Am I right?*

She'd nodded, feeling both mollified yet chastened.

Hugo wasn't rude, was he? Vector's expression went from smarmy to smarmy concern.

He was fine. That wasn't the problem, Chiren told Vector. *I was just surprised. I didn't think unaccompanied children were allowed in the pits.*

Vector had laughed heartily. *Oh, my dear Dr Chiren! Hugo's a* kid, *not a* child.

Then Ido had shown up with Claymore, whose left arm had been hanging by a wire, and Vector had made himself scarce, as he usually did whenever Ido was around, unless he had something to tell both of them. That had been Ido's fault—she could tell by the way he looked at Vector that Ido was only tolerating him for the sake of the job and, some days, Ido's tolerance was pretty low.

Chiren had asked Ido how he could feel any hostility towards someone who paid as well as Vector did. So well, in fact, that Vector practically financed the clinic singlehandedly. Without him, they'd have had to close up shop long ago. Ido had said something about getting help for the poor and marginalised from the person who kept them that way. Chiren had told him self-righteousness had always been his least attractive feature.

Privately she'd thought he was jealous. Ido had never been the jealous type, nor had he ever envied anyone for their belongings or talents.

But that had been in Zalem. In Iron City even a saint would have felt at least a little threatened by an attractive and obviously affluent man in handmade suits and supple leather shoes, who was chauffeured around in an armoured limo. Vector was always so impeccable, just the way she and Ido had been once.

Vector was also well-spoken—for Iron City, that was. After more than a few words, it had been obvious to Chiren that he was doing his best with comparatively little formal education and above average street smarts. But that was only because she had a basis for comparison. To anyone born in the dirt, Vector probably seemed like a higher form of life. Most of Iron City seemed to look at him that way. She was impressed with what he'd managed to do for himself with the resources available.

If they'd been in Zalem, the Dyson Ido she had known and loved would have outshone him in every way. Down here, however, Vector showed her how much Ido had deteriorated. Long before *that* night, Ido had been shrinking and fading in her eyes. Maybe Ido had thought she'd been withdrawing from him. But, really, it had been the other way around.

Day after day they'd worked in the clinic but she hadn't been *with* him, she'd only been in the same location. In accepting exile, Ido had given up. He lost all his power, his magnetism, and there had been nothing to keep the two of them from drifting away from each other, not even their daughter. Ido had been completely unaware; he'd never seen what was happening.

Chiren got up from the scratched, uneven kitchen table—one of her apartment's ineffably sad, shabby furnishings—and made herself another cup of tea, using the teabags and bottled water Vector had given his pit crew as gifts after the last game. Supposedly the tea was the same stuff they sent up to Zalem and the bottled water was from Vector's personal distillery, but it tasted a little off to her. Maybe it was the crappy air.

She opened the window by the table a little more and put on the floor fan. It helped a little; the humidity was awful tonight, even for Iron City. Poking her head out of the window, she looked up at the overcast sky, not at the clouds but at the darker shadow that was the disk of the floating city. The weather down here had three main settings—rain, pre-downpour and post-downpour. With occasional brief periods of blue sky. God, she missed Zalem.

She could not forgive Dyson for this, and she never would. *He* had been the one who bowed his head and accepted Nova's judgment—delivered by bureaucrats!—without a fight. *He* had built the stupid pod so they could land in the *trash heap*—as if they belonged there! *He* had insisted they open the clinic and help those who were even worse off than themselves. As if there really *was* anyone worse off! No one else in this godforsaken town had lost as much as they had.

But did Dyson even *try* to get any of it back? Of course not. He was too busy being St Dyson, ministering to the so-called less fortunate. Looking back on it now, she wasn't sure how much longer she'd have been able to stand being under the same roof with him anyway. He'd seemed content to go on living in a wasteland, having nothing, being nothing, doing nothing—well, nothing that really mattered—even though he knew she was unhappy. He'd probably thought he was being patient; in truth, he didn't know the difference between patience and apathy.

At least his famous insomnia had allowed her to rest undisturbed. They worked so hard all the time, she was too tired, either to be intimate or to explain why she didn't want to be. For the first time in her life, she'd been glad of his sleeplessness.

And then their daughter—

Chiren had taken to blanking the whole thing out. It was the worst thing that could ever happen to a parent, and she avoided reliving it. When her daughter's life had ended, her life as a mother and wife had ended too. Yet she had gone on living.

But not with Ido, not in the home they'd shared with their daughter, not in the clinic where the girl had scooted around helping them, laying out clean instruments and sterilising used ones and chattering to the patients in the waiting room. Not in the place where Dyson had put all those holos with them looking like they really were a happy family.

They were so absurd and unacceptable, those holos, with their daughter smiling because she didn't know any better and Ido grinning like the fool he was. Ido had even made *her* look happy in some of them—as if she weren't revolted by the very air she was forced to breathe, as if she hadn't hated the dirt that soiled her shoes, her clothes, her life. Looking at those holos, anyone would have thought they were a happy little ground-level family.

Not hardly. Not even close.

The one holo that irked her most of all was the one Ido had smuggled out of Zalem. It was a close-up of the three of them, showing nothing that would reveal anything about the floating city. Well, unless you counted the fact that all three of them were clean, well-dressed and obviously better off than they could ever be on the ground.

She hated that one most of all because she didn't look happy *enough* for it to have been taken in Zalem. That woman in the holo with her daughter on her lap and her husband's arm around her, that woman was stupid and clueless and vacant. She didn't know anything bad could ever happen to her, even though the toddler on her lap was obviously too thin and pale to be normal. That woman had been too obtuse to know misfortune when she was actually holding it in her arms.

And Ido—the son of a bitch *wasn't* smiling as broadly as in a lot of the holos taken in Iron City. He didn't look sad, just a bit thoughtful. Like he didn't have brains enough to know that he was in the best possible place and he should appreciate it.

Ido probably hadn't learned his lesson either. For all she knew, he was grinning like a damned fool right now, as if there really were something in this ugly, dirty world to be happy about.

CHAPTER 5

The bruises on Hugo's face had faded enough to be practically unnoticeable. People no longer winced when they looked at him or asked him if he'd taken the license number of the ass-kicking machine that hit him.

He still hadn't told his crew what had happened, not even Tanji and Koyomi. Tanji would have been all for getting everyone together for some payback, not caring how much bigger those guys were. That was Tanji all over. Tanji had been on the street longer than Hugo or anyone else in the crew, and he didn't back down from anything or anyone. He didn't go around looking for fights but he wasn't afraid to square off against someone if he had to. Most of the time he came out on top, but even when he didn't, his opponents always knew they'd been in a fight.

Tanji had taught him a few moves, good for both Motorball scrimmages and self-defence. Hugo's preferred strategy for either was simply to be faster than everyone else, but that only worked if you remembered to stay alert, especially on someone else's turf.

So now here he was: back in south-town a week and a half later, staying very, *very* alert as he stalked the guys who had handed his ass to him and walked off with his mother's bracelet. At the moment he was parked at the mouth of an alley, watching the crew hang out in the southie version of a market. It made him glad he lived in midtown.

The market wasn't really small, but everyone was squashed together with the vendors practically on top of each other, like south-town wouldn't give them any more space than was absolutely necessary and they were lucky to get that much. The forced togetherness didn't bring out the best in anyone's disposition.

The food area didn't have as many different kinds of foods. The falafel looked good, but the woman behind the counter never stopped yelling at the kid working prep for her. Worst of all, in Hugo's opinion, there weren't any buskers, which might have made the general atmosphere a bit less grim and prickly and generally unpleasant.

Or not, Hugo thought, watching one of his attackers harass a woman who'd had the poor judgment to get within arm's reach of him while searching for a place to sit down and eat the sandwich she'd just bought. The other guys jeered and hooted as she slapped his hands away. She left the market altogether, ignoring the calls and kissing noises. As she passed Hugo, she gave him a dirty look. He didn't blame her. She was around thirty, a bit plump, dressed in a Factory jumpsuit. Just coming off the early-bird shift at the nearby distribution centre, packing shipments for Zalem, and she couldn't even eat a sandwich in peace.

She had cyborg legs—Hugo recognised the gait. Everyone with cyborg legs attached to their torso walked the same way. Like his father, but only until he'd replaced more of his body. Then he'd walked like all the other machines.

The woman could have kicked her harasser into a pulp with her cyborg legs. She could have stomped the whole crew, and everyone in the market would have cheered her on like a Motorball hero. Didn't she know what she could do? Or was she too afraid of payback?

The strong didn't just prey on the weak, Hugo thought, they made sure no one knew their own strength too.

Not me, you assholes, he told them silently. *You might get a piece of everyone else but you won't get me. Not again.*

Two guys Hugo didn't recognise joined them. They were just as big, possibly a little older than their fearless leader. Or maybe they just had more mileage. They had more scars and one of them had a mouthful of crooked broken teeth. Hugo was surprised to find he actually felt a little sorry for them. Sad bastards—they had nothing going for them but following a bully. Tanji would have told him he was stupid to feel sorry for a couple of meat-bags who would have joined in stomping him if they'd been there.

The crew ambled out of the market, heading farther south; Hugo paced them on a parallel street a block away. Even at that distance, he was taking a chance. He knew what Tanji would have said: *Are you crazy or do you just have a death wish? What do I tell Vector if they beat you again— you can't help it, you're addicted to tough love?*

The Tanji in his head was as big a pain in the ass as the real one, Hugo thought ruefully. He was also right. If Vector knew he was doing exactly what he'd been told not to, he'd kick the whole crew to the curb, even though they'd delivered two orders on time since the late one.

Tanji might even go looking for another crew and take the others with him, leaving Hugo with no one to watch his back. People who tried to make it alone, without a crew or family or anybody to care what happened to them, didn't last long.

The thing was, Tanji and Koyomi and the others, they all still had family. Even if they didn't live with them, they had blood relatives—

parents or aunts and uncles, cousins. Koyomi had so many cousins it seemed like half of Iron City was related to her. People with family didn't know what it was like to be related to no one, and they didn't know what it was like to have the only thing you could remember your mother by taken from you like it was nothing. Like *you* were nothing.

Hell, Hugo didn't even know where his parents were really from. They'd never talked about their families except to say they were all dead. Now that they were gone too, Hugo might have just sprung up out of the ground or dropped out of the sky from nowhere.

Or from Zalem? Hugo looked up longingly at the city floating overhead.

If only.

The south-town crew wandered through the neighbourhoods in no particular hurry, taking a route that arced west as well as south, and all they did was hassle and harass everyone they met, shaking them down for money and anything else that caught their eye. It was a protection racket, Hugo realised—*pay up and we won't kick your ass.* Some people gave them credits without being asked. Sometimes the crew would leave them alone; more often they'd hassle them for more money.

They collected from a few businesses too, mostly small grocers or cafés or sad little hardware stores or junk shops. Why did those people go along with it, Hugo wondered; why didn't anyone do something, or ask someone for help?

Like who? A Hunter-Warrior? Hunter-Warriors only went after someone if there was a price on their head. The Factory wouldn't bother putting a marker on these guys; they were too penny-ante. No marker, no bounty; no bounty, not a bounty-hunter's problem.

The crew kept moving until they came to an open-air café four or five blocks west of the market where Hugo had first picked up their trail. They went in and commandeered the place, driving out the other customers while getting grabby with the waitresses. They were so full of themselves, Hugo thought he could have ridden his gyro right through the centre of the café without any of them noticing, or at least not right away. Hugo parked his gyro around the side of the building, put his hood up and sat on the curb in front to watch them surreptitiously.

The leader was really stuck on himself. He had gold tips in his hair now and there was more to the design tattooed on the right side of his neck. And, Hugo saw finally, he was wearing the bracelet.

At first he was surprised—he'd have thought the guy would give it to a girlfriend or sell it. Nope, not this guy—it was all for him, everything they did, the whole operation. He was just going to keep doing whatever he wanted until somebody stopped him. The guy probably couldn't even imagine that happening. He was like a robot, not even a cyborg. He was a meat-robot and all he did was all he knew how to do.

Hugo decided he'd had enough: of the crew, of south-town—of Iron City, for that matter, and of everyone who just stood by and let any kind of shit happen, whether they were people who got victimised on the street, or Factory slaves who replaced their bodies piece by piece so they could die with almost nothing left that made them human.

CHAPTER 6

"I wanted to do this months ago," Vector said, sitting across from her at the small table set up in his office, which was ridiculously large and luxurious to the point of vulgar. "But I thought it would be… unseemly. Uncouth. As if my interest in you were less than worthy."

Chiren didn't quite smile at him over the top of her wine glass. He was talking the way he thought people talked in Zalem. Wanting her to believe she wasn't the only highly evolved intellect marooned in the dirt with lower forms of life. He was trying to make the whole evening as much like Zalem as possible—the brilliant-white tablecloth, the wine obviously pilfered from a shipment meant for the flying city. It made her glad she was wearing the cream-coloured tunic and trousers she'd had on the day they had been exiled. They were the only things she had from her lost life, and she hadn't worn them again until tonight. Vector knew her clothes were from Zalem and he couldn't take his eyes off them, his gaze running over her arms, her shoulders, her chest with an eagerness and avidity that veered between wonder and lust.

"I've worked on your Motorball players for years." Chiren took a sip of wine, refusing to let herself enjoy it. She had to keep her wits about her. She was a sheep eating dinner with a wolf posing as a shepherd; she couldn't let her guard down for a moment. "In that time you've always treated me with respect. I have no reason to expect anything else." *Expect respect, expect respect*; the words echoed in her mind nonsensically, as if she were already drunk.

"You and your husband were a package deal," Vector said. "Two highly skilled cyber-surgeons, turning my Paladins into winners while funding your work with the less fortunate. Of which there's no shortage in Iron City. I so admired what you two were doing that I could never bring myself to take offence at Ido's—oh, lack of warmth, call it. I put it down to overwork."

"That's very kind of you," Chiren said, looking into his eyes. She could do sincere.

Two flunkies in formalwear came in with appetisers—baked Camembert, or what passed for it in Iron City, with small round pieces of garlic toast. Chiren noticed Vector waited a fraction of a second to see what she did, then copied her exactly. The observe-and-mimic strategy was probably how he'd survived for so long.

"You've always been more approachable," Vector told her. "No matter how hard you've been working, you remain even-tempered. I put that down to your innate character."

"That's very kind of you," Chiren said again, letting herself smile. "But I think it only means you weren't around when I bit someone's head off."

Vector chuckled. "If you bit anyone's head off I'm sure they had it coming. Actually, I'd wanted to invite both you and Ido to dinner to show my appreciation. *And* my admiration. But you were both so busy, working so hard all the time. If you weren't at the track, you were at the clinic. There never seemed to be any time in your schedule to relax.

Although I wasn't so sure how relaxing it would be for you to have dinner with the boss." He paused, looking at her expectantly.

"Well, that really *was* all Ido and I did together," Chiren said. "Work, I mean. At the clinic, at the track. Ido never learned how to shut it off. In all the time I knew him, I don't think he ever slept more than four hours in a night, and usually not that much. I'd wake up and find him at his workbench, fiddling with a circuit or a chip."

"Really." Vector was gazing at her more intently now. "What kind?"

Chiren was about to tell him about the integration chip that had been Ido's obsession when the flunkies came back for the empty dishes. Vector raised a subtle finger and she nodded to show she understood. She'd finished the Camembert without even noticing. It had been a long time since she'd eaten anything that good.

"Sorry," he said when the flunkies were gone. "I do trust my staff, but I also do my best not to add to their burden of discretion. They work hard enough as it is."

If Vector had ever cared how hard his employees worked, it hadn't been in this lifetime, Chiren thought. "As I've pointed out already, you're very kind," she said.

Two different men brought in the main course: Filet mignon for her and a very large, very bloody prime rib for him, accompanied by baked potatoes with sour cream and butter, and green beans. The butter was too yellow and the green beans looked like they might glow in the dark. Vector had added colour to his filched foodstuffs to match his idea of how fancy food would look in Zalem. Chiren found it both absurd and pathetic.

"Is that all right?" Vector asked, nodding at her steak. "I thought it was something you would like. Unless you'd rather have the prime rib?" He put on a mildly concerned expression. "Or have I guessed wrong altogether and you're a vegetarian?"

"I'm most definitely not a vegetarian and filet mignon is exactly right," she assured him. "The name means 'dainty filet' and it comes from the tenderloin area on either side of a beef animal's spine. It's cut from the smaller end, where the lesser-used muscles are located, which is why it's so tender." She smiled at the bodyguards as they arranged the other dishes on the table for them. They were also in formalwear. It made her wonder how he'd found suits to fit them with their enhancements. Lots of alterations, she supposed—unless he'd actually had them made. If so, he'd gone to a great deal of trouble and expense for her. What did he want, besides the obvious? Was it real and, if so, could she actually give it to him?

"The term filet mignon was first used in a story by some writer way back in the early twentieth century," Chiren added as the bodyguards marched out of the room, "but the story title and the author's name escape me."

"Maybe more wine will help," Vector said, giving her a refill she didn't actually need. They were drinking from crystal wine goblets Vector claimed he'd found in a stash hidden in the Factory before the War three centuries ago. He made the same claim about a lot of things, but he might have been telling the truth about these.

Chiren forced her wandering mind back to the situation at hand. "I hope hearing about my steak didn't overburden your men," Chiren said.

"It's probably the most education they've had for—" Vector made a face of mock-concentration. "Ever. I had no idea you were so knowledgeable about cuts of beef."

"Well, I *am* a surgeon," she said.

Vector surprised her by throwing back his head and roaring laughter at the skylight above them. "That one hit me square on the funny bone," he said when he wound down.

Chiren smiled. She was tempted to give him a lesson about the humerus and decided to save it in case he annoyed her. His cultured mask had begun to slip a little; he was starting to look at her the way he looked at his prime rib, and it wasn't just her clothes he was appreciating now.

She had to admit she was surprised at how well the dinner had been prepared. If it wasn't as good as anything she had ever had in Zalem, it was close enough. Did Vector have an exiled chef chained to the wall in the kitchen? Maybe someone Nova had thrown over the side for burning his toast?

"This really is excellent," she told Vector. "My compliments to your chef."

He laughed again. "I'll pass your compliments along." Then he sobered. "I wanted so much to please you, to make everything perfect. You deserve the best of everything—the best food, the best clothes. And a palace to live in, rather than three rundown rooms with a view of nothing."

And he was just the man to give them to her, Chiren thought. The only man who could, anyway. She took a sip of wine and Vector poured more into her glass as soon as she put it down again. Like magic, the bodyguards appeared with another bottle. They poured the last of the old bottle into Vector's glass, then opened the new one and added an inch to hers before they left.

"Please tell me you don't eat like this every night," Chiren said with a small laugh.

"No, I don't. I couldn't even if I wanted to," Vector replied, sounding a bit wistful. "I have so many responsibilities that I can seldom take this much time for a meal. Besides, I'd feel silly doing this alone." He paused, staring at his wine glass with a thoughtful expression. "As I get older I find I'm becoming less and less content to be by myself. An active mind needs stimulating company. Someone to talk to. I'm starved for conversation that has nothing to do with business, Motorball or making sure everyone's doing their jobs right." His gaze slid away from the glass to her. "I can't even imagine what it's like for you."

Chiren tensed a little. If he started talking about her daughter, if he even said her name aloud, she would throw her wine in his face.

"As I said, I did want to reach out to you before now," he went on, "to let you know that I was thinking of you, that I felt for you after such a terrible tragedy."

Chiren kept her face neutral as her fingers tightened ever so slightly on the stem of her glass.

"When I found out you were alone, I wanted to reach out to you even more, to say—" His voice trailed off and he frowned. "To be frank, I had no idea what to say to you. I still don't. What you've been through is completely outside my experience. I was afraid if I said the wrong thing to you I might lose you as well as Ido. I didn't want that. At the same time, I didn't know if this was a permanent break or if Ido might want to reconcile—"

"He won't," said Chiren. "Ido is where he wants to be, doing what he wants to do. As far as I know, anyway. We haven't spoken since I left."

"So *you* left *him*," Vector said. He added more wine to her glass; she didn't remember drinking any but apparently she had. "I was afraid you were going to tell me he'd thrown you out. I might not have been able to stop myself from, ah, talking to him about his bad manners. Even if it's not my place."

"No, I left of my own free will," Chiren said, keeping her tone light. "Motorball gave me—gives me—what I need. Work I can throw myself into. It's been—well, practically a lifeline."

"I'm glad it's helped you." Vector had on his compassionate face now. "But if I'm honest, I've benefited greatly." Pause. "Which almost sounds as if I'm reaping rewards from your pain."

Thanks for letting me know, Chiren told him silently, keeping her face neutral. Spinning pain into gold was a succinct description of what Vector did for a living. "Of course not," she said.

Last chance to run, said a little voice in her mind. *If you don't go now, you may never get out. If you do run, don't stop till you get to the clinic. Dyson will take you back like you were never gone, and you're still in your child-bearing years—*

Chiren killed the thought and shoved it away as hard as she could. Bring a child into *this* world—down in the *dirt*? Doom an innocent soul to the tender mercies of Iron City, watch a pure spirit become tainted with corruption? And for what—a no-hope future as either a Factory slave at best or a Hunter-Warrior's bounty at worst? Had she lost her mind?

Maybe. But she wasn't brain-dead. She was going to stay right where she was, finish this incredible Zalem-worthy steak dinner courtesy of the most powerful man at ground level, a man who was willing to go to a lot of trouble to keep her happy—or at least keep some of her appetites satisfied—while satisfying his own, of course. But what the hell, it was more than she'd ever get anywhere else.

"I'm afraid I'm full," she said as she finished the last bite of her steak. "I've barely touched the baked potato, and it's awful to let it go to waste, but—"

"But nothing," Vector said, waving one hand, and for the first time Chiren noticed his fingernails were manicured. "My chef is brilliant. Nothing will go to waste." He smiled. "Would you prefer to delay dessert and just have coffee for now?"

"You read my mind," Chiren said, reading his. She was tempted to ask what they'd be having for dessert but she didn't think he'd get the joke.

The coffee came in a silver service that made Chiren gape openly. The only other time she had seen something like this had been in the apartment of the man who had told her and Ido why they had to leave Zalem.

"I think I've impressed you," Vector said, studying her face. "Have I? Yes? Pardon me for feeling pleased with myself about that."

"I shouldn't be surprised at anything," Chiren said. "Not after that meal, anyway."

"Like the crystal wine glasses, I found it hidden away in the Factory. Stashed by someone before the War but never retrieved for reasons that are only too easy to imagine." Vector's pleased expression had turned to smugness. Chiren supposed he'd never needed to know the difference between the two.

"I *am* impressed," she told him. "So little from before the War survived. It's amazing—a work of art."

"Then please allow me to give it to you as a gift," Vector said. "A work of art for a woman who is herself a work of art."

You know, of course, that after tonight he will never talk to you like this again, said the voice in her mind. *This is just to get you into—*

She shut the voice out. It wasn't telling her anything she didn't know.

As soon as they finished their coffee he led her to his bedroom. There was no explanation, no suggestion. This was simply what came next on the schedule, and since she hadn't talked even vaguely about leaving, he'd assumed they had come to an understanding.

His bed was enormous, about as large as the living room in the dump she called home, she thought. He took his time undressing her—he'd waited all night to get his hands on her clothes and now the magic time had come. He rubbed the material between his fingers, marvelling at the softness and the subtle glint from threads that were neither metallic nor cloth but something else.

She moved to undress him but he told her to climb into bed and feel the sheets instead. The product of nano-machines that were his and his alone, he told her, unavailable even in Zalem. No one else had sheets that felt so good against bare skin.

Then he had dessert.

She had expected to be disappointed, and he delivered with no surprises. Vector knew what he liked and he knew what a woman's body was supposed to like, or at least respond to. He handled her expertly. It was all so impersonal, she wondered whom he was really in bed with. Maybe a composite created from different experiences.

And all without a word. He didn't speak to her at all. When she started to say something to him at the beginning, he had looked meaningfully into her eyes and pressed his finger to her lips. *Hush.* She had listened to the sound of his breathing and her own and the whisper of the sheets, and that was all.

When he finally fell away from her he looked pleased and gratified; mission accomplished. If she had broken his concentration with pillow talk it might have taken him forever to get himself back into the right frame of mind.

The ceiling in his bedroom was high, not like the one in her miserable, cramped flat. Fortunately, she'd never have to go back there again. He'd send his flunkies to collect her things for her. She lived here now, in the penthouse atop the Factory. Not really a palace but as close as she'd ever get in this lifetime.

And this was the best bed she would ever sleep in, with its miraculously soft sheets. He would dress her in handmade designer clothes, which she would wear even when she was working on his Paladins at the Motorball track. As long as she made champions for him, he would make sure she stayed shiny, elegant and in good repair, just like everything else he owned. She was going to live better than she ever had since her expulsion from Zalem.

The food would be great too, just like the clothes and the sheets on the bed. And the sex would be sex. This man would never make love to her, but that didn't matter; she was pretty sure he'd never made love to anybody.

Well, she hadn't come here for love or great sex or even good sex. Vector had much more than that to offer. A man who wasn't afraid to skim from shipments intended for Zalem obviously knew the authorities were looking the other way. Which meant he had some seriously important connections—the kind that might know how to get her out of the dirt, off the ground, and back up to where the air was clean and bright.

Why else would the sex be so bad?

CHAPTER 7

When the distinguished lady cyber-surgeon finally dropped off, Vector got up and put on his silk pyjamas and robe. The pyjamas were adorned with alternating bands of silver; the robe was the colour of excellent Shiraz. Someone had once told him they made him look like old-time royalty, the lord of the manor. Vector no longer remembered which of the various women who had passed through his bedroom had come up with that insightful description of his appearance. Memorability wasn't a trait he looked for in the women he invited into his bedroom. Chiren was the lone exception and only because she was useful.

Since the first moment he'd seen her Vector had been curious as to what she was like in bed. As he became better acquainted with her he formed his own ideas about it, and she hadn't surprised him. Had she been a very different person up there in Zalem, that Dyson Ido would fall in love with her? Or was he one of those sad fools who had a type? Maybe they were all the same up there—neurotic, pretentious and unreachable. He wouldn't have been surprised.

Vector took a few moments to de-opaque the window and look out at the night view of Iron City. Seeing it like this, he could almost forget it was really just a toilet for the aristocrats in the sky.

Okay, that was a bit harsh. Trashcan was more like it, or junk yard. He had come to this place very young, but even then he had wondered what kind of people built a city around a better city's rubbish.

It hadn't taken him long to learn the answer—he was a quick study— and it was the same now as it had always been: people with the souls of jackals and hyenas. Carrion eaters that survive on some better, stronger animal's leavings.

And what did that make him?

He smiled; that was an easy one.

I'm the King, baby. I'm the Emperor, the Lord High Commander, and the jackals and hyenas worship me as their god. Anyone screws with me, I don't have to kill them—I have someone to do it for me and I pick my teeth with their bones.

There was only a partial view of Zalem from here but it included the waste chute. Refuse poured out of it as he watched.

More riches for me. The Emperor acknowledges your tribute. Thank you and good night.

Three centuries since the War of Whatever and still no one knew much about the place—well, almost no one. The one in his bed wasn't talking, but she didn't have to. Vector knew people and he knew life, and he was pretty sure that things up there probably weren't a whole lot different than they were on the ground. The only difference was, up there they had nicer things and no one went hungry unless they wanted to. In Vector's opinion, any place where people starved themselves in the midst of plenty was corrupt all the way through.

Vector knew little about Zalem; most of his contact came by holo from Factory bureaucrats who looked too wispy to cast a shadow, although that may have been his screen. They called to tell him what Zalem wanted—more avocados, not so many grapefruit, larger cucumbers. But Vector knew damned well *they* weren't in charge.

The first time he'd seen the man in charge was shortly after he'd taken over in Iron City, which the man in charge had helped him with. Even then they hadn't had much contact but he'd known the man had been watching him and he liked what he saw. Vector hadn't merely known that, he'd *felt* it, especially after he'd consented to letting the Factory install the identity chip. The chip saved a lot of time and trouble—it was like having a universal master key to all the locks that mattered. In some cases, literally—he no longer had to carry key cards or remember entry codes.

But even better, the chip provided a connection between himself and the man in charge, whom he thought of as the Watcher, even after learning his name was Nova. The first time Vector had seen the Watcher on his screen had been on a conference call about quarterly production figures; the Watcher had been sitting silent, off to one side, but Vector had known who he was. It wasn't hard to guess why—he and the Watcher were two of a kind. He knew the Watcher had been around for a very long time—an impossibly long time, if the stories were true. Maybe he'd been waiting for someone like Vector, someone who saw things from the same angle, heard what he heard and knew how the music was going to change, and knew what to do when it did.

Although to be honest, Vector thought the Watcher had it easier. When he gave an order, everybody up there gladly went along with it so they could keep all their nice things. What had happened to the distinguished lady cyber-surgeon in the bed behind him was their worst nightmare.

Thinking about it that way, Vector could almost have felt sorry for them. But he'd never been able to muster up any pity for people who were happy to serve in Heaven when it was so much better to rule in Hell.

He turned to look at the distinguished lady cyber-surgeon—correction: *his* distinguished lady cyber-surgeon, she belonged to him now just like the view, the penthouse and anything else he cared to call his own. Iron City itself was, for all intents and purposes, his. From his penthouse atop the main Factory building, he ran the show—any show, every show, all shows great and small, from Motorball to marketplaces. Nothing happened without his say-so. And so it would continue, because he knew how to keep things functioning. It was actually very simple, down here in the dirt: just enough bread and a plethora of circuses. Circuses made people forget they wanted more bread. Keep the circuses coming thick and fast, and after a while people would choose circuses *instead* of bread.

Bread was expensive, but you could make circuses out of anything. Even a pile of trash.

It was well after one A.M. when the supervisor from the Factory's south-town distribution centre called to say she had skimmed another load of plums from the fresh fruit bound for Zalem. She'd swapped them out for green apples and altered both the packing list and the requisition form, so it would look like someone up there had a green-apple habit. Concord grapes, however, still weren't available anywhere, and wouldn't be for another couple of months.

"So what's the problem *now*?" Vector demanded testily. "I thought you said they finally developed a strain that'll produce all year round."

"Yeah, they did," said the supervisor. She was a middle-aged woman named Frida who was high up on his go-to list as someone who got results. She wasn't conventionally beautiful but Vector had found her very attractive, so much so that he had nearly made the mistake of going to bed with her, which would have completely ruined her as an employee.

"They got the grapes to grow just fine," Frida was saying. "But they can't get them to ripen faster without losing all the quality. I tasted the fast ones and they taste like nothing. They don't even *smell* like Concord grapes. They smell like—well, nothing. Not even grass. So we gotta wait till they're ready."

"And they call themselves scientists," Vector said, his voice dripping with contempt. "Meanwhile the gutless wonders in Zalem aren't complaining. How are any of them still alive?"

"Nobody told them to die," said Frida.

That jerked a surprised laugh out of Vector in spite of everything. "You're probably right," he said, and told her to keep him posted before he hung up. God, why couldn't *she* have been a distinguished lady cyber-surgeon, he thought just as the phone rang again.

This time it was Myrtle, one of the pit bosses at the Motorball stadium. There had been no game tonight, just a practice session for the jobbers. Myrtle told him they had enough parts and equipment to cover everyone's repairs tonight—but *only* for tonight.

"As of now, the cupboard's pretty much bare," Myrtle said. She sounded tired, but she always did, even when she wasn't. "After tonight we need a whole lotta inventory or we gotta figure out how to make servos from cardboard and spit. And we're all outta cardboard."

Vector groaned. "Make a list, then copy it two dozen times and hand it out to our best suppliers, including what's-his-name—the kid with the crew that's always hanging around."

"You mean Hugo?" Myrtle said.

"Don't ask me, I'm not your secretary," Vector snapped. "Just get going on this. If we come up short, it's *your* head I'll be yelling for." He managed not to crush his phone's screen. Then he sat and glared at it. "Go ahead, ring again," he muttered.

It did, making him jump. This time it was Gamot, calling from the Kansas Bar with the news that one of Vector's Paladins had busted up most of the furniture then stormed out without paying his tab, leaving the owner close to apoplexy in the wreckage.

"Who was it?" Vector asked wearily.

"Wheelstein," Gamot told him.

"He's a *menace!*" yelled the owner in the background. Vector knew his voice; he'd heard it in the background of a lot of phone calls.

"Tell the owner he's not one of mine any more; I just cut him from the team," Vector said. "Which means Wheelstein's responsible for his own expenses."

He listened as Gamot relayed the message to the owner.

"Is he about to burst a blood vessel?" Vector asked Gamot in the ensuing silence.

"Oh, I'd say about half a dozen," Gamot replied, making it sound as if he were talking about damage. Gamot had a lot of cool. If only he didn't dress like he lived under the causeway. "All right, put him on."

A moment later the bartender's strained voice said, "Hello?"

"As my associate just explained, Wheelstein is no longer one of my mine," Vector said smoothly, "which, I'm sorry to say, means he's uninsured." He waited a beat to let the bar owner's blood pressure hit three hundred over two hundred, then added, "*However*—as a goodwill gesture because so many of my guys drink there, send me the bill and I'll cover half of it."

The bar owner made a strangled noise that could have been "Yes".

Gamot came back. "Anything else?"

"No," Vector said. "Now get out of there before he tries to make you call back and ask for more." He hung up and called the pit boss back to tell her to cut Wheelstein and backdate the paperwork by twenty-four hours.

"Sure thing, boss," Myrtle said. "What about all the stuff in his locker? Guy's, like, a hoarder."

"Can you eat it?" Vector asked.

"Hell, no." Myrtle sounded incredulous now as well as tired.

"Then whatever you do with stuff you can't eat, do that."

"Oh." Myrtle sounded a little sheepish. "Okay."

Vector hung up and made a note to pay only a fourth of whatever figure the bar owner sent him, which would be about half of the actual cost. Bar owners were always trying to bleed him. Next case.

He sat at the desk and waited. A minute went by in silence, and then another. He checked the time. It was after two-thirty. Stupid o'clock, sometimes known as suicide o'clock, when things usually went quiet and stayed that way until sometime between five and five-thirty.

Vector swivelled around in his chair and looked out of the big windows. They had the best view of Zalem. When he first got the desk he'd put it facing the windows, then realised it would put his back to both doors. It made him feel too vulnerable.

By contrast, putting Zalem behind him felt like it was not only his but it was backing him up as well. Which, considering his arrangement with the Factory, wasn't too far from the truth.

While he and Chiren had been having dinner in here, she hadn't been able to go more than a minute without looking at the view, and he knew that it wasn't Iron City she'd been so captivated by. She obviously had no idea how much her longing showed. She was homesick. Poor thing. Who could have blamed her? Iron City was a hell of a comedown from what she was used to. He was going to have a hard time making her see that just because you lived at ground level didn't mean you were in the dirt. Handmade designer clothes, fancy food and the penthouse would have turned any other woman's head. But Chiren was homesick.

Of course, maybe he could use that to his advantage, he thought suddenly. If she thought he'd send her back to Zalem in exchange for

making his Paladins into champions and his champions into winners—
that just might do the trick and put a little more hustle in her bustle. Or
even a lot more.

She wouldn't be the first person he'd promised to send to Zalem. He'd
never have to deliver—he always found a way to show an eager would-
be traveller how they'd failed to keep their part of the bargain, rendering
the deal null and void. With Chiren, he wouldn't have to worry about
that for a long time. Meanwhile, he could work the hell out of her and
she'd be only too glad to do it. He probably wouldn't even have to pay
her except in clothes and food and a place to live—oh, and act like he
cared just often enough to make her think he did. He could even say *I love
you* if he had to, although he doubted it would ever come to that.

Chiren was so bitter and wrapped up in herself, she might not catch
on for *decades*.

Damn, how could someone so brilliant and intelligent be so blind and
stupid? Maybe it was losing her kid that had ruined her. But that wasn't
the whole story. If her daughter had still been alive, she'd have still been
miserable because she wasn't in Zalem.

And even if her daughter had been alive and she'd still been in Zalem,
she'd have found something to be unhappy about. Maybe that was what
Dyson Ido was for. Except things hadn't worked out that way.

Which was his lucky break, Vector thought, smiling at Zalem's shadow
in the night sky.

High overhead, above the clouds, the man leaning on the railing at the
very edge of Zalem smiled. He was enjoying the show.

CHAPTER 8

Ido hoped this would be one of those rare nights when he was tired enough to sleep. He'd kept the clinic open an extra three hours for everyone in need, triaging them into three categories: *Urgent!*, *Today For Sure* and *Mañana*. Chiren had done him no favours by leaving. She hadn't even offered to find someone to fill in for her. If he didn't get some help soon, he might have to put Hugo in a nurse's uniform.

Although the little scoundrel hadn't been around since the night he'd limped in all beat to hell. After treating him Ido had told him to come back the next day for a check-up but he hadn't. Well, he was a kid. He'd probably been distracted by something shiny. Or maybe he'd annoyed somebody else and he'd got his ass kicked again. Ido hoped not but he wouldn't have been surprised.

Once his too-long day was over, he'd considered checking the scrapyard to see if Zalem had thrown out anything useful. But then he'd taken a quick look at his accounts and his accounts said he needed to put in some time at his second job.

The Rocket Hammer was in its case, ready for use. No matter how tired he was he was always careful about how he put it away: taking it apart, cleaning the components and inspecting them for cracks or worn places, making sure the controls were stable and there was plenty of fuel to fire it up, ensuring none of the little vents were blocked so the power was there when he needed it most and he wasn't just holding a fancy stick in his hands. He closed the case, went to the bureau to get his gloves, and remembered he'd left them in his coat pockets. As he turned away he caught sight of himself in the mirror.

Damn, he looked *cold*. It was hard to believe the man he saw there was a doctor. He looked more like someone who killed people for money and never gave it a second thought.

Not entirely true. He thought about everything he did.

Then he put on the dark coat and the gloves, pulled his hat low, set his glasses for night vision and wheeled the Rocket Hammer case into the elevator. He wouldn't be the only one out hunting—he never was—but there were plenty of marks to go around.

He was lucky—he picked up two marks in a row, both highly rewarding. They put up a fight, but he'd got good at this. Using the Rocket Hammer, he bagged the first one in ten minutes, and the second in fifteen, including the time it took to remove their heads. Both were wanted for home invasions in which a total of five people had been killed. Ido presented their heads at the Factory redemption counter and came away with close to fifty thousand credits for the night's work. That would keep the clinic open for another week, the good Lord willin' and the creek don't rise.

Yeah, right. The good Lord was only willin' to be absent these days, and it had been raining so much the creek had turned into a rushing river that was halfway up its banks. Any more rain and there'd be flash-flooding around the bridge again. Ido had sent a message to the Factory telling them they had to do something about the drainage upstream in the eastern part of town. They'd paved over too much land and it didn't allow adequate run-off. He'd have thought that in this climate they'd know better. His answer had been a form email thanking him for his input. Did Iron City even have a civil engineer, he wondered.

Ido came back from the Factory redemption centre bone-weary after fighting, hoping he'd used up enough energy to drop dead for a few hours. The second mark had given him a hard punch in the ribs, which was going to hurt more tomorrow. Ido didn't care. All he wanted was an intermission that would divide tonight from tomorrow instead of it being all one long today.

The spirit was willing but the insomnia was stronger and the flesh was collateral damage. Dr Dyson Ido could heal everyone but himself.

Not long after they'd opened the clinic together, Chiren had suggested he let her give him a mild sedative and he had absolutely refused. A drug would only make him high, not sleepy. He'd be sleepless and stoned, and he'd like the stoned feeling too much. Then he'd have a problem much worse than insomnia. Insomnia, for all its faults, was free.

Chiren hadn't argued; she'd seen as many addicted ex-Paladins as he had. They kept all the drugs that felt good locked up in the cellar safe and set an alarm that would notify both of them whenever it was opened. That way neither of them could yield to temptation without the other knowing. Ido was sure Chiren didn't need the safeguard. Addiction was a loss of self-control. Chiren would never let that go. Not just for a cheap high, anyway.

Ido had muted the alarm on his own phone but never shut it off completely. It still sent messages to her phone whenever he opened the safe; her phone rejected all of them. She'd probably thrown the phone away by now, or maybe she'd buried it in a drawer or a closet to keep the number, because it was *hers*. Chiren had a strict policy—whatever was hers *stayed* hers.

Well, except him.

He sometimes thought about actually calling her old number to see who, if anyone, would answer. He never did though—there was an ever-so-slight chance that Vector would answer, and Ido didn't know what would happen if he heard that slick bastard's voice answer the number she'd had when they'd still been together. He might scream or tear out his hair, break down and cry; his head might even explode, or he might just hang up without speaking. But no matter what he did, Vector would know that he'd got to him and that was the last thing Ido wanted. Vector had come out on top, just like he always did. He could ride around in his limo and tell himself he was the king of the world in his Factory penthouse. But he would never hear Ido say it.

At least he never had to work for the son of a bitch again. No more long hours in the pits putting Paladins back together and Vector coming by supposedly to say, *Nice job, you can expect a bonus*, but in truth to stare at Chiren's shapely behind like it was a steak and he hadn't eaten for three days. Only when Chiren wasn't looking, of course; it was a courtesy Vector hadn't extended to Ido.

Well, Chiren was on the menu now. Ido wondered if Vector had moved her in yet or whether he would go through the motions of courting her for a few days. No, he wouldn't waste any more time locking down her services for his Motorball players. He probably hadn't done sooner just to allow what he thought was a decent period of time since "the tragedy". That was how Vector referred to their daughter's death: "the tragedy".

Ido thought if he had ever heard Vector speak his daughter's name, he'd plant the Rocket Hammer in his face. How smooth would he be after that?

God, he needed something else to think about, something that wasn't Vector or Chiren.

"Shut *up*," Ido told himself. "Work."

He had four replacement arms laid out on his largest workbench. Most of the components in each one were of the same generation or close enough that hesitation and drop-out wouldn't be a problem for the cyborg. He'd found a way to make newer parts more backwards compatible with older parts, but some parts were just too old. He'd had some luck with rebuilding the older parts to fool them into thinking they were newer by resetting some of the interrupts. That was a new skill he'd taught himself quite recently. Dr Dyson Ido, cyber-surgeon, heavy on the cyber.

The chip he was working on would make all the old fiddles and tricks unnecessary—he hoped. At the moment the chip was installed in a double arm he'd been upgrading for a musician. Hector played double-necked guitar and he made brilliant music with the vintage instrument. But then the signals for his fingering began scrambling on him. *I know it ain't life and death, Doc, and maybe nobody really needs to hear me playing classical pieces in the marketplace all day. But it's a living—it's* my *living, anyway. And if I can't play, I might as well lie down and die.*

Without music, we all *might as well lie down and die,* Ido told him, meaning it. And it was a relief to work on something that had nothing to do with the Factory or bounty hunting.

The guitar player's double arm was highly complex; whoever had designed it had been a cut above the usual techie hard-head. This was the product of someone who knew something about music and musical instruments. When Ido had asked the musician about it, however, the man had been vague and obviously uncomfortable. Ido hadn't pressed the matter. People in Iron City knew that talking too much never ended well. Ido could relate—he didn't like answering questions about himself either. Besides, all he needed to know was right there in the arm.

The chip worked well in the arm but only on the short term. Hector said he improvised a lot when he played; tests showed the chip would speed up the signals from his nerves a little too much, so that it would be more like the chip was playing the guitar than the man. A fast chip didn't belong on a slow job. Ido had fixed the hardware to operate virtually free of conflicts, but Hector still had to come in and play while Ido fine-tuned him so he could get the kind of movement he wanted.

The chip itself needed a lot more work. Speeding up nerve signals so movement felt as natural as it did for someone fully organic was a good idea in theory, but the chip kept jumping the gun. It would anticipate the next signals in the sequence, a little earlier each time. That was okay for a robot programmed to do one thing repeatedly. For a cyborg—a human being—the chip could get so far ahead of the nerve signals that it took over and the person lost autonomy and control.

Chiren probably would have accused him of letting his perfectionist tendencies sabotage tech that was acceptable if not quite up to his lofty benchmark. *The pursuit of perfection is the enemy of good*, she'd told him more than once. He might have been more inclined to her point of view if she'd been talking about art, where there might be a million right answers or none at all. But Ido had always operated on the basis that there was an ocean of difference between *good* and *good enough*; settling for the latter when you could attain the former with more time and effort was—well—*not* good enough.

Now Chiren could have everything her way. Good, good enough, functional for now—it was her call and no one would argue with her; Vector would just tell her to hurry up. Other than that, Vector would spoil her rotten with a laboratory full of nothing but the best, all stuff he'd skimmed from shipments bound for Zalem. He'd be as ostentatious about it as possible, to make sure Ido would know what he was missing now that he wasn't working in the pits any more.

And he *did* miss it. At first he hadn't been sure he wanted to work on giant armoured cyborgs that dismembered each other while chasing a quirky motorised ball around a snaking track. He'd never watched any of the broadcasts on Zalem. But the game had hooked him faster than he cared to admit even to himself. Some kind of testosterone thing, he supposed; there were no activities in Zalem that involved extreme violence at high speed, nothing that would induce a man to feel like standing up and pounding his chest while he bellowed a challenge to the immediate world.

Of course, this didn't take the female players into account. Or Motorball's popularity among people of any sex who weren't given to displays of brute force.

For Chiren it was pure escapism—she stopped thinking about where she didn't live and what she didn't have. If Vector had somehow been able to get his limo into the pit, Chiren would have turned it into a Paladin, no questions asked. She really was that good—better than Ido was. She liked having to think fast in the pressure cooker. She liked being the Paladins' only hope, Hero to the Motorball Heroes, not the mother who got kicked out of heaven for producing a defective child.

Ido wondered how much she had amped that up since she'd left him. How manic did she get? What did she have to do to get herself up there, and how did she come down afterwards?

If she hadn't been crazy before, she probably was now.

Dammit, he'd sat down at the workbench to put her and Vector out of his mind. Ido took the chip out of the guitar-player's double arm and replaced it with a more conventional type of controller, one that wouldn't get ahead of the musician. He ran a brief diagnostic, with a sheet music subroutine, just to see the movement. Watching the fingers play invisible frets was a bit trippy but everything looked good.

The next arm on the table had a hand that could be swapped for an array of surgical instruments. This one was for a nurse who'd been sideswiped by a truck; it had taken her left arm off at the shoulder. He was briefly acquainted with Gerhad—she'd sent a few patients from the ER his way, but that wasn't the only reason he liked her. She was a very good nurse—you had to be to work in an emergency room—and she thought her career was over. What she made at the hospital wouldn't have bought her so much as an elbow joint. Would she ever be surprised when he showed her what he'd cooked up for her. Ido really hoped she liked it, because he wanted to offer her a job too. What he made as a bounty hunter would be enough to tempt her with a better income than she had at the hospital.

Getting a good nurse in to work with him would make his life so much easier. He could train Gerhad as a full nurse-practitioner so she could prescribe lower-level drugs and prep patients for surgery. Together they could help more people than he could alone.

Yeah. The Dyson Ido clinic: one-stop shop for all your cyber needs, lifeline for indigent cyborgs. Lives would not only be saved, they'd be improved; and all he'd have to do was collect one or two extra bounties per night—one or two extra heads. Dr Dyson Ido, life-saving cyber-surgeon by day, deadly Hunter-Warrior by night. Licensed by the Factory to kill. Where would you end up, under the knife or under the Hammer? Cure or kill? No refunds, all sales are final.

Ido put his head in his hands. He could not let himself spiral. The last time had been *that* night, when he'd spiralled right out of his mind.

He had been spiralling when he'd marched into the Factory to get a bounty hunter's license. He'd looked calm enough to pass for normal, but then "normal" in Iron City was an extremely broad and highly vague designation. In any case, the deckman hadn't challenged him and the Centurians hadn't pointed their weapons at him. Apparently they hadn't picked up on the fact that he was a hair's breadth from losing his shit and screaming his grief and rage until his voice gave out. Or they'd determined that would pose no threat to the Factory.

It probably wouldn't have mattered if he'd come in stark naked, covered in mud and calling himself the Queen of May. As long as he directed any homicidal tendencies towards criminals with prices on their heads, he wasn't their worry. Or maybe he was wrong and the Centurians would have shot him if he'd put a foot out of line. You never really knew with Centurians; you weren't supposed to.

In any case, they'd given him his license and told him to read the fine print on the back, which was the Hunter's Code. That was all he needed to become one of Iron City's Hunter-Warriors. Some of them were good men, like Master Clive Lee and McTeague with his Hellhounds. Others were cruel and violent, like Zapan, who seemed to spend all his money on plastic surgery.

The rest were mostly ex-Motorball players, which answered a question he had never thought to ask—namely, what happened to those who washed out or got cut from the team?

Back when he and Chiren had been busy building bigger and better Paladins, he'd never wondered about the players who never made the big time. Now he knew: if they didn't end up on the street selling off parts for a fix of the performance drugs, they might get work as hired muscle in the ever-popular security industry. (If they were really lucky Vector would put them on his payroll.) Or they pulled themselves together and became Hunter-Warriors.

Ido was one of the very few residents of Iron City who knew any real history—not just about the War, but also how things had been before that, when civilisation had been more orderly and regulated, and civil servants protected the weak and, if possible, prevented the strong from victimising them. Sometimes it worked, sometimes it didn't. There had been problems—the haves had so much more than the have-nots, and corruption had kept it that way. Other problems were inherent to the system—bureaucracy slowed the process of justice. People were convicted of crimes they hadn't committed and spent years trapped in overcrowded prisons, and if they hadn't been criminals when they'd gone in, they were when they came out... *if* they came out.

Now there were only Hunter-Warriors and Centurians. Crimes against persons all had the same penalty, carried out either by a Hunter-Warrior or a Centurian. Case closed.

With very few exceptions, Hunter-Warriors were only allowed to take the heads of those with markers on them. Once the identity was verified by the Factory, the hunter could collect the bounty and spend it at a Hunter-Warrior hang-out like the Kansas Bar. Poaching another hunter's mark was expressly forbidden by the Hunter Code and was grounds for execution. That was as complicated as it ever got.

Under this streamlined system, however, there was no provision specifically for the protection of the weak. In Iron City the best thing you could do was not be weak and hang around other people who were also not weak.

As for the question of what Hunter-Warriors could do if they sustained any damage or serious injury in the course of taking down a mark, that was an easy one: you went to Doc Ido's clinic and he'd fix you right up, even if you'd lost the bounty and couldn't pay.

This was quite a recent development, but it was in keeping with the original idea behind the clinic. Ido had met a lot of Hunter-Warriors that way, even before he became one of them—putting them back together, rewiring nervous systems, replacing ribcages and pelvic connectors. They were grateful and paid as and when they could, even tipping him off to an especially profitable mark to support the clinic.

He was the total package: healer of cyborgs and killer of criminals. Dyson Ido, cyber-surgeon and professional contradiction. *First, do no harm.* That wasn't actually part of the Hippocratic Oath. Neither was kill or cure.

Well, it could have been worse, Ido thought, reaching for the third arm on his workbench. That was another feature of life in Iron City: no matter how bad anything was, it could always be worse. No matter how far down you fell, you'd find there was at least one more level lower than that.

Well, unless you ended up with your head in a bag. Then you were done. You couldn't fall off *that* floor.

His daughter's face appeared in his mind's eye, pale, her lips a little blue from the exertion of pushing herself around in her chair. *I'll use the motor later, Daddy. I want to build up my arm muscles. Check it, my biceps are already bigger!*

Oh, yes, it could have been so much worse. His daughter hadn't lived to see what a sorry pass he had come to. If she had, Ido wouldn't have been able to look her in the eye.

He put his head down on the workbench and let himself fall apart. It had been some weeks since the last time; he might as well get it over with so he could pull himself together and get back to work on these damned arms.

Three hours later he woke to find he'd been tightly gripping one of the cyborg hands with his own, as if he'd needed to hold on for dear life. He raised his head and slowly let go of the cyborg hand. He uncurled his fingers slowly, absently aware his ribs hurt a lot more now.

Thanks for the helping hand, he told the cyborg arm silently. *Otherwise, who knows how far I would have fallen?*

CHAPTER 9

"He lives!" Tanji said as Hugo joined him and Koyomi outside the CAFÉ café. "Your face looks better. More like a human's."

"Thanks," said Hugo. "Can't say the same about yours."

Koyomi laughed. "Ooh, he gotcha!" She ran a hand through Tanji's frizzy halo of hair. "And the 'do isn't even warm after a burn like that. It's a miracle!"

Tanji pushed her hand away but without much effort. How much longer were the two of them going to dance around each other, Hugo wondered; they were starting to drive him crazy.

Koyomi turned Hugo on the sidewalk so he was facing the late-afternoon sun. "Yeah, definitely a lot better," she said, peering at his face. "I'd never know just by looking at you that you got beat up for your lunch money." She frowned slightly. "Are you ever gonna tell us what really happened? Jealous boyfriend? Pissed-off cyborg?"

Hugo grimaced. "Something stupider," he said, then hesitated. Tanji and Koyomi were his closest friends. If he didn't tell them about it, he'd never tell anyone. He hadn't even told Ido the whole story; the doc had just patched him up, no questions asked, for which he'd been grateful. Some things he didn't want to talk about. But he didn't need one more thing to carry around all by himself.

"Okay," he said after a bit. "But this stays between the three of us. The rest of the crew doesn't have to know."

Koyomi mimed locking her lips with a key while Tanji raised his left hand and put his right over his heart.

"I was down in southie—" Hugo began.

"On *purpose*?" Koyomi made an incredulous face. "Did your brain fall out of the holes in your head?"

"If you *wanted* to get beat up, you coulda just asked *me*," Tanji said. "I'd've punched you out and saved you the trip. Unless you wanted to pick up lice too. That's all they got in southie—beat-downs, lice and some incurable skin diseases."

Hugo sighed heavily. "Let me know when you guys are done."

"Gimme a second." Tanji frowned as if he were thinking hard. "Yeah, I'm done. You?" He tugged one of Koyomi's skinny braids.

"I'm good for now." She turned back to Hugo. "You were saying?"

His friends listened as Hugo told them about the bracelet, although he left out the part about going to live with his brother and Nana and the drone that never was, saying only that he'd run away from home after his mother died. Tanji had already known Hugo's father had been a TR but the whole thing was new to Koyomi. She looked so upset, Hugo was afraid she might cry. Neither of them gave him any grief about his swiping the bracelet off the woman's arm, which surprised him. He'd expected Tanji at least to say something about the kind of people who took other people's stuff, but his friend didn't look even slightly disturbed by what he'd done.

"I know, I shoulda stayed outta southie," Hugo added after he finished the story. "I didn't even really know where I was, just that I was by the trash pile, and that belongs to everybody."

"The south-town crew's been trying to stake a claim on that part of the trash pile," Tanji told him. "They've been hassling people picking there. They got into it a couple of times with the westies after they chased off one of their aunts or cousins or something."

Hugo winced. "Well, geez, don't you think you coulda maybe mentioned this? Because if I'd've known, I'd've been more careful."

"You didn't ask," Tanji said coolly. "But you being our fearless leader and all, I'd've thought you already knew. Because you know everything, right? Including everything they do in southie."

Hugo gave him a look. "No, that's *your* job. *I'm* your fearless leader. You're supposed to tell me things."

"My mistake," Tanji said. He was deadpan, but Hugo could see he was getting tense. Tanji ran hot sometimes; you had to know when he'd had enough.

"Hey, I'm just bustin' your chops," Hugo said. "Getting caught in south-town's on me alone. I feel stupid."

Tanji relaxed visibly. "That was lousy, you getting worked over and losing your mom's bracelet to some punk-ass southie garbage-eater. I know you got nothin' from your folks." He put his hands in his pockets, looking self-conscious and awkward.

No one spoke for a long moment. Then Hugo said, "Well?"

"What?" Tanji's eyes narrowed.

Hugo spread his hands. "I'm waiting for the insult. Unless you've gone soft on me?"

"Hey—dead mom," Tanji said, his expression slightly appalled as well as surprised. "You don't rag on a dead mom, everybody knows that. Oh, wait—I forgot, they adopted you from one of McTeague's hellhound litters. You're doing good just walking on your hind legs."

"That's better," Hugo said. "For a second there, I was afraid you were gonna start talking about your feelings."

"Aw, do you need a good cry?" Tanji asked.

"Jeez, get a room, you two!" Koyomi stepped between them and pushed them farther apart. "Or one of you buy me an iced coffee for making me listen to that crap." She went into the café and they followed.

The three of them waited out the rest of the day at the far end of the counter that ran along the front window. A month earlier Hugo had done a deal with the café owner on some hard-to-get parts for some kind of fancy coffee machine. The owner was attached to it for some reason and didn't want to get rid of it. Hugo found the right replacement parts and offered him a discount if he'd let Hugo and his crew hang out. The owner agreed, as long as they didn't screw up his business. Tanji had told him he should have gone for the money, but having a place to get in out of the rain twenty-four hours a day turned him around. Besides, Vector paid them enough to make up for it.

In fact, Hugo had just had another meeting in the back seat of Vector's limo, which had gone better than the last one. Vector still wasn't quite over Hugo's delivering late. *A man with as many responsibilities as I have counts on a certain level of excellence*, Vector had said, *and it's no small thing to be let down*. Hugo knew he'd be hearing some variation on that from Vector for a long time.

Today, however, Vector had something he was a lot more pissed off about. It seemed there was a Total Replacement cyborg walking around not designed or built by anyone Vector controlled. There was a new designer-engineer in town, which was why Vector couldn't get his hands on the specs. But from what he'd heard the TR was superior to anything Vector had.

No one seemed to know where this new designer-engineer had come from, except that her forehead was unmarked, so she hadn't fallen from Zalem. Somewhere out in the Badlands was about as specific as it got.

The Badlands lay beyond the area surrounding Iron City where the Factory ran its arming operations. Out there the contamination from the War had decreased enough that fields and forests and even some wildlife had come back but it was deemed by Zalem's authority to still be too high for human habitation. There were people living in the Badlands, although no one was sure who or how many or even where, as no one was sure how far the Badlands extended before becoming the wasteland that the Factory said made up most of the planet. If anything lived out there it was probably mutated creatures that roamed the poisoned landscape looking for things to eat alive.

The Factory wasn't actually responsible for that last bit of speculation but it didn't discourage it; fear of the unknown made people less whimsical and thus more easily controlled. All anyone really knew was people who left Iron City never came back, and no one thought that was because they'd found something better. There *was* something better, but it wasn't out in the Badlands—it was floating in mid-air and Iron City lived in its shadow.

Sometimes people did come to Iron City from elsewhere—not often, but once in a while. They arrived without fanfare, unnoticed except by the Factory, which regulated every part of life in Iron City, and Vector, who kept track of anyone with an unknown pedigree because there was no such thing as a nice surprise.

Ms Cyborg Designer had arrived ten or eleven months earlier, a slightly dumpy woman nearing the upper boundary of middle age. Vector had thought she looked like a schoolteacher but he never made assumptions. In fact, she did teach for a while, in a private elementary school in northland, although she actually lived in a two-room dump on the edge of the Slum District.

After six months she quit and seldom left her sorry little apartment. Vector put her under surveillance, using a special team that none of his other employees knew about. They reported she seemed to be tutoring a select group of northland children who went to her place in the Slum District. Anyone else on Vector's payroll might have left it at that, but this particular team operated on the premise that all behaviour was deceptive.

Eventually, after a lot of patient observation and some undetected breaking-and-entering, the team reported to Vector that the schoolteacher was a cyborg designer and engineer. She had built a Total Replacement cyborg with a number of improvements to the central nervous system. Said cyborg had registered for the next Motorball tryout session.

Vector was no engineer but he'd picked up a few things. Looking at Ms Designer's schematic, his first impression was that the cyborg was too over-built to function—it was packing three times as many nerves in each part of the body. Everything fed into the spine, which had been completely reconfigured in a way Vector had never seen.

He'd told Hugo his new Tuner had been impressed. Chiren said it must have taken years of trial and error to get it right, which he figured explained why she hadn't made one of these for him already. Thank God someone already had; it would save them years of work.

The problem was, Ms Designer didn't want to sell Vector her design and she didn't want to go to work for him. She had a group of six financiers looking after her expenses and they didn't interfere with her work or try to boss her around. They didn't even make her move to northland.

This little cabal apparently thought their TR was going to wipe the floor with everyone else at tryouts. Maybe he would or maybe he'd blow up on his way to the starting line. But the only way to be sure was to take him *before* he got to the stadium. Vector wanted that spine and all its connectors, along with anything else they could dig out of him. But the spine was the priority, backbone included.

Once he got the cyborg, Vector said, he wasn't too worried about the northland bunch. Apparently they'd thought they could use the cyborg to take control of Motorball before knocking Vector out of his position with the Factory. As if they had a chance. The Factory didn't want half a dozen people doing a job currently handled by one. One man, one word was all it took to get the job done. Any job.

All of this was far more than Hugo had ever wanted to know. Normally, Vector told him what he needed done and, one way or another, he did it. But since Hugo had been late—just that *one* time—he supposed Vector felt the need to explain why the job was important. Maybe if he got this one right, Hugo thought, he might regain all the ground he'd lost and everything would be okay again.

At least Vector hadn't called off the other deal they'd made, and Hugo knew Vector could never have got where he was now by making promises he didn't intend to keep. If the Factory could take Vector at his word, Hugo could too. And he'd never let him down ever again.

Hugo didn't share all the details with Tanji and Koyomi. Tanji would have been bored and Koyomi would have asked what all that had to do with how they were going to do the job. He did explain that the cyborg might be more difficult to take down, but Tanji only shrugged.

"I'm at full charge," he said, patting the sleeve where he kept his paralyser bolt. "I'm good for the next two days and I don't think it'll take that long. Unless he's shockproof."

"Not that I know of," Hugo said. "I don't think even the doc could do that."

"You sure like him, dontcha?" Koyomi said. "Doc Ido, I mean. You're always hanging out there."

"Not lately," Hugo said. "I haven't seen him since he patched me up. And I only went to him because I didn't want to sit in the emergency room for seven hours with my split lip the size of a salami."

"The size of a salami," Tanji said. "I'll believe it when I see it."

"Are you asking to see it?" Hugo asked, deadpan.

Koyomi rolled her eyes. "When's the wedding? I want to save up for your gift."

"Tanji wants a salami," Hugo said.

"Hugo doesn't have one," said Tanji.

"You guys are *killing* me," Koyomi said. "Just kiss already, will ya?"

The three of them slipped out of the café shortly after eleven. The traffic in Iron City was starting to segue into late-night calm. Iron City was at its quietest in the dead of night, though it was never completely still. The Factory never slept; there was always a shipment to be packed or inspected, or things to be cut, sewn, glued, stamped, etched, painted, hammered, polished, assembled, inspected, and sent up through one of the supply tubes that extended from one of the distribution centres to Zalem like long spider legs. If you were close enough to one of the tubes, you could even hear a shipment whooshing upward.

But you could see and hear the sound of Zalem dumping their trash from almost anywhere in Iron City. Even at the busiest times of the day, when Iron City was wall-to-wall engines, blaring horns, kids yelling, and all kinds of business getting done, you could always hear Zalem flush the toilet.

Well, that wasn't really what it was, of course; Hugo had heard Ido mutter the phrase and the expression had stuck in his head. If it wasn't real excrement that came out of Zalem's waste chute, it might as well have been for the way it felt at ground level.

And maybe from up there the feeling was mutual.

This only made Hugo more resolved. Just because you'd been born in a trashcan didn't mean you had to stay there. People might think those were the rules. So you had to make your own rules.

"What are we doing here?" asked Koyomi as she got off the back of Tanji's gyro. They were in the loading area of an abandoned warehouse behind the ruins of the old cathedral. "I thought you said the cyborg would be at some place back in the Slum District or near there, and it's three or four blocks back that way."

"He is," Hugo said. "But he won't be out on the street where we can get him for another two hours."

"How can you be so sure?" Koyomi asked him.

"Yeah," said Tanji, "what if he's early? Or late? You got his schedule for the rest of the week?"

Hugo made a face at him. "I've been told where he'll be and when. He won't be out on the street before one A.M. It's two blocks to the stop for the all-night bus to northland. We can pick him up on the way."

"Then what?" Tanji asked. "Do we just take him apart on the spot and wave at anybody watching us? Or do you know any deserted streets on the bus route?"

"That's the good news," Hugo said. "We've got something even better." He took them down to the end of the loading dock to something with a tarp over it. Hugo pulled it off.

"Oh, great," Tanji said sourly, folding his arms. "You got half a truck. Did it come with half a sandwich? How long till you get the other half?"

"Oh, lighten up," Koyomi said, walking around the narrow green-and-white truck. "Skinnies look weird but they're good for getting through traffic. As long as it runs." She looked at Hugo.

"It runs fine," Hugo said. "How do you think I got it here?"

"Only you could buy half a truck." Tanji jumped up on the step to look through the driver's-side window. "It's got a back seat. I guess it has to; you can't fit three across."

"The best part's back here." Hugo led them around to the back of the truck and opened the rear door. There was a winch with a lot of thick cable as well as heavy-looking restraints screwed into the floor. "We hook the guy up to the cable and pull him in, then strap him down and take him someplace else to part him out." Hugo pointed. "There's enough room for both our gyros too."

"You got a place we can keep it between jobs?" Tanji said. "Like, in a whole truck, maybe?"

"We don't have to use it for *every* job," Hugo said. "Just tough ones. Like when there's only three of us. And we might want to use it for other things, not just jobs."

Tanji gave a short, incredulous laugh. "Like what?"

"I dunno," Hugo said. "Maybe take it out to the Badlands. We could find something out there we couldn't carry on a gyro."

"Like what?" Tanji laughed again. "No, I know what you're thinking. That thing in the lake wouldn't fit in a *whole* truck, let alone this one."

"There's still lots of other stuff inside it," Hugo said.

"Underwater." Tanji looked appalled. "*You* can dive for treasure if you want. Count me out."

"Something coulda floated to the surface or washed up on the shore," Hugo said. "We haven't been out there in a while."

"Where'd you get this thing anyway?" Koyomi asked.

"Vector," replied Hugo.

"*Vector* gave you a *truck*?" Tanji looked even more incredulous.

"Don't you mean half a truck?" Hugo said. "And he didn't exactly *give* it to me. He said I can use it whenever I need it."

"He probably got tired of trying to find a place to park it," Tanji said.

"What do you care, as long as he pays?" Hugo asked him evenly.

Tanji shrugged. "Good point. So Vector gives a truck. Can I drive?"

The cyborg finally came out of an apartment building in the middle of the block just before three A.M. The guy was larger than Vector had led them to believe. Anyone trying out for Motorball was going to be on the big side, but this cyborg was seven feet tall in his street body, with big, over-built shoulders and long arms shaped as if they were muscles. He reminded Hugo of Grewishka in his early days, before everything had gone bad for him and he'd been banned from the game for life.

That had to be why Vector wanted him so badly. A lot of people had lost big money on Grewishka's last game, Vector included. Not enough to clean him out, but Vector hated losing. Hugo wondered what had happened to Grewishka, if he'd really gone back into the sewer like everyone said.

They were parked in an alley off the street a little over a block away from the bus stop, with Koyomi in the driver's seat. She turned to say something to Hugo and he shushed her, telling her to cover up. Obediently, she pulled down her goggles, tied a bandanna around the lower half of her face, then pulled up the hood on her jacket. Hugo and Tanji did the same.

"Should I pull out?" she whispered. "He's gettin' close—"

Hugo shushed her again. "I'll bang on the door. And don't stall it too soon!" He and Tanji slipped out of the passenger-side door and watched the guy approach. When he was about ten feet away, Hugo banged the door twice and Koyomi pulled the truck into the street in front of the cyborg with a jerk.

"What the hell!" Hugo heard the cyborg yell.

"Sorry!" Koyomi said in a shrill, little-girl voice.

"Watch it!" the guy snapped. His footsteps went towards the rear of the truck. Tanji moved quickly around the opposite end to sneak up behind him. Hugo stepped out in front of the cyborg as he cleared the back of the truck.

The cyborg stopped short with an expression of bewildered surprise. Hugo felt the same—the cyborg looked so much younger in person. He couldn't have been more than sixteen, Hugo thought. Or maybe that was just the curly ginger hair and the freckles, because he was *big*, husky as well as tall. Maybe they should have had two more of the crew with them.

"What the hell are *you* supposed to be?" the cyborg said.

Hugo tapped the cyborg's knee with his paralyser bolt. He went down with a yell and Tanji hit him in the back of the neck with his own paralyser. The cyborg flopped on the pavement, arms and legs thrashing; he tried to call out but only made grunting noises. Tanji hesitated, then hit him again in the same place. Now the cyborg shuddered violently, as if the whole street were vibrating, and went limp.

Alarmed, Tanji touched a finger to his neck. "He's alive," he whispered to Hugo.

Hugo knelt down to take a close look at his face, lifting one of his eyelids. "Let's get him in the truck."

"Some super-cyborg," Tanji said as he opened the back door. "Vector better not ask for a refund if his big deal turns out to be a hunk of junk."

Hugo worried that the cyborg might start coming around after they got him strapped down in the truck, but he remained limp and unconscious.

Some cyborgs never lost consciousness, but those were the really tough guys. The adrenaline rush kept them wide awake, even if they were drunk or high. Hugo hated jacking one of those because they never shut up the whole time they were being separated from their body. They kept cursing and telling you all the ways they were going to kill you and you could barely hear yourself think. Sometimes they were still cursing when you dropped their core on the street. Hugo imagined they were still running their mouths when the Prefects picked them up and put them on life-support. Hugo always tipped off the Prefects after he dumped a core—anonymously, of course—but sometimes he thought the Prefects could find them just by the sound of their nonstop bitching.

Tonight, however, he'd have almost preferred to have the guy cursing and swearing at him. He really looked dead. Young and dead—whoever had built him had really messed up. Maybe it was all that extra stuff Vector said he had in his spine; the engineer had enhanced him, but it looked to Hugo like she'd forgotten to make a fighter out of him.

And the way he'd reacted to Hugo—*What the hell are* you *supposed to be?*—like it never occurred to him he would get jacked, like he didn't even know what a jacker was. As he and Tanji worked on severing the first set of connections between his core and the cyborg body, Hugo couldn't help feeling sorry for him.

Hugo insisted they leave the core near the market district where the Prefects would find him quickly. Tanji didn't argue; Hugo could tell he also felt funny about the way things had gone down, although Tanji would never have admitted it to anyone, especially Hugo. But Tanji made a point of keeping Koyomi out of the chop process this time, telling her to stand watch instead. Anything that could spook Tanji had to be bad.

The delivery address Vector gave them was an old annex to the Factory building. When they pulled the truck up next to it, Hugo was afraid for a moment that Vector had set them up to be eliminated as loose ends. But as it turned out, Vector had made the annex into a fancy laboratory for his new favourite Tuner, Doc Ido's ex-wife.

Hugo had never seen anything so elaborate and lavish. It was at least four times the size of Doc Ido's clinic, with a lot more equipment. Some of the machines were upgrades of things he'd seen the doc use, but others he couldn't identify at all. Chiren's instruments were in display cases, like they were supposed to be admired when she wasn't using them. She even had a small staff, although they looked a lot more like bodyguards than nurses. The doctor herself looked more like she was going to one of Vector's fancy parties; Hugo had never seen a Tuner in stilettos.

Normally Hugo would simply have dropped the requested parts off, collected his payment, and gone home. But this time he felt compelled to tell Vector how clueless the cyborg had seemed and how easily he'd gone down.

Vector's Tuner Chiren had shown a great deal of interest, asking him to tell her exactly what happened, making him go back over certain details about how the cyborg had behaved. Her face was intensely serious, her ice-blue eyes looking hard into his as if she could *stare* information out of him. Hugo had only seen her at a distance when she'd still been with the doc—before their daughter died—but even then she'd looked like she never found much to smile about.

She interrogated him for something like half an hour. Then Vector paid them and added a small bonus for "useful information". The sky was getting light when Hugo finally made it back to his single-room apartment. Maybe it had been the job or having to answer so many questions about the TR cyborg for Chiren or simply the fact that he'd been awake for over twenty-four hours but he was suddenly overwhelmed by a mix of pity and anger—pity for people who got victimised and anger at those who benefitted by it.

Normally Hugo didn't think about this sort of thing if he could possibly avoid it. There was no point in agonising over anything—he couldn't do anything about it. He was doing well just keeping himself together. But now he was too tired to resist.

Then he remembered the bag of credits in his jacket pocket. He dug a dented metal box out from behind the loose board on the floor of his one and only closet. It was a little over half-full now. Not enough yet for what he needed—but he was getting there. He added most of the night's take to it, keeping only the bare minimum he needed for the next day, and felt a little better as he put the box back in its hiding place.

As soon as he lay down he fell into a deep and mercifully dreamless sleep.

CHAPTER 10

The woman in the plush chair on the other side of Vector's enormous desk was beautiful when she wanted to be. Vector was very pleased Soledad had made the choice to be beautiful this afternoon. He preferred his women beautiful, especially when he met with them in his luxurious office. Not everyone got to meet beautiful Soledad. In her line of work, being forgettable paid better.

They didn't make them like Soledad any more. Having a mutable facial structure was now a criminal offence. But the Factory allowed her to retain the ability to alter her appearance as long as she was useful and didn't engage in unauthorised deception.

The fact that she'd managed to swing such a deal made her beautiful *and* smart, something Vector greatly respected. You could get away with a lot if you were beautiful, but if you were beautiful and smart, you could get away with anything.

Soledad was one of Vector's most closely held secrets. Virtually everyone else on his staff thought she was a "janitor"—i.e., someone's mentally impaired relative Vector employed as a favour, doing manual labour for minimal pay. It wasn't so unlikely, as Vector actually did employ a few mentally or physically disabled people as a favour to their loved ones. It made him look good, like he actually had a heart; better yet, however, it kept said loved ones continuously in his debt, making it impossible for them to refuse whatever he asked of them. Soledad moved among all of them unnoticed, observing and listening and reporting anything of interest.

She was also highly accomplished at breaking and entering. If there were any places Soledad couldn't gain entry to, they weren't in Iron City. Once inside, she could search the whole place thoroughly and leave no trace. She stole only on request and took only what she had been asked to take.

Which made her beautiful, smart and strong-willed, a combination that was so rare in Iron City as to be non-existent. It was rarer even than ex-residents of Zalem, neither of whom Vector thought of as strong-willed. He was very glad Soledad worked for him, although he didn't kid himself. She worked for him because the Factory wanted her to. But as long as she took orders from him, it didn't really matter.

Vector got up and went around to lean on the front of his desk, leaving his glass of Scotch where it was. He wasn't sure looming over this woman would have any effect on her but it was always good to remind employees he was above them.

"You understand it's crucial that we get this chip and that Ido not know we've taken it for as long as possible," Vector said. "I'm sorry we don't have an exact image of what you'll be looking for—"

"The sketch Dr Chiren made is detailed enough," Soledad said.

"I'm glad Chiren could be helpful. She's quite the intellect," Vector said with the stiff formality of a superior praising hired help he more often had to reprimand. "Looking after my Paladins is an enormous responsibility, one that has forced her to narrow her focus. If there were more hours in the day and more days in the week, I'm sure she would already have developed this chip herself. As it is, I'm sure Dyson Ido used a great deal of her work. So really, what I'm asking you to do is to retrieve property that is rightfully Chiren's."

Why did I just tell her that? Vector thought as Soledad nodded. "I'm sure, given world enough and time, Dr Chiren could master any skill, even breaking and entering," Soledad said. "Although I doubt she'd want to."

And why did she just say that to me? Vector wondered. Pushing the thought away, he said, "You have the latest reports on Ido's daily movements?"

Soledad tapped her phone. "The gentleman is a creature of routine. But I have contingency plans in the event he takes a walk on the wild side. Breaks his pattern," she added in response to Vector's slightly perplexed expression.

"Very good," he said. "And you're sure you won't have a drink with me before you go?"

"Another time, thank you." Soledad stood up and Vector immediately followed suit. She was several inches shorter than he was but sometimes she seemed taller.

"Then don't let me keep you, my dear," Vector said, dismissing her before she could leave the room without his permission.

"Oh, I wasn't," Soledad told him. "I stopped by in case you needed to say anything else to me. I'll call you when the job's done."

"Don't bother," he said as she started to turn towards the door. "Just bring me the chip."

She nodded. "As you wish."

Vector stared after her as she strode out of his office. He wasn't used to feeling relieved when a beautiful woman left his office, and he didn't like it.

The open-air taqueria across the street from the clinic was getting busy, Ido saw as he locked up. For a moment he stood and listened to the sound of cheerful voices calling to each other over the sound of the highlights of the latest Motorball game, whenever that was.

One of the waitresses hollered something to the bartender and he hollered back. Ido couldn't make out what either of them had said over the noise but it made everyone sitting nearby laugh uproariously. Ido smiled. People were people were people—no matter where they were or what was going on, they'd find some way to have a good time, at least for a little while. The idea made him feel hopeful. Maybe when he was done picking through Zalem's refuse, he'd have a couple of tacos before going out to his second job.

So that was Chiren's ex-husband, Soledad thought, staring after him as he headed for the scrapyard. It was the first time she'd seen him in person. Unless she was mistaken, he almost had a spring in his step. Maybe something almost good had happened to him today. That would be a nice change; tormented soul seemed to be his default setting. Either way, he'd be gone for at least an hour.

She could have hired a lookout to text her when Ido headed for home but that meant involving someone else in the job, even if she didn't give them any details. The fewer people who were connected to you by way of a job, the less likely it was to come back and bite you on the ass. You never knew who might add two and two and get you.

No one had seen Soledad leave the taqueria. Since departing from Vector's office she had shifted her cyborg bone structure so that her eyes turned down at the outer corners, as did her mouth, which now had pronounced marionette lines and incipient jowls to go with her double chin. It was the face of any older woman who had spent most of her life trying to be useful, knowing she would be singled out only for admonition, never for applause. This face was a composite of many different women: familiar enough to pass unquestioned, unfamiliar enough to be ignored.

Even after so many years, Soledad was still amazed at how easy it was to be invisible. Sometimes she stood right in front of someone without being noticed.

As for her clothing, everything she wore was reversible. Turning her clothes inside out was effective, simple and far less uncomfortable than shifting the bones in her face.

Ido lived above his clinic, so there were two separate entrances. Soledad decided the entrance to his home would be safer. There would be less chance of bumping into a patient looking for out-of-hours treatment.

Traffic was heavy in this part of town. There seemed to be virtually no time when the streets were completely clear. Very useful; no one paid any attention to her on Ido's porch. Ido used a standard lock and key set-up, which Soledad thought matched his image as charmingly retro and eccentric. He was too smart to use an electronic lock, which could easily be disabled just by cutting the power.

In her extreme youth, Soledad had learned to pick just about any kind of mechanical lock with patient manipulation. Having a superior set of lock-picking equipment was a definite advantage, especially when there was a clock on the job. And when it came to burglary, there usually was.

Once inside, Soledad stood in the dark for a few moments, listening to the way things sounded in the house, the muffled traffic noise, her breathing, the air contained in the place, the lonely darkness. She committed all of it to memory, then put on her night-vision goggles.

To her left was the living room, to her right, the kitchen and, beyond that, the clinic. She went soundlessly through the kitchen to a hallway and was surprised by a spiral staircase. Chiren hadn't mentioned it was a spiral staircase. Soledad leaned on it slightly; there was no movement or rattling. Pretty solid for such an old house. The place looked like it could be pre-War. There were a surprising number of pre-War buildings in Iron City. Vector claimed parts of the Factory predated the War but Soledad took everything he said with a grain of salt.

She memorised the layout of the clinic, at first seeing it all at once, as a whole, and then in smaller sections, until the room was as much in her as she was in it. Not a very large room at all, crowded and, though not tidy, not disorganised. As she moved into the space, she passed a tray table on wheels with an arrangement of surgical instruments laid out on it, still in their sterile wrap; Ido liked the convenience of having anything he was actively working on within easy reach when he returned to it. Like those two arms on the table.

They were definitely for two different people. One of them was a strange creation she'd never seen before, with a forearm that divided in two at the elbow, opening like alligator jaws. The double forearm connected to an even weirder extended double hand, both sections with five finger-like appendages. She couldn't imagine what it was for—some kind of special sex aid, maybe? Ido wasn't known for that kind of thing, but maybe with his wife gone he was branching out.

Soledad bent over the table and set her vision for extreme close-up. She found a chip right in the spot Chiren had said was the controller position but it was plain old tech, not the super-chip Chiren had described. No super-chip in the other arm either, which was a standard labourer's device with attachments for tools.

If it's not in the clinic, try the cellar safe. It's set into the floor, Chiren had said, giving her the combination. Ido might have changed it but she didn't think so.

He hadn't.

The safe was full of drugs, in bags, in bottles, in bundles of flat patches, in pre-measured ampules. Everything the average Motorball wash-out needed to keep the party going. Soledad was afraid she was going to have to remove at least half of it to find what she was looking for. Then she spotted what looked like a small paper envelope stuck to one side of the safe.

There it was, and so thin she was afraid she'd snap it in two by accident. But it was oddly strong, like a small steel plate. She saw lines on both sides but they were indecipherable to her eye.

God, how the hell did something like this work?

Soledad put it in the small, plastic container Chiren had given her, started to put it in one of her pockets, then tucked it into her bra next to her right breast. If anybody reached for that, they'd come away shy one hand, regular or cyborg.

She made her way back upstairs quickly but without haste, careful to be as soundless as before. Stowing her goggles, she put her hand on the front door, then stopped. Something was off. She ran through her mental checklist but no flags went up—the house sounded right, felt right. She'd left both the cellar and the safe just as she'd found them. Ido wouldn't know it was gone till he went looking for it, and even then he wouldn't know when it had been stolen, or how, or by whom.

Soledad actually sorry for him. Life was hard all over—

That was it, she realised, running her hands over her face. She had let her face revert. Damn, she had to watch that.

It was just that changing her facial contours was uncomfortable at best, sometimes even painful, not just at the time but sometimes for a day or two after. It came with getting older. She'd been warned morphing wouldn't get easier with age, and the time was coming when she'd have to give it up and live with whatever she had.

But not tonight. She felt the bones and muscles move under her skin and knew when it was right again without checking her appearance in a mirror. Every face had its own unpleasantness, some more than others. But it could have been worse—this drab mask could have been her actual face. While the one the world called beautiful could have been too painful to maintain.

She slipped out of the house and went back to the taqueria. Ido returned an hour later with what looked like a bag full of servos and a preoccupied expression. As she watched, he stopped at the bottom of the steps to his front door and looked directly at her.

Soledad caught her breath, waiting for something to happen, for him to come over to her and say something. But he kept on staring and she realised he was staring at the taqueria, not her. Maybe he was hungry.

Ido wasn't all that bad-looking, Soledad thought. Too pale—too pale by half, even his *hair* was pale. But the lines on his face suggested he had smiled a lot in the past. Now he had an intense look, but that could have been the eyeglasses. He moved more gracefully than the average

Iron City male. Vector had said he wasn't from around here, but that was obvious. She wasn't sure she believed Vector's claim that Ido and Chiren were from Zalem, even with that gem in the middle of Chiren's forehead. If they were from Zalem, why would they leave? And why would they stay in Iron City, of all places? It made no sense.

Vector said Chiren had left Ido and that *did* make sense. Ido certainly hadn't thrown her out; Soledad knew men who threw women out and Ido wasn't one of them. Although he must have been pretty sick and tired of her bullshit to let her go. That woman was high maintenance; only Vector was rich enough to afford her.

Chiren, on the other hand, didn't have the look of someone who had traded up. More like someone who was convinced she had nothing because her life wasn't perfect.

Soledad chuckled silently. Maybe she was from Zalem after all.

CHAPTER 11

"If I'm lyin'—C major—" Sitting on the treatment table with his legs dangling over the side, the dark-skinned older man played a single chord using only the guitar's upper neck with easy skill. "I'm dyin'—C minor." He played another chord using only the lower neck. "And I don't play those lightly, Doc."

"I wouldn't either," said Ido, watching the movement of the adapted metal fingers on the frets. "How do you feel? Any conflict with your strumming hand?"

"Nope. You did a beautiful job. I'm playing better than I have in years." Hector's snow-white moustache spread with his smile. "But with one of those super-chips, I could play flamenco duets with myself."

"You can already play duets with yourself. You play flamenco just fine. I've heard you," Ido said. "I told you, every cyborg part would mean re-learning some things."

"*Si, si, si,*" Hector said, flexing the long extendable fingers of his right hand. "If not for you, I'd be sitting around with knuckles the size of hen's eggs, wishing I could still play. That was gross, man. I don't miss the old meat hands even a little bit. But if I had a super-chip—" His face looked pained. "I dunno how to make you understand what it would mean to me if I could keep improving. I could pour my years into my music instead of fighting physical decline."

"There comes a time for all of us when we stop improving. You'd have to face that even if you went Total Replacement," Ido told him, trying to be as gentle as possible. "Everybody faces decline in performance, not just musicians. Cyber-surgeons too."

"But don't you want to put it off as long as you can?" Hector asked.

Ido smiled. "Of course."

"Yet you're not enhanced," Hector said, gesturing at Ido's body. A moment later he looked embarrassed. "I didn't mean anything bad by that."

"No, actually, you've got a point," Ido said with a small laugh. "I suppose it may seem a bit strange that all my patients are enhanced but I'm not. Does that bother you, Hector?"

"Hell, no," said the guitar player.

"Do you think it bothers the other patients?" Ido asked him.

Hector thought for a second. "I never heard anything like that. Mostly we talk about Motorball in the waiting room. This time next year Jashugan is gonna be everybody's hero, better than Grewishka ever was because he won't get all debauched."

"I hope not," Ido said, momentarily serious. The last time he'd seen him, Grewishka had been climbing down an open manhole into the sewer, which was, according to legend, where he'd been born.

"You want me to ask around, see what anyone thinks about your not being enhanced?" Hector asked.

"Don't bother." Ido lowered the table so Hector could get off it more easily. "What I'd *really* like you to do is get back to your usual spot in the market. Then when I'm shopping for servos, I can brag to everyone that I know you personally."

Hector's smile turned apologetic. "As soon as I can make up for the time when I couldn't play—"

"Pay me as and when," Ido said kindly, talking over him. "You know where I am. And if you get any more drop-out, or if you have any problems at all, come back and I'll take care of it."

Ido would have forgotten about what Hector had called the super-chip if it weren't for his next patient, who couldn't talk about anything else. Tonio was a skater for a messenger/delivery service; he was still in his twenties and had had his feet replaced in his late teens. If Ido had found the person who had done the work, he might have gone after him with a weapon.

It wasn't simply that the work had been poorly done; it was also that Tonio had never been told his high-performance feet would put so much strain on his organic hips and knees that he would have to have his legs replaced altogether. Fortunately, Tonio wasn't upset at the idea of swapping out so much of his organic body for hardware.

"My boss says Mercury'll cover, like, three-quarters of the cost," Tonio said. "Even though I'm not going to their guy to have the work done."

"'*Their* guy'? Is that the same guy who replaced your feet?" Ido had to make an effort not to show his anger.

"Nah, a different guy," Tonio said. "The first guy went out of business and took off. Nobody knows where he is."

"Lucky for him," Ido muttered. He had Tonio lie down on the treatment table, which he elevated so he could take a close look at the connections. Tonio's feet had been attached at the base of his ankles with the bare minimum of connections; he was lucky they hadn't broken off. As it was, Ido could tell Tonio had significantly reduced sensation, to the point where he could have stepped on a spike without knowing it. Ido had done what he could to keep Tonio going for a while, but the poor guy couldn't go on for much longer.

"You send Mercury an invoice," Tonio was saying. "Although they'll probably pull their sixty-day billing routine on you. They make customers pay up front, but when *they* pay, it's always sixty days. Some kind of bookkeeping thing."

"You need to hold very still for this," Ido told him, rolling a small scanning machine over to the table.

Tonio lifted his head to see what he was doing. "You're not takin' 'em off now, are you?" he asked as Ido placed his feet in the scanning box.

"No, this is a scanner," Ido assured him. "This will give me a full three-hundred-and-sixty-degree image so I can see all the connections from the outside all the way down to the bone."

"But you're just gonna cut my legs off anyway," Tonio said.

"Yes, but not today. I want to see what kind of shape you're in now. Lie flat, Tonio, and don't move your feet."

Tonio obeyed. "I hope we can do the surgery soon. I'm not planning to skate for Mercury forever. That's no job for a grown-up."

"Oh?" Ido said. "What's a grown-up's job?"

"I'm gonna hire a trainer and try out for Motorball. And if I can get one of those super-chips, I'll have it made."

Ido paused in the act of rolling the scanner away from the treatment table. "What super-chip?"

"This guy who was at the last tryouts at the stadium had one and it was unbelievable. He was so fast everybody else looked like they were in slow-motion."

"What about his coordination?" Ido asked.

"This guy could probably juggle chainsaws and dance ballet—*real fast.* I'm definitely getting me one of those."

"Where?" Ido asked.

"Well… here, I hope." Tonio looked a bit puzzled. "You got stuff like that, right? New hardware and software, I mean. Even if you don't work in the pits any more, you get all the latest stuff, don't you?"

Ido took a breath. "If you want to go pro, you'll have to go TR," he told Tonio. "All Paladins are Total Replacement cyborgs. Flesh and blood wouldn't make it once around the track, even skipping the obstacle course."

"Fine with me," said Tonio. "A super-chip wouldn't work with meat anyway, would it?"

Ido winced at the term. "But it's not enough just to be a TR." He scooted the stool he was sitting on up to the head of the treatment table. "Not every TR is cut out for the game. And not every Paladin makes it big. Plenty end up as jobbers on the Factory practice team." *Or wash out before they play a single game*, he added silently.

"I know," Tonio said, raising himself up on one elbow. "You gotta be athletic and you need a competitive spirit. With a super-chip, I'd be the whole package, with whipped cream and a cherry. I mean, talk about physical enhancement! This is what it must have been like back when everybody had to walk everywhere and then somebody invented the car."

Ido decided giving Tonio a history lesson wouldn't help either of them.

"I dunno who made it, but Vector's got the chip now," Tonio went on. "This guy went through the practice team like they were wet paper. Vector signed him to one of his teams."

"And Vector would never have paid the Factory team to take a dive," said Ido sceptically.

"Sure he would!" Tonio laughed. "But not that night. You can bribe someone to go slow but not to go faster—not *that* much faster. Guy was so fast, they had to replay him in slow-mo so we could see what he did."

Ido was still sceptical. There were always rumours and gossip going around in Motorball, about new drugs, new players with unheard-of talents, new hardware that could make a statue into a contender for Final Champion. They always turned out to be exaggerations or wish-fulfilment fantasies from the fevered brains of hard-core fans who still missed the days when Grewishka's career had been on the upswing.

Ido made a few adjustments to Tonio's feet and worked out a schedule for the Replacement surgeries. Tonio was still talking about the super-chip as Ido saw him out.

The next patient was a twelve-year-old girl named Courage who had lost her right arm to bone cancer and needed her cyborg replacement resized after a growth spurt. She came in with her older sister, Spirit, who had lost her own right arm to the same cancer but had then chosen to replace her other arm and both legs. Spirit's torso was holding up well, and she had expressed no desire as yet to replace anything else. Eventually, aches and pains in the organic part of her body might change her mind. Ido kept her chart up to date, just in case. Both sisters were tremendously girly, which Ido enjoyed. It was as if something of his daughter's essence came with them, and for a little while she was slightly more present. Today he thought the sisters would provide a respite from all the talk about a hot new Motorball up-and-comer with hardware that couldn't possibly be real. But he'd forgotten that even the girliest girls could be Motorball fans.

"So I see the tryouts on the JumboTron in mid-town," Spirit said, perched beside her sister in one of the reclining chairs. She had dark-brown skin and thick waist-length braids held back by a wide gold-lamé hairband. These patients were too recent to have met his daughter, but

Ido knew she would have begged Spirit to braid her own, much thinner shoulder-length hair. Or maybe she'd have wanted locs like Courage.

"And I can*not* believe my *eyes*!" Spirit was saying. "I call Courage and tell her to meet me at the stadium before they wise up and start charging admission!"

"You can watch tryouts for free," Courage put in.

"Yes, I know," Ido murmured, making sure her shoulder was positioned correctly in the stereotactic frame. He could have put her on a treatment table but he'd discovered his younger patients tended to squirm less in the chair.

"I was *so glad* she called me," Courage said, "because I wouldn'ta believed her. I've never seen anybody that fast. And he's *dreamy*!"

"He's got it going on," Spirit agreed. "But I'd still like to meet Jashugan and Kinuba—"

"Dibs on Kinuba!" Courage giggled.

"No *way* would I *ever* let that guy get near you," Spirit said. "You can date Jashugan."

"No way! Going out with Jashugan would be like going out with *Dad*."

"I need you to hold still," Ido told her. "Unless you want your arm coming out of your ear."

"Just don't hook it onto my boob!" Courage giggled, her short locs bouncing.

"Courage! Shame on you!" Spirit said. "Talkin' to the doc like that! Look what you did; you made that nice man blush! I'm sorry," she added to Ido, who felt as if his face had burst into flames. "We're tryin' to raise her right, but kids these days. It's a losing battle. That's what our mom says, anyway."

Ido smiled; his face was still hot. He really had to get a nurse in here, he thought. In a civilised society, doctors never saw patients without a chaperone. Gerhad's arm was ready—he'd pay her a visit, either tonight before he went to his second job or tomorrow morning, before he opened the clinic.

"He's got the best name too," Courage said. "The guy with the super-chip."

"Oh?" Ido said politely, adding connectors to both the girl's shoulder and the cyborg arm.

"*Chase*," the girls said in rapturous unison.

"Vector's already signed him," Courage added. "Vector hogs all the good players."

"Kinuba won't sign with him," Spirit reminded her. "Hey, Doc, you used to work at the track, didn't you? I bet they miss you in the pits. You still go to games?"

"Nope," Ido said without looking away from what he was doing. *And please don't ask me why*, he added silently as he finished resizing the end of Courage's arm to her shoulder. Most people knew what had happened to his daughter, and almost all his regular patients knew Chiren had left him. Some thought the former had caused him to quit Motorball while others thought it had been the latter. He didn't care what they thought as long as he didn't have to talk about it.

"Courage, I'm sorry but you're still moving around too much," he said. "Please try to keep still. If I make a mistake with the wiring, you'll raise your hand every time you blink."

"Sorry, Doc," said Courage. "I'll be good—well, I'll *try*."

"Oh, Doc, I bet you never made a mistake in your whole life," Spirit chuckled. "You must be the smartest person in the world, or at least in Iron City."

"That's very nice of you, Spirit." Ido felt his face grow a bit warm again. "But there are many highly intelligent people around, and by the law of averages, a few of them would be smarter than I am."

"Doubt it," Spirit said, and laughed some more. "At least *I* never met any. Are they all hiding?"

"Yeah," Courage said. "From *you*. Anyone with half a brain sees you coming and they run for their lives."

"You're dead," Spirit promised her sister. "Seriously. As soon as your ass is outta that chair, your life is *over*."

Ido had to take a break from Courage's arm to re-wire part of a Factory worker's autonomic system to stop sudden bursts of hyperventilation. After ascertaining the man wasn't suffering from an undiagnosed anxiety disorder, Ido found the problem quickly—a faulty stretch of wire. He replaced it and all the wires immediately adjacent as well, just to be sure, then had the Factory worker remain in the clinic for another two hours for observation.

"If you say so, Doc," the man said, settling down in another of the reclining dental chairs. "But I can feel the difference. For a while there, I thought maybe some of the clowns at the southie distribution centre stuck a super-chip in my lungs or something."

Both Spirit and Courage perked up immediately. "You saw the tryouts too?" Spirit asked.

"Sure did," said the Factory worker. "I don't usually stay on for them but I'm glad I did. I couldn't believe it! Fastest thing I ever saw in my life. Some are saying this guy's gonna be as good as Grewishka, but I say he's gonna make everybody *forget* Grewishka…"

Ido managed to tune them out, but he couldn't do that with everyone. By the end of the day, which he had extended by two hours, he'd heard more gossip and rumours about super-chips than he could keep track of: the guy was a beta test for a whole new breed of super-Paladins; the super-chip had actually been swiped from a medical facility where the Factory were developing super-soldiers for the next war; the guy with the super-chip was a lost, mythical soldier from the United Republics of Mars; the Factory planned to replace Centurians with super-chipped cyborgs.

Ido finally gave up and took a look at some of the video from the tryout, figuring he was going to see what looked like someone doing gymnastics on a high dose of amphetamines, possibly with a psychedelic sweetener. What he saw made all the tiny hairs on the back of his neck stand up.

The cyborg on the track looked to be about twenty, with short, spiky black hair and tan skin. It was hard to get a good look at his face because he moved as if he were on fast-forward, but without the jerkiness of a speeded-up video. If this wasn't some kind of trick, someone had done what he had been trying to do. Someone else had made a chip that would match the cyborg body to the speed of thought in the organic brain.

Ido had become so frustrated with the runaway problem that he'd decided he needed a break and locked the chip in the safe for a while. Using it to integrate only one or two cyborg parts with an organic body had worked well, but only for a while. The early results from the first virtual experiment had made him hopeful. But then, with no warning at all, the chip began anticipating movements *too* quickly, until the chip was guiding movement rather than a human will. Ido tried different configurations and settings but the chip kept rushing ahead of the human brain.

Giving the chip an entire cyborg body to integrate with an organic nervous system seemed to work better—but again, only temporarily. It simply took longer for the chip to reach the runaway state. How much longer seemed to vary. In virtual experiments, it might function for the autonetic equivalent of two months, but that seemed to be the maximum amount of time. Virtual experiments in different neural configurations showed it might be only a few days before the chip went into runaway.

Normally when Ido took a break from a project, it was for a week at most. It had been two weeks since he'd put the chip in the safe and he still thought he needed a bit more distance. He was starting to think he was attempting the impossible—the materials to hand just weren't good enough. But apparently he was wrong. Someone had done what he couldn't.

Chiren, of course. It had to be Chiren.

The chip hadn't been a collaborative project but she'd done a little work on it with him. She'd known what he'd been trying to do and what materials he'd been working with. Vector could provide her with much better materials and a better-equipped lab. As a result, anything Ido could do, she could better. And sooner. And probably in an array of attractive colours too.

Ido wouldn't have minded so much except she'd done it for Vector, as if there was nothing more important than pleasing him. The way she was going all out for the king of Zalem's trashcan, anyone would think he had more to offer her than trash.

But he did—he already had. Vector could give her what he skimmed out of Zalem shipments. He could give her *pre-trash.*

After the last patient left, Ido decided to postpone seeing Gerhad till the morning and go directly to his second job instead.

Tonight's big bounty was on a nasty piece of tin who had been preying on couples. Any kind of couple—old, young, same-sex, hetero. Two friends walking together were safe. But any display of affection, whether it was kissing or even just holding hands, called for the death penalty.

So far the Un-Coupler, as the marker called him, had attacked six couples. Only two people had survived—a man from the second couple and a woman from the fifth. Neither remembered much about what had happened, although the woman had been able to provide a vague description of the attacker.

Looking at the locations of where the victims had been found gave Ido an idea of the Un-Coupler's preferred territories. He used a few different places but his favourite killing ground was near the ruins of the old cathedral. He hadn't dropped any bodies there lately but he was bound to go back there soon. Ido decided to see if that would be tonight.

The Un-Coupler was good for 55,000 credits, a nice sum that would sustain the clinic as well as a nurse's salary. There might even be enough to spare for new materials so Ido could start over with the chip.

Damn that squeaky wheel, Ido thought as he wheeled the case through the late-night streets. He could resize a twelve-year-old's cyborg arm, give a guitar player a new start, and fix a man's autonomic nervous system. But he couldn't get that goddam wheel to stop squeaking. Someday it was going to drop him in the shit in a way he never saw coming.

Ido paused to get his bearings, then headed towards the jagged silhouette of the ruined cathedral. The Un-Coupler liked the cathedral because of the stones. They were nice and heavy, good for crushing heads. Ido wheeled his case around to the far side of the cathedral and found a patch of scrubby grass in the shadows near an outside wall where he could lay the case on its side to open it.

One of the other Hunter-Warriors, that vain son of a bitch Zapan, had told Ido any weapon that had to be assembled was a ridiculous waste of time and effort. Death could creep up behind him before he could stick tab A into slot B. He advised Ido to get himself either another weapon or another line of work.

Ignoring Zapan had never got anyone killed, so Ido went with that. He already had another line of work. As for weapons, there were an astonishing number of devices made for the express purpose of taking people out of this world. Ido had tried just about all of them from every arms dealer in town, legal and illegal. Then he'd gone home and made the Rocket Hammer.

Constructing an instrument for killing went against everything he stood for as a doctor. However, the murder of his daughter had gone against everything he had stood for as a father, so maybe that evened things out.

Well, no, not really. The clinic was supposed to even things out, but there was nothing that could ever balance the murder of his daughter. He was simply doing the only thing left for him to do. He took her killer off the streets. Then he took other killers off the streets and hoped that would save other parents from the miserable perversity of having a child die before them. Only a Hunter-Warrior could cure that condition, not a doctor.

Ido wasn't sure where the idea of the Rocket Hammer had come from or what had suggested it to him. He'd sketched it on paper, then used a design-engineering program on the computer. It had been hard to construct, harder than anything else he'd ever done—well, until the chip.

Ido took the two main components out of the foam-lined case. The lower part of the handle had the controls; the upper part included the hammer head. As he put them together, he felt the handle vibrate in his grip. The sensation made him feel strong. He tightened his grip on it as he looked up its length to the head.

The head had come to him practically in a vision. One side was blunt, like a mallet, made for smashing. The other side was a shiny, extra-hard, thick piece of metal that tapered to a nasty point, made for irreparable damage. The blunt side had vents for propulsion, so that when he swung pointy side first, there was more in the blow than the power of his arms. There were also a few small motors on the blunt side; a control on the handle would turn one blow into several, like a jackhammer.

The Rocket Hammer was heavier than he'd intended, and the controls made it more complicated than almost any other weapon save for McTeague's cyborg Hellhounds. It was easier to transport in the case, but that was all right. It made him look like some harmless eccentric rather than a Hunter-Warrior. Marks ran from Zapan and others like him, but they seldom gave Ido a second look; he could take them by surprise.

Some marks never ran from anyone; they thought they were invincible. Ido heard the voices coming through the cathedral, a man and woman pleading and a loud, jeering laugh, high and shrill enough to break glass.

It never ceased to amaze Ido that, although killers came in all shapes and sizes, they all had a compulsion to play with their victims for the sheer sadistic pleasure of it.

Ido moved the suitcase up against the cathedral wall and waited to see if the cyborg planned to kill his victims inside or drag them outside and work them over a little more. Holy places and hallowed ground weren't things most psychos worried about. The Un-Coupler probably didn't even know what a cathedral was. Just that it had lots of heavy stones for crushing skulls with.

A man suddenly flew through one of the arched gaps that had once been a window and landed on the ground with a cry of pain. As he struggled to get up, Ido saw he was at least sixty-five. He got to his knees but he was too off-balance to make it to his feet. His shoulder was dislocated. Ido winced in sympathy—it must have hurt like hell, even more than his broken nose which was bleeding so much, the man had to be on blood thinners. He needed a hospital *now.*

The man spotted Ido in the shadows and opened his mouth. Ido shook his head emphatically and put a finger to his lips, then hefted the Rocket Hammer so the man would know he was a Hunter. A second later, the woman tumbled out of the window onto the ground. She made a low grunt but didn't cry out. The man tried to stand up again but she got to her feet first and went to him with the tell-tale movements of someone with cyborg legs. She could have run away easily, gone for help, but she wouldn't leave him. Ido felt a pang and told himself to toughen up; these people needed him to save them, not envy their relationship.

The Un-Coupler leaped out of the window and landed directly in front of them. "I don't know if I've tenderised you enough yet," the cyborg said in a high-pitched demented squeal. "Old meat's so *tough*—like beef jerky with metal. That'd be *you*, sweetheart," he added, gesturing at the woman.

She picked up an irregularly shaped chunk of stone almost as large as her head and held it in both hands, getting ready to heave it at him, for all the good that would do.

"*Ooooh!* I can *use* that!" enthused the Un-Coupler. "Toss it to me!" His fingers clicked as he flexed them. He was going to kill the woman first— Ido could see that as plainly as if there was a glowing sign over his head spelling it out. He'd kill the woman first to torment the husband, tearing her limbs off like a nasty kid with a fly. Then he'd crush her head with the rock she was holding. The sound would be obscene.

And the guy wouldn't budge. She hadn't left him; he wasn't going to leave her either. Not that he could. He was in agony, trembling, his knees about to buckle. They'd die for each other and with each other, and the

Un-Coupler hated them so much for that he could barely contain himself.

They'd suffered enough. Ido stepped out of the shadows with the Rocket Hammer. "Hey, tin can!" he yelled. "How about you and I go a few rounds instead?"

The Un-Coupler whirled on him and Ido's heart jumped and accelerated into high gear. The cyborg was a piecemeal mess. No part of him matched any other part—even his eyes were two different colours and sizes. One arm was an exposed framework that seemed to have been jerry-rigged in a hurry; the other was carved to resemble organic musculature, ending in a scythe rather than a hand. His right leg was such a mess of cobbled-together parts, Ido was surprised it worked. His left leg was a single limb that Ido had seen before, on a member of the Factory Motorball practice team. The player himself had vanished the day he'd been cut and never reappeared. He must have parted himself out... or the leg was actually the last original part. Ido really hoped it wasn't.

A fragment of history popped into Ido's mind: the notion of spontaneous generation. The people of a less knowledgeable time had believed that mice sprang into existence from a dirty shirt in a box and mud at the bottom of a lake turned into fish. Ido could almost believe that the Un-Coupler and others like him congealed out of the trash pile combined with bad air and hopelessness in the shadow of Zalem.

Ido shoved the thought away as the Un-Coupler squealed and lunged for him.

He swung the Rocket Hammer blunt end first and knocked the cyborg's legs out from under him. "Go! Run! To a hospital!" Ido yelled at the couple who were just standing on the sidewalk, transfixed. The next blow brought the blunt end down on the cyborg's composite leg, which came apart in an explosion of metal pieces.

"I'll kill you!" the cyborg screamed and made a swipe at him. Ido ducked and gave him a jackhammer blow to one shoulder. The cyborg's arm popped out to reveal wires and cables.

Ido glanced at the spot where the couple had been. Correction: still were. *Dammit.* As the Un-Coupler tried to get to his feet, Ido gave him another jackhammer blow, this one to the centre of his torso.

"Go to a hospital!" Ido yelled at the couple angrily.

The woman started pushing the man down the sidewalk. They were in shock, Ido knew, but he couldn't help feeling a little annoyed anyway. Did they really think they were safe just because he was there beating up their attacker? Didn't they know they needed medical attention? Didn't they know they had to get to a safe place?

A safe place? As if there really were such a thing.

Ido slammed the cyborg's chest again and the armour fractured into pieces. But he was still threatening to kill Ido, as if he had a chance of doing such a thing. Ido smashed the other knee, breaking his leg in half.

The Un-Coupler was on his back now, still making swipes in Ido's direction with his good arm. Ido smashed his hips, destroying the pelvic connectors, and raised the hammer to smash his lower torso.

Now *who's playing with his prey?* a small voice whispered nastily in his mind. *Or is this really your idea of fun?*

Ido turned the hammer around and brought the pointy end down onto the Un-Coupler's neck with propulsion. The cyborg's head separated from his body with a wet, meaty noise that made Ido queasy. He put it in his bounty bag, then cleaned off the Rocket Hammer and put it away.

He dropped the case at home before going to the bounty headquarters at the Factory to turn in the Un-Coupler's head. The deckman didn't thank him or compliment him on a job well done for getting a dangerous killer off the street. Deckmen never did. They looked like trashcans with cartoon-like faces on them, and no one knew what they were for other than to creep people out. Ido didn't care, as long as he got the promised bounty.

He thought he'd been out all night, but there were still some dark hours left.

There always were.

CHAPTER 12

"What else do you work on?"

Chiren looked up from the 3-D schematic floating over her worktable to the young guy standing beside it. Which assistant was this, Dave? George? Oh, right—Theo. He was the one with the freckles across the bridge of his nose.

"Excuse me?" Chiren asked, her tone stiff and formal.

"I was just wondering," said Theo. He was hairless—all the assistants were, lacking even eyebrows and eyelashes. Vector had told them it was the only way to maintain proper laboratory hygiene. As if that were real and not something Vector had made up to assert his ownership. "Her" assistants were in fact *his* property; his property didn't even grow hair without his permission.

If the assistants ever wondered why she could have hair without violating proper laboratory hygiene, they kept it to themselves. They seldom asked any questions that weren't essentially some form of *How high?* or *What colour?* For all the personality they showed, they might have been deckmen, and if Vector could have figured out how to make them serve the same purpose, he'd have replaced all the humans already. Except her, of course—unless the Factory developed a special lady-faced deckman with both cyber and bedroom skills. Then she might be out of a job.

"What were you 'just wondering'?" she asked the assistant, even more stiffly.

It wasn't always easy to read people who had no facial hair, but she could tell Theo wished he'd just kept his mouth shut and enjoyed the boredom instead of finding something to do.

"Uh, what you thought you might need for tonight's round of upgrades," he said, trying to look like the kind of helpful employee she wouldn't ask Vector to get rid of.

"No, it wasn't," Chiren said firmly. "What else do I work on besides Paladins—that's what you meant, isn't it?"

Poor Theo couldn't help squirming under her gaze. "I know you used to do a lot of general cyber-medicine," he said.

"At my ex-husband's clinic," Chiren prodded. "Before I came here full-time. Before I lost my daughter."

"I didn't mean to get so p-personal with you," the assistant said, his expression a mix of misery and desperation, "or to bring up things you don't care to talk about with people like me."

"People like you? What kind of people are those?" Chiren asked, deciding to be merciless. "People I barely know? People I employ to wash beakers and sterilise instruments? Or people who have the bad judgment to try getting familiar with their betters?"

Theo was staring at the floor. "Um… I'm gonna go wash some beakers now."

"Good idea. We have lab hygiene to maintain." She turned back to the schematic. "Wash *all* the beakers. When you're done, wash everything else."

"Yes, Dr Chiren." The assistant practically ran for the storage closet.

That had been mean even for her, Chiren thought. Nonetheless, every cat needed a scratching post, and every soul needed to know which they were—cat or post.

It was good to know where you fit in, where you stood. Vector was king of the trashcans. She was here to keep him on his trashcan throne and to be rewarded later for a job well done. The assistants were merely tools, and it was best for all concerned that they didn't get any stupid ideas, like thinking they knew her just because they worked for her. Breaking in new shoes didn't mean the shoes *knew* you.

Which reminded her: after seven straight days of wear, these damned stilettos were still pretty rigid. This was the most uncomfortable pair yet, but Vector loved her in stilettos and kept giving them to her. She was tired of them; if you'd seen one pair of stilettos, you'd pretty much seen them all.

This was true of a lot of things in Iron City. Only Motorball held her interest. Building champions was the only thing that didn't bore her stupid, the one thing that she could stand to do while she waited for Vector to make good on his promise to send her home to Zalem.

Sometimes, however, even that could be a pain in the neck; the shoulders too. Chiren sat back and rolled her head slowly around on her neck to loosen the muscles. Without having to be asked, Ido would have come over to rub her shoulders, starting with the muscles at the base of her neck and going all the way down to her shoulder blades. Just remembering how it felt made her sigh. The only person she allowed to touch her physically now was Vector and he didn't do massages outside the bedroom. He'd have hired a massage therapist if she'd asked but he wouldn't have allowed Chiren to keep one on standby in the lab.

What she really needed, however, wasn't a massage. She needed help from someone who was her intellectual equal and, in terms of lateral thinking and application, her superior. There was only one person like that in Iron City and Vector wasn't going to like it. She didn't like it herself.

On the other hand, she knew Vector still wanted Ido back. If Ido had come to him asking to work the pits again, Vector would have gladly taken him back. He would have hemmed and hawed to see if he could make Ido beg for it, and he'd have shorted him on salary, but he'd have taken him back.

Maybe if Ido saw her fancy set-up, he might even change his mind about Motorball. Ido was still grieving, and he would never stop blaming himself. But maybe the idea of having the right equipment, the latest tech, and the best materials and resources, would get through to the scientist in him. Nothing could extinguish that spark—he'd be Dr Dyson Ido, cyber-surgeon, until the day he died.

Chiren dialled her phone.

Ido had wanted to say no and hang up on her like a sane, sensible person. But Chiren would never have called him unless she'd truly needed help and had no other choice—this *was* Iron City after all. The lonely man he was still craved to be a husband, even if he could no longer be a father; that man was also hoping Chiren had called because she missed him.

The sane, sensible man in him said this was a sad, futile hope that would only enlarge the sucking chest wound that was his grief. But the lonely man wasn't listening.

Even if he did say no, she would only call back and keep calling until she got him to say yes. As a result, he would go to her believing even harder in the fairy tale that she wanted him and he'd be in even worse condition when she eventually thanked him for his help and sent him away. Better he should go to her while he was strong enough to recover without it affecting his work in the clinic. His patients shouldn't suffer for his foolishness.

But he refused to work at the stadium. He hadn't been there since losing their daughter and he couldn't, wouldn't, go back.

Chiren told him it wasn't a problem. There was a practice going on tonight. It was impossible to work properly with trainers yelling and players complaining and then pestering her about some new tech they'd heard about that didn't even exist. She gave him the address of her new laboratory.

Ido wasn't thrilled about going to the Factory, even if her lab was actually in an outbuilding and not the main headquarters. But at least he wouldn't be carrying a couple of severed heads in a bounty bag. Plus, Chiren's lab wouldn't have Centurians lining the walls waiting for a threat they could shoot to pieces.

Ido arrived to find Vector's top team on the premises. Apparently it was Upgrade Night before the next game. Ido no longer kept track, so he had no idea if it was a season game, an exhibition, or a play-off. The Paladins were their usual rowdy selves and Chiren had curtained off half the lab to make a waiting area, where they could hang out, watch videos and bullshit each other while her weird, bald assistants waited on them hand and foot, or hand and wheel, and made sure they didn't bother her.

There was an actual waiting room outside the lab that looked a lot more comfortable. Chiren told Ido she no longer used it because she couldn't trust the players to stay there. When they got bored or restless, they decamped for more interesting environs. Keeping them in the lab made them feel less like they were waiting.

The lab certainly was big enough. Even with a third of it given to keeping Paladins amused, it was four times the size of his clinic, not counting closet space, and equipped with things he hadn't thought were available in Iron City—probably because they weren't. How the hell did Vector get away with all that skimming? Apparently the man had low friends in high places; somebody up there—in Zalem—liked him.

Which made Ido wonder what Vector could possibly do that would make them so generously grateful. What could Vector give them that they couldn't get faster or bigger or in customised colours and styles?

Not "them"—the man in charge. Nova. All Nova wanted was gratification and, right now, he was getting it from Vector.

Ido's stomach rolled over. Eventually Nova would get bored with him. Someday Vector would reach into his bag of tricks and come up empty—there would be nothing else he could do to entertain Nova. That wouldn't be a good day for Vector.

But that day hadn't arrived. Vector was still the king of the trashcan and Nova's favourite toy. Dance, puppet, dance. Ido's gaze fell on Chiren, who had a ribcage and spine set up in a stereotactic frame. *That's entertainment.*

"Have you heard a word I said?" Chiren asked him, but not unkindly— Ido knew she wouldn't bite his head off while she needed him.

"Yes," Ido lied, "but it's pretty complicated. Let's go over it one more time, in case there was something I missed."

She knew he was lying but she also knew he would have asked her to go over everything again anyway so he could pick out mistakes and inconsistencies. Chiren hated when he did that, but tonight this was why he was here. She turned the frame around so the spine was facing them and opened each section of the backbone.

As she began to explain what she wanted to do, Ido realised he'd heard a lot of this before. Chiren had been trying to do something similar back when he'd first met her in Zalem's medical training programme.

He'd told her at the time that changing the spinal cord required changing the brain, and that was where the whole thing became a mess. The vertebrate brain had evolved to work with the spinal cord in a certain way, and the spinal cord took its form from the brain. It was a chicken–egg case of mutual influence further complicated by the neocortex. And if that wasn't enough, every brain–spine configuration was unique; no two people had the same one.

This was, in part, why neural enhancements for sensory organs like eyes and ears weren't possible for everyone; even those who could adapt to enhanced vision and hearing sometimes had side effects like synaesthesia. Supposedly, only the United Republics of Mars had ever succeeded in making extensive changes to the brain and spinal cord, and that was Lost technology now. The closest anyone had come in three hundred years was the Zalem bio-engineer who had successfully grown a spinal cord in a vat.

It took some time for Ido to argue Chiren into just extending and increasing the number of connections to and from each area of the spine. It would be painstaking work but it could be done without destroying brain architecture and disabling the person. In the meantime, the Paladins became rowdier in their little corral. They had no way to blow off steam. If they'd been at the stadium, they'd have hit the track, and each other. There was a gym, Chiren said, but it had been flooded when one of the Paladins had used a water pipe as a chin-up bar. She had no idea who—they had knocked out the surveillance on the first day and no one was talking. Vector had shrugged it off; at least it hadn't been a waste pipe.

"Who's here tonight?" Ido asked her, jerking a thumb at the other end of the room.

"The usual suspects," Chiren said. "Ajakutty, Crimson Wind, Claymore. God, Claymore is always in for repairs. The Jay, Low-Rider, Baby, and a few others."

"Not Wheelstein?" Ido said.

Chiren shook her head. "He trashed the Kansas Bar one too many times. Vector had to cut him from the team. Why? Is he some special interest of yours?"

"Just curious," Ido replied, frowning. Without the safety net of a team, Wheelstein was all too likely to end up living under the causeway and selling off parts of himself for the drugs he wasn't entitled to any more. It wouldn't end well for Wheelstein or anyone around him. "What about the new guy—Chase?"

"He's at the track with his trainer." Chiren's tone was still pleasant, but now it had an ever-so-slight hint of impatience. "Come on, are you still with me here? That *is* what I'm paying you for."

Paying? Ido blinked at her. "I thought you just wanted me to help you out."

"Yes, but I hardly expect you to work for free. We *are* professionals, after all."

"That we are," Ido said with false cheer and busied himself with connecting the first layer of dermis to the left side of the ribcage so Chiren wouldn't guess from the expression on his face that he had come to her with no thought of payment.

"This is superior skin," he said as he worked. "Did you develop it yourself?"

"I used some of our research," she said, "but it needed a lot of work to make it into what you're handling now."

"We'd give you the name of a supplier," a man added, "but there isn't one. The skin's proprietary."

Ido told himself he was too busy to turn around and look at Vector, who had entered the room quietly for a change. And really, applying the first layer of dermis wasn't the most difficult procedure in the world but it was fiddly. Leaving bubbles would be uncomfortable for the cyborg, an itch that couldn't be scratched.

"Vector, I *told* you: this is a *scientist-only* area tonight," Chiren said archly. "I'm sorry but you'll have to leave."

"Just passin' through," Vector told her. "I'm here to see how my champions are doing."

"Make it brief, and use the exit down there, please," Chiren said, a superior speaking to a clueless warm-body breathing air meant for the elite. "This work takes a lot of concentration."

"I beg your pardon," Vector said in a pleasant, easy tone that told Ido Chiren was going to pay for being high-handed with the king of the trashcan in front of her ex. "It's just that I expected you'd be further along." Vector strolled towards the curtained area, and Ido was unable to resist a quick glance. The king of the trashcan had a sense of style that wouldn't have been out of place on Zalem and the looks to carry it off. Ido considered this proof positive that the world had gone too far wrong to ever go right again.

"It's his team," Chiren said to Ido in a low voice as the Paladins gave Vector a hero's welcome.

"His lab too," Ido replied before he could think better of it. He turned to her, intending to apologise, and heard himself say, "Is this what you want?"

Her gaze seemed to bore into him; blue ice, so cold it burned. "It's exactly what I want." Pause. "You're doing it perfectly. Keep up the good work."

"I will," he said, faintly emphasising the *I* as he turned back to the dermis. That would teach him, he thought.

"Vector has been extremely generous," Chiren said in a lofty tone. "His generosity has allowed me to develop some amazing things besides this dermis."

He considered trying to talk her out of a few sheets for his burn patients—there weren't many, but this would have been miraculous for them—and decided against it. It would be just like Vector to find the patients, throw them in the back of his limo, and bring them here to have Chiren remove the stuff. Because it was *proprietary.*

To Ido's relief, Vector honoured Chiren's request. He must have felt it was more important to keep Chiren sweet than it was to assert his dominance, at least for the moment. He'd probably take it out on her later, Ido thought with a pang; men like Vector always did. And, he realised, with another, more intense pang, Chiren knew it.

Vector's arrival perked up the Paladins. They had been quieting down, but their collective energy level rose immediately as they bombarded him with questions about the line-up for the next game: would there be a new training schedule now; was the new guy gonna start right away or would he still be in training; and when could they all get their own super-chips because imagine what they could do with that kind of speed plus their skill and experience, they'd be *unbeatable.*

The super-chip discussion continued after Vector was gone, with the players talking about the new player's unprecedented speed. Chase was a good name for him—but it wasn't just skating speed on the track; it was reaction time and reflexes, and those new parts he had probably helped a lot. Sure was getting quick to anger, though.

"Pay them no mind," Chiren said as they finished covering the ribcage area with the first metal layer. "Gossip is the real fuel the Game runs on. If they couldn't gossip, they couldn't play."

That went without saying, Ido thought, and they'd both been around long enough to know it. He smoothed away a few small bubbles near the bottom of the ribcage, listening to the Paladins. No wonder Chiren had been happy to keep him out of the stadium, even though it meant having a lab full of rambunctious Paladins running her assistants ragged with requests for food, drink and entertainment. She didn't want him checking out the new guy's hardware.

And now she was telling tell him not to pay attention to Motorball scuttlebutt. The thing about scuttlebutt, though, was it tended to range far and wide. These guys could barely talk about anything else except the new guy's super-chip that gave him super-reaction time, super-reflexes, and super-coordination to match. Like he was born living at a faster rate than everyone else.

"Sounds like you've really outdone yourself with your latest enhancement," Ido said to Chiren after a bit.

"I outdo myself every day," Chiren said absently. She was running a diagnostic on the part of the torso they had just finished applying skin to.

"I'm referring to this chip you've developed," Ido said. "In case you need me to narrow it down."

Chiren finished the diagnostic, then paused. Ido could practically see the wheels and gears turning in her mind while she decided what to tell him and whether she should lie a little or a lot. Sometimes Ido wished he'd never come to know her so well. Maybe they'd have had more to talk about.

"It's just a little something I've been working on with this spine," she said finally. "When I'm not making repairs or doing upgrades or swapping out lungs and livers. Right now I'm testing a prototype." She beckoned him to join her at her desk and put up a 3-D display. "Since you're here anyway, let me ask: do those numbers look right to you?"

Ido felt himself go cold as he stared at the display. Well, he'd expected her to lie to him, he told himself. She'd done a lot to disguise it, rearranging some things and adding others that didn't seem to belong, but he knew he was looking at a partial schematic of his own chip. She had already installed it in the spine, and the discussion about brain–spinal cord arrangements had actually been her way of getting advice on the best way to utilise it.

Had she really thought she could fool him? And how could she have possibly known he'd gone back to work on it after she left?

Hugo.

Ido's heart sank. Chiren might have overheard him talking about the chip to his friends, trying to show off how much he knew. Or maybe Vector had taken advantage of Hugo running his mouth the way kids do.

He tried to remember what he'd told Hugo in all the thinking out loud he'd done. He'd just been running his mouth too, talking it up like it was a miracle. Hugo hadn't known about the problems. Ido had never gone into detail about those, just extolled the possibilities. Because nobody ever waxed rhapsodic about all the things they couldn't get right.

That'll teach you—again, said a small voice in his mind; it belonged to the sane, sensible man who hadn't wanted to come here.

"You can, can't you?" Chiren was saying.

Ido looked at her blankly.

"Stay a little longer?" she said with exaggerated patience. "You can stay a little longer and help me with these upgrades, can't you?"

Ido gave a weak laugh. "Are you putting in super-chips?"

"Don't *you* start." Chiren rolled her eyes. "If I hear the term 'super-chip' one more time I'll go nuts and kill everyone I see."

But he could only get through two upgrades before he could no longer stand to be in the same room with her. He apologised, telling her his lack of sleep was finally catching up with him.

"But you're an insomniac," Chiren said, frowning. "You never sleep."

"Sometimes I do," he replied. "I'm sorry, but I'm ready to drop where I stand. And I don't think Vector would like it if I spent the night with you. Even if it was in your lab."

Chiren looked as if she were about to argue, then shrugged. "You helped me with the main problem. I can handle the rest of the upgrades myself."

"Great." He headed towards the exit at the other end of the room, where Ajakutty was just letting himself out.

"Hey, *wait!*" Chiren called after him.

He stopped and turned. Did she know he was onto her?

"Send me an invoice," she said.

Ido was blank again. An invoice for what—the chip?

"We'll pay your going rate," Chiren went on. "Whatever it is. I'll round up to all night. I'm sure you—the clinic can use it."

"Oh, yeah. Thanks," Ido said and hurried out, hoping he hadn't lost Ajakutty. Fortunately, the Paladin had gone only half a block. Definitely not equipped with a super-chip, Ido thought as he caught up with him.

"Hey, Aja," Ido said. "What about this new guy and his so-called super-chip?"

"What do you mean, Doc?" Ajakutty looked mildly puzzled. "You musta seen the videos."

"Yes, but how does he seem to *you*?" Ido asked him. "You know, up close and personal."

Ajakutty shrugged his big shoulders. "He's a whole new brand of fast."

"Yes, I saw." Ido tried not to show impatience. "What else can you tell me about him?"

"Other than he makes the rest of us look like we're standing still?" Ajakutty said. "Not much."

Apparently that was all he was going to get tonight, Ido thought. He thanked the cyborg and started across the street.

"Hey, Doc, wait," Ajakutty said. "Is there any chance—any chance at all—you might come back to the pits? We sure need you."

"Sorry," Ido said and walked swiftly around the nearest corner before the Paladin could say any more.

Ido told himself he was too tired to think straight about anything, that he could open the safe after a few hours' sleep. Whatever he'd find now would be there tomorrow. His resolve lasted all of fifteen minutes before he went down to the cellar.

He found only what he already knew. The chip was gone. But he had no way to know when it had been taken—

Wrong—he did. It would be logged to his phone, even though he'd muted the alarm, which was the stupidest thing he'd done lately. Or ever. If he hadn't, he'd have known the very moment it happened. Ido looked at his phone and decided that he didn't have to know now. Maybe tomorrow or the next day, or next year, when he could better withstand one more thing to feel bad about.

CHAPTER 13

"Some people you only have to tell once and they get the message," Vector said to Hugo as they sat in the back of the limo. The clink of ice in his glass as he took a sip sounded rich somehow and the amber liquid looked even richer. Hugo sipped from the small bottle of soda Vector had given him, unconsciously mirroring the man's actions. So far he was still on the seat and he intended to stay there.

"Sadly, our northland friends don't know what's good for them," Vector went on. "Not even after I put two of them out at Farm Forty-Three to pick asparagus." He looked at Hugo with pleasant curiosity. "You like asparagus?"

"I love it, sir," Hugo said. He'd never had any.

Vector nodded approvingly. "It's a food for the discriminating palate. It can be harvested by machine but it bruises the stalks and damages some of the nearby plants that aren't ready to be picked." Vector leaned towards Hugo and lowered his voice a little. "The Factory are all cheapskates, tighter than a duck's ass. They won't spend money on a better harvester. They'd rather cross their stingy fingers and hope some labourer has a hardware brainwave and builds them one for free." Vector sipped again. "But you never heard that from me."

"No, sir," Hugo promised, shaking his head solemnly.

"But asparagus is best picked by hand anyway," Vector said, sitting back. "It's the only way to really do justice to it. You know, in ancient times—" Vector paused for another sip "—asparagus was reserved for kings. Commoners weren't good enough." Vector smiled at Hugo. "But I doubt I'm telling *you* anything you don't know."

Hugo dipped his head in a non-committal way. For all he knew, Vector was spinning him a line. But it was his limo. If he wanted to tell fairy tales about vegetables all day, Hugo was all ears; it might make Vector feel generous.

"It's hard work, even for a cyborg tailored to the job. But hard work makes people feel *good*." Vector had another sip from his glass and Hugo had a drink of his dark-brown soda. Hugo was a bit leery of drinks he couldn't see through but this tasted pretty good. Vector said it was from his private stock of something called "coke". Weird name but it had a nice bite.

"Anyway, two of the cabal are picking asparagus," Vector said. "And waiting to have their lumbar regions replaced while they contemplate the folly of their misdeeds. I thought this would make their cronies do likewise." For a long moment Vector stared down at his glass. Hugo hoped he wasn't supposed to contemplate the folly of his own misdeeds. He was tired of thinking about all the ways he'd screwed up.

"I was wrong," Vector said after a bit. "I'm not wrong often and I don't like it. But when I am, I have to take action. I may not want to, but it's my responsibility. People in Iron City have been let down too many times. Their leader can't be one more big disappointment." He looked at Hugo with an expression so serious it was frightening. "You see what I mean, don't you?"

Hugo nodded, trying to look like he knew something. "If there's something I can do to help, sir, just ask."

"Good to know I can count on you, kid." Vector's heartfelt tone only increased Hugo's anxiety. People always sounded like that right before they threw you under a bus for your own good. Whoever had talked his father into his first cyborg replacement had probably sounded like that.

"Our northland friends have regrouped, even though there are only four of them now. Five, if you count the cyber-surgeon."

Hugo was confused for a moment. "You mean the one that built the TR—"

Vector put up a hand and Hugo promptly shut up. "A designer with a lot of potential but no judgment whatsoever. Speed doesn't mean much if a person can't stand up to the aggression and, ah, physical demands that make Motorball what it is."

"I agree completely," Hugo said.

Vector looked at him with a faintly surprised expression and Hugo realised that hadn't been a cue to speak. Mortified, he dropped his gaze to his nearly empty bottle.

"The northland cabal's learned nothing," Vector continued after a moment. "I thought their pet cyber-surgeon would have taken her act on the road, off to the Badlands. Instead, she's hiding out in somebody's cellar, working on their new project. Unfortunately—for them—*I* know what that is." Vector put down his glass and held out his arm so Hugo could see the pictures on his phone screen.

Hugo wasn't sure what he was looking at as Vector scrolled through the photos, whether these were real, or extremely detailed artist's concepts. Vector kept scrolling, and eventually Hugo saw these were photographs of an actual cyborg, with on-board attachments coming out of his forearms and biceps and even his thighs. This cyborg didn't swap out tools—it carried extra limbs with whatever gear was required. One foldaway arm-within-an-arm was equipped like a standard all-purpose toolkit.

"You see the problem, don't you, Hugo."

It wasn't a question, but this time Vector wanted a response. "Well, yeah," Hugo said, wondering how to bluff. "All that stuff—"

"Is too damned much. Exactly! Got it in one!" Vector gave him an attaboy-punch on the arm that almost knocked him over. "It's *far* too much for the average person." He sat back and turned off the phone display. "Our hapless northland friends have no idea what life is like for the average person in the Iron City workforce. They never considered what this would cost. Nobody could afford a body this elaborate."

Hugo took a moment to let out a relieved breath while Vector poured himself a refill. "Or maybe they thought a TR like this shouldn't cost any more than a standard TR," he said, returning the decanter to the holder next to his seat. "But it would put vendors out of business in a week. Vendors aren't deckmen, they're people. With families, mouths to feed, employees to pay. Who also have families and mouths to feed. You see where I'm going?"

Hugo nodded, hoping he did.

"And that's leaving aside the fact that it's also beyond the average person's biology." Vector showed him the phone screen again. "All those things—it would take a brain twice the size of normal to coordinate all those extras!"

Or a super-chip, Hugo thought. A super-chip would speed up a brain so it could handle all that and more.

Vector was looking at him expectantly. "Yeah, that's bad," Hugo said, trying to think fast. "I dunno what to do. Maybe warn people that this is a super-expensive TR that could kill them?"

"How?" Vector asked, as if he really thought Hugo could tell him. "I could release a statement, but would anyone read it? Have my Tuner read it in the stadium before every Motorball Game? She's prettier than I am, some people might pay attention instead of just chucking bottles and cans at her." Vector gave a short humourless laugh. "Don't worry, I'm not serious." Now he sighed. "I'm telling you, Hugo, I see a future where the streets are littered with the bodies of people whose heads have exploded."

Hugo didn't think that sounded terribly plausible. If people couldn't afford the souped-up TR in the first place, their heads were in no danger of exploding. But it was Vector's world; Hugo was just living in it.

"I want to do whatever I can to help," Hugo said finally. "But I don't know what that is."

"I do," Vector said promptly, giving him a big smile. "This cyborg is already running around loose, a living advertisement for our northland friends. We need to get him off the street before things get out of hand. And there's only one crew I know of that's good enough to take him down."

"You got it," Hugo said.

"Hold out your phone," Vector ordered him. He obeyed and Vector tapped it with his own. "There. Now you've got photos and a list of his hangouts. I've also included a map of northland, in case it comes to that. You needn't worry about, ah, turf. I've put it out that if you're in northland, you're on a job from me. You shouldn't have any trouble, but if you do, tell me and I'll fix it. I couldn't offer you this same protection in south-town, as you weren't there on *my* business."

Hugo felt heat rush into his face. Was there ever a time when he wouldn't be reminded about that?

Vector gave him a friendly slap on the shoulder. "But all that's in the past, okay, kid? Just do this job right and it's all good. Because we don't have much info on the target, I'll give you a week to deliver."

"Maybe if you hear more about him, you can text me—" Hugo started.

"Are you nuts?" Vector snapped, making him jump. "We can't

communicate while you're on a job. Anyone finds out I'm giving you special treatment, I'll have every goddam snowflake in town after me, wanting special this and special that." He looked furious a moment longer, then relented. "If I find out anything useful, I'll get a message to you. But *you* don't call *me*. Clear?"

Hugo nodded. Vector's glass was empty again and Hugo could tell he wanted another refill. But he wouldn't let himself have it until Hugo left, because he was tipsy, Hugo realised. One more and he'd be drunk, and Vector couldn't be drunk in front of people like Hugo.

Vector nudged him. "Any questions?"

"No, sir," Hugo said. "I got everything I need."

"Great!" Vector said. "So go out there and do what you do. Make me proud, kid. You got five days."

Hugo almost opened his mouth to tell Vector he had originally said a week and then decided he'd better get the hell out before Vector cut it to three days.

The moment the door shut behind the kid, Vector reached for the decanter.

"Rear view," he said as he poured, and a small flatscreen folded down from the limo ceiling. It lit up to show the street behind him. Hugo was running away like a good little jacker, not looking back or stopping to talk to anyone. Vector considered having someone check on the kid, just to make sure he was behaving himself, then decided he didn't need to spend the money. He could tell Hugo wanted to please him. Maybe it was some kind of father thing. The kid *was* an orphan, after all.

"*That* is a *big guy*," Koyomi said. She sat between Hugo and Tanji in their usual spot in the CAFÉ café. Hugo had tapped the info Vector had given him to both her and Tanji's phones, and she was studying the screen with a nervous expression.

"The last guy was just as big," Hugo said.

"No, this guy's bigger," Koyomi insisted.

"He isn't any bigger than the biggest guy we ever took down," Hugo said and looked at Tanji to back him up.

Tanji, however, looked as apprehensive as Koyomi. "She's right, Hugo. That's like a tank, heavy all the way through. Thick."

"Lots of mass," Koyomi put in helpfully.

"Yeah, that," Tanji said. "After he's down, we'd have a lotta trouble moving him."

"That's what the *truck* is for." Hugo was starting to get impatient. "Remember the truck? With the winch in the back? If you're feeling puny, have another coffee. We got time. It's still early."

Koyomi slid off her stool. "Anybody want anything? I'm *not* treating," she added as Tanji opened his mouth.

"No, thanks," Tanji said, looking slightly disappointed.

Hugo waited till Koyomi was at the counter before he turned to Tanji and said, "Man, you're such a boob sometimes."

"I'll tell my shrink," Tanji replied. "But she's right. This is a big job. As much as I like splitting three ways, I think we need two more on this. Dif and Louie—they've both got muscle."

"Dif?" Hugo made a sceptical face.

"Dif's kind of a lump," Koyomi said, materialising between them. She was holding a cup of something hot crowned with a small peak of ersatz whipped cream.

"He's solid," Tanji corrected her.

Koyomi gave a short laugh. "You practically have to tell him to put one foot in front of the other to get him to walk."

"Then he can drive the truck," Tanji said.

"Does he know how to drive anything?" Hugo asked.

"He can learn by doing," Tanji replied.

"No, we stick to the plan," Hugo said. "Vector gave me five days to bring this guy in. We can do it in one night."

"Five days is time enough to make a new plan," Koyomi said. She had licked off most of the whipped cream; what remained gave her a white moustache as she drank.

Hugo shook his head emphatically. "Originally he gave me a week. Two seconds later, he says five days. I was afraid if I hung around any longer, he'd say he wanted it yesterday and why was I late again."

"He might say that anyway when we show up tonight," Tanji said.

"If he says tomorrow he wanted it yesterday, that'll mean he wanted it today," Koyomi said.

"Just what is it you're trying to say?" Tanji asked her.

"I guess that's why we ought to get him today. And I'm not *trying* to say it, I *said* it." Koyomi frowned. "Sometimes I really don't know about you two."

It seemed to Hugo as they left the café that the streets were emptying more quickly than usual. He looked up; clouds were rolling in, promising rain as they obscured Zalem's ever-present disk.

"Hey—" He elbowed Tanji. "Is it supposed to rain tonight?"

Tanji grimaced and pointed at the sky. "Looks like it's gonna, whether it's *supposed* to or not."

Hugo frowned. Rain made the streets slippery for gyros. They'd done a lot of jobs in the rain but he was tempted to call the whole thing off and do it tomorrow. Of course, it might rain even harder then, so what the hell. Doc Ido had called Iron City's climate "tropical"—good for growing orchids and rainforests in the wild, and mould and mildew in town. Hugo had offered to take him out to the Badlands so he could see a rainforest in person but the doc said he was too busy. It was too bad because that wasn't the only thing he wanted Ido to see.

Tanji gave him a shove. "I *said*, do you wanna check the Widow Shins bar first?"

Hugo stared at him blankly.

"Earth to Hugo, where the hell did you go?" Tanji asked, annoyed.

"I'm right here," Hugo said defensively.

"You *better* be," said Tanji, glaring at him. "This is *your* show."

"You just worry about checking Widow Shins," Hugo told him.

"*Hey!*" Koyomi snapped her fingers between their faces. "Guys! I don't know what's your damage but shake it off. This is a job, not a *telenovela*!"

"You *still* watch those?" Tanji said scornfully.

"Only for pointers on how to handle you two," Koyomi said. "Widow Shins is *that* way." She pointed at a place where the main road curved away from the flyover remnants, and she moved towards Tanji's gyro. "Hey, can I drive?"

"The truck is *that* way," Hugo said, pointing in the opposite direction, towards the cathedral ruins. "I'll go pick it up and meet you guys at Widow Shins."

"I'll drop Koyomi at Widow Shins and stake out his other bar," Tanji said, climbing on his gyro and starting it up. "If he shows up, I'll text you. And you: don't ask stupid questions," he added to Koyomi as she climbed on behind him and put her arms around his waist.

Hugo rode to the abandoned warehouse's loading dock, pulled the tarp off the truck and put his gyro in the back. No one ever came down here—no one who would care what was under a very grungy-looking tarp, anyway. But just in case, he'd switched around some of the wiring under the dash, making it impossible to hot-wire normally. He got the idea from listening to Ido tell one of his patients how he was re-wiring his legs.

Driving the truck past the cathedral reminded him that he hadn't climbed up to the platform around the spire for a while. It was the only spire completely intact and the platform was solid. It was probably the highest point in Iron City, higher even than Vector's Factory penthouse, which was supposed to have killer views from every window.

Hugo doubted any of them were really as good as the one from the spire platform. But then those were probably views of Iron City. He only wanted to look at Zalem, seeing the setting sun hit the skyscrapers at the edge of the disk, making the glass flash like it had burst into flames—and the light lingered on the buildings even after it was dark in Iron City. Zalem was up so high, sunsets happened a lot later for them.

When this job was over, he'd get back up the cathedral spire. Until he had a million credits in his lockbox, that was as good as it would get for him.

Hugo backed the truck into an alley three blocks from Widow Shins and rode his gyro to the bar. He'd never been to this particular bar, but then he seldom went to bars—booze cost money he had a better use for. The place was a dive, which meant it wasn't as clean as a joint, but it didn't have as many brawls as a hell-hole.

No one gave him a second look as he went in and made his way to a table in a far corner. There was a glass on it half full of something slightly darker than the coke Vector had given him. Hugo moved it closer to himself so he'd look like a paying customer and noticed there was a layer of something in the bottom that looked like mud. It figured, he thought; when you ordered something on the rocks, you had to specify still water. Otherwise you got industrial tap, with real rocks frozen in it.

The table gave him a good view of the rest of the bar, which was full but not overly crowded. Hugo looked around and didn't see Koyomi. Irritated, he phoned her.

"Where *are* you?" he asked.

"Across the street watching the front door," she said. "I don't have to be *in* the bar to watch for the target."

"Why?" Hugo said impatiently.

"If you'd ever been a pretty young girl alone in a bar, you wouldn't have to ask," she snapped.

Hugo felt like an idiot. "Sorry, I didn't think anyone would bother you."

"*Seriously?*" Koyomi squeaked with disbelief. "Half of them are creeps whose wives don't understand them, half are *northland* creeps whose husbands ignore them, and you don't wanna know what the rest of them want. Don't expect me to come back in just because *you're* there now."

"No, it's okay. Call me if you see him. Or I'll call you." Hugo hung up as a waitress came towards him. She was holding a dozen dirty glasses in an enhanced cyber-hand and a small order tablet in the other; she looked so exhausted Hugo felt tired just looking at her.

"Another?" she asked him in a flat, nasal voice.

"Still workin' on this one, thanks," Hugo said.

"You been nursin' that for so long, I swear you look younger." She looked at the glass. "Dontcha like it? That's Iron City Black Tar."

Hugo squirmed a little. "It looks like it."

The waitress leaned over and stirred it with the pinky of her normal hand. The dark swirl in the glass looked even more like mud. "There," she said. "Now you can't see it. Outta sight, outta mind. Down the hatch. You're welcome."

Hugo pushed the glass farther away as she stumped off. His phone said it was after two A.M. He should probably wait till two-thirty before giving up, but what the hell. He got up to leave, thinking the guy might have gone to the other bar. Once he got outside he'd call Tanji and, if the cyborg was still a no-show, they'd call it a night. Vector should have given them more information, he thought, making his way through the room towards the door.

He opened the door and immediately bounced off something solid and unyielding. He staggered back a few steps, trying to regain his balance. But something shoved him hard in the centre of his chest and he flew backwards several feet, going down hard on his tailbone. The room erupted in screams of laughter, as if this was the most hilarious thing the happy clientele of Widow Shins had seen lately, or ever.

"Young people today!" boomed a jolly male voice. "They just can't stand up to a drink."

More laughter. Wincing with pain, Hugo started to push himself to his feet. He was on one knee when he looked up at the man standing over him and nearly fell over again.

"Hey, little fella!" The cyborg looked exactly like his photos. He bent over with his hands on his knees, grinning hugely. "If you can't hold your liquor, you oughta watch where you're going!"

Koyomi and Tanji had been right, Hugo thought, unable to move. This guy was *enormous*. Why hadn't he seen that?

Because he'd only seen what Vector was paying, and he'd wanted to show Vector he could do the job right. The money and the need to prove something had made him stupid when he should have been observant and cautious.

The cyborg's biceps opened and shiny mechanisms unfolded from each one. Both had large pincers on the end. They grabbed Hugo under his arms and lifted him up until he was eye-to-eye with the cyborg, his feet dangling freely above the floor. The pincers squeezed so hard Hugo felt as if his flesh were being crushed. He jammed his lips together, refusing to cry out in pain.

"Better go home, kid." The cyborg ruffled Hugo's hair with his regular right hand in a parody of affection. "I bet your momma's worried *sick* about you." Still holding Hugo up, he turned around and tossed Hugo against the closed door. Hugo rebounded and fell on his tailbone for the second time.

The pain was actually blinding. Hugo couldn't help crying out and didn't care. Ignoring the jeering laughter, he scrambled to his feet and fled. His tailbone was still throbbing as he stumbled across the street, looking for Koyomi.

"What the hell did you do in there?" Koyomi demanded, materialising out of the shadows. "You always said we shouldn't call attention to ourselves on a job. By the way, did you see the cyborg? He went in just before you came out. I called Tanji. He's on his way."

Hugo groaned, barely aware of the sound of Tanji's gyro coming towards them as he rubbed one armpit and then the other. The cyborg hadn't had to hurt him *that* much; he'd simply enjoyed it. *Bastard*, Hugo thought, biting back tears from the pain under his arms.

"Where you want to take him?" Tanji asked. "I saw a couple places—"

"It's off," Hugo growled, straightening up. His tailbone gave an intense throb, as if to remind him it hurt too. "Go home. We'll meet up tomorrow and make a new plan."

"Really?" Koyomi blinked at him.

"Why?" Tanji asked, looking equally baffled.

"Because I said so, that's why," Hugo said testily.

Tanji's face lost all expression. "Oh, so it's like that now?"

"No, it's not," Hugo said in a heavy voice. Tanji was unmoved and Koyomi looked wary. "You guys were right. He's *big*. We need a couple more people with us."

Tanji looked from Hugo to the bar and back again. "What happened in there?"

"Nothing," Hugo said. "I just got a good look at him and my gut said not tonight."

"Okay," Tanji said. "I never argue with the gut either." Koyomi nodded in agreement, climbing on the back of Tanji's gyro so he could give her a ride home.

Hugo waited until they were gone before he got on his own gyro. Then he got off again and walked it to the alley. Driving the truck was marginally less painful, but he certainly couldn't park that at the curb in front of his apartment.

Covering it with the tarp at the loading dock proved to be a serious challenge. Hugo had to climb up on the cab, then onto the trailer to cover it properly, and even that hurt. Then he had to ride his gyro home, unless he wanted to sleep in the back of the truck with it.

He was seriously tempted, but he could see there wasn't much ventilation. He'd wake up sick. And his ass and his armpits would be worse. It always hurt more the next day.

Hugo started to walk the gyro away from the loading dock towards the cathedral and suddenly heard voices—familiar voices. He couldn't quite place them, but he knew they weren't any of his friends. They were coming from inside the cathedral, which wasn't good. Everybody around here knew better than to go in there.

It was the crew from south-town who had kicked the shit out of him.

He moved behind a partially broken-down wall and watched the front entrance through a gap in the bricks. He didn't have to wait long before three guys came out, all hopped up on what they'd found stashed inside. The first one was the guy who had given Hugo a farewell kick in the kidneys. The second one Hugo didn't recognise; the third had gold-tipped hair.

"Hey, guys," the leader said cheerfully as the other two leaped up to bump chests. "Muffle it till we get home, will ya?"

Abruptly the flatscreen mounted on a building across the street lit up, making all three of them jump. The screen turned on whenever its sensors detected more than two people at the cathedral. Hugo chuckled silently as they stood transfixed by the images. Apparently they didn't have a lot of outdoor flatscreens in southie.

"Jeez, do bounty hunters hang around here?" asked one of the guys. "Look at all those marks!"

"If you see a mark, call the Factory," said the leader, running a hand through his silly hair. "Right now, they could hear you without a phone."

Hugo spotted a gleam of copper on his wrist.

"Why would a dealer keep their stuff here?" said the second guy. "Where a screen lights up with marks for bounty hunters? That's nuts!"

"That's *awfully* good stuff!" said the first guy. That was the signal for the two of them to jump up and bump chests again.

"You took too much. I'm gonna have to throw you guys in a cold shower," said the leader, impatient now.

"I don't see why we don't just take the whole thing and sell it ourselves," said the first guy.

"Because they'd find out we stole it and come after us," said the leader, speaking slowly and distinctly, as if to a small child. "And nobody'd lift a finger to help us."

"We could kick their asses. And then shut out everybody who didn't have our back," said the second guy.

"Then who would we sell to?" the leader asked. The other two guys looked sheepish. The leader threw his arms around their shoulders. "Listen, do I keep you guys around to think?"

They shook their heads.

"That's right. Why do I keep you around?" He waited a beat. "To party with! That's why you're here and why we're keeping this little treasure to ourselves—just us three. Nobody else in the crew needs to know about it."

"How'd you find out about it anyway?" the second guy asked him. "Just tell us that."

"I can't betray a confidence." The leader made a sad face. "All I'll say is, drug dealers oughta be a lot nicer to the people they cheat on their main squeeze with and not break up with them by text. Because that really hurts their feelings and makes them tell a friend about where the dealer stashes their goodies. Now, c'mon, the bus stop's a block away and I wanna get home before dawn."

"When're we coming back?" the second guy asked plaintively.

"Two, three days," said the leader magnanimously.

"Make it two?" the first guy said hopefully.

Hugo stared after them as they ambled up the street. All jacked up on stolen drugs and they were going back to south-town by *bus*? These guys were *geniuses*. He stifled a laugh. In southie they probably were.

After a bit, he straightened up; his armpits and tailbone let him know what they thought of that, but now he didn't feel it quite so much. He knew what they'd been sampling. The Duchess had been stashing inventory in the cathedral for ages. Hugo wasn't especially fond of her or any other drug dealer. However, she'd never hassled him about climbing up to the spire platform.

Hugo discovered there was no riding position that didn't hurt. Taking pressure off his tailbone put more pressure on his armpits and vice versa. He managed to make it home trading off one pain for another. It was just his luck to get hurt in two of the most laughable—and inconvenient—places on the human body.

And, once again, he couldn't tell anybody. *Oh, yeah, the guy had me by the armpits. Hurt? I thought I was gonna die.* Tanji would laugh till he peed. Koyomi would probably have the decency to try not to. God only knew what they'd say if he told them it hurt to sit down. They'd be forwarding him ads for spanking dominatrixes for the rest of his life.

Dammit.

When he finally made it home, he took a few moments to make sure the lockbox was safe. Then he took a few more moments to count his credits, just in case he had miscounted last time and he actually had less than he thought. Or in case some miraculous increase had occurred courtesy of a Guardian Angel, or a Good Fairy, or a Secret Agent of the Universe on a mission to Make Life Fair—none of which he believed in, but what the hell did he know.

He hadn't miscounted either way.

After putting the box back in its hiding place, Hugo stripped to his underwear, dropping his clothes on the floor around the bed. His tailbone objected to his lying on his back; his armpits didn't much care for either side. When he rolled over onto his stomach, his armpits reminded him not to raise his arms or try to hug his pillow. Curling up into the foetal position was also no go, he discovered.

Eventually he found a position that gave him the least amount of pain and might actually let him get some sleep. He dozed off sometime after the sun came up, thinking that, for the first time, he could see how people might decide to swap out the parts they were born with for something less sensitive.

CHAPTER 14

"He's intractable," said Chiren.

"What's *that* supposed to mean?" Vector asked, annoyed.

She had definitely spoiled tonight's special dinner, Chiren thought with bitter satisfaction. They were both having prime rib to celebrate the start of what was supposed to be Vector's ongoing success with their super-chipped Paladin. She had barely touched her food, which also irked him. Any time she didn't grovel in abject gratitude, it put his nose out of joint. The way things were going, he'd have to swap it for a cyber-nose.

"*Well?*" Vector said impatiently.

"He's stubborn," Chiren said. "Unmanageable. Doesn't play well with anybody, even himself. Whatever team you put him on will walk out. Including the Factory practice team."

Vector paused with his hand on the wine bottle. "You're kidding."

"I lost my sense of humour ages ago."

Chiren heard the door behind her open—a bodyguard/waiter coming to see if they wanted anything. The service in Vector's office was impeccable.

"Get out!" Vector barked. The door shut quickly. That would come back to bite him if there were any justice, Chiren thought. But there wasn't; never had been.

"Talk to me," Vector ordered her. "You're at the stadium all the time. You know what's going on better than I do."

"He's intractable," Chiren said again. "Refuses to cooperate even when it's in his best interests."

"I got that the first time," Vector said. "Unmanageable, people threatening to quit. What does he want?"

Chiren shrugged. "He wants what he wants when he wants it."

"Ah." Vector nodded knowingly. "Gratification."

Sometimes she forgot how intelligent Vector was. She had to remember not to underestimate him.

"So get a handler to wrangle him and fetch whatever he wants."

"That would be okay if he wanted lollipops," Chiren said, cutting a piece of prime rib. "He wants the world to not be so slow. For everyone to love him. To win *all* the time without even trying, and not just Motorball."

"Then get him a harem and a chorus of yes-men," Vector said, exasperated.

"I tried that," Chiren said. "Some things you can't even pay yes-men enough to withstand."

Vector threw up his hands. "What do you want from me? I got you the chip. You said you'd only put it in a cyborg sophisticated enough to handle that kind of acceleration, otherwise the chip would probably blow out all the nerves. So I got you sophisticated cyborg parts to save you the trouble of building them from scratch—you're welcome, by the way—"

"So what do *you* want—a gold star?" Chiren gave a single hard laugh. "Those parts needed a lot of work before I could install the chip."

"And you said you'd make him the best ever, even better than Grewishka before he crapped out and went back to the sewer. You made a lot of promises, and I put up with a lot from you—"

Chiren's jaw dropped. "*You* put up with a lot, from *me*?"

"—and suddenly you can't deliver because you've got all these *problems*," Vector continued, as if she hadn't spoken. "I don't pay you to have *problems*. I pay you to build champions. Get him on the track for tomorrow's game."

Chiren cut some more prime rib for herself. "Well, there's just a tiny little prob— difficulty," she said.

"So? Fix it."

"I'll need a lot of help," she said. "I mean, a *lot*."

"So get a lot of help!" Vector was dangerously frustrated with her now. He had never hit her but sometimes he grabbed her arm and left a hand-shaped bruise.

"I said a *lot*. Everyone you can spare and everybody else."

For a moment, Vector just glared at her. Then light dawned. "Oh, God." He leaned his head back and closed his eyes. "You can't find him."

"We have a winner," Chiren said flatly.

"I just saw him last night at the stadium with his trainer. What happened?" asked Vector, his voice heavy.

"You did," Chiren replied. "You inspired him. You left to go somewhere else more interesting, and he decided to follow your example. To go some place that didn't piss him off so much, was what he told Ed on his way out."

"So he *rolled* out?" Vector asked in disbelief.

"No, first he got Ed to put his feet back on." Chiren glanced at Zalem; a wave of intense longing ran through her.

"Ed's a moron," Vector said, disgusted.

"No, Ed's *observant*. He's *observed* what happens when Chase doesn't get his way. But don't take my word for it. Let's look at the highlights. Screen, please."

A screen on the wall to Chiren's left lit up. It was one of the very few things in Vector's office that he allowed her to control. The videos she wanted were already cued up and waiting.

The first one showed Chase, in red-and-orange armour with a flame design, skating behind a group of Factory practice players. They barely qualified as Paladins, but they'd once been serious contenders for a championship before hard living, injuries and age had eroded their abilities. But they weren't pushovers either—anyone who practised with them felt it the next day.

It didn't take long for Chase to catch up with the practice team, who were obviously trying like hell to pull farther ahead. Chase began playing with them—letting them think they were getting away, then speeding up so he was practically on their heels before dropping back as if they were too fast for him.

"Is that new armour?" Vector asked.

"That's what we told *him*. He won't put on anything 'pre-used' or 'pre-worn'." Chiren made air quotes with her fingers.

On the screen, Chase had lowered his upper body and leaned forward, preparing to charge the Factory team. A second later there seemed to be an explosion that sent them flying in all directions, most of them parting company with at least one limb. Bright-blue cyber-blood splattered the track, the safety rail and the players themselves.

"Now *that's* what I want to see my players doing on the track—taking apart the opposition," Vector enthused. "How soon can we get more chips for all our Paladins?"

"As soon as they all get upgraded CNS and spinal cords. Oh, and I have to figure out how to fix it so they don't go insane with rage," Chiren said casually. "So not for a while yet." Pause. "Maybe never."

"Paladins have tempers," Vector said, irritated. "They gotta be aggressive to play."

God, for a smart man he could be so *stupid*, Chiren thought. "The chip accelerates aggression so it runs wild. Jashugan has the most self-control of any Paladin I ever saw, but with that chip in him, he'd go homicidal before he could get a grip. The chip would ruin him and his CNS."

"Then we'll have to develop a better chip and a better CNS," Vector said, in a maddeningly reasonable tone. He might have been suggesting she carry an umbrella when it rained. "Whatever that is."

"Central nervous system." Chiren sighed. "You barge into the lab so much I'd have thought you'd picked up a few things."

"Sometimes you think too much," Vector said, glowering.

"That's what you pay me to do—think. There's more. Skip to Juggernaut," she told the screen.

Juggernaut had four arms and, instead of legs, three wheels—a large one in front and two smaller ones behind. On the screen, he was racing along the track, visibly straining to go faster. Abruptly, the Motorball flew into the back of his head. If he'd been on skates, he'd have gone down immediately. Instead, his wheels shifted to counter his fluctuating balance. His upper body lurched, swayed and all four arms flailed as if he were attempting semaphore.

"Maybe we should've put the chip in Juggernaut," Vector said. "All those arms and wheels would've kept it busy."

"That's not a bad idea, but the extra limbs would still have to be more complex than just arms and wheels," Chiren said. "Limbs within limbs, motion within motion."

Vector nodded. "Okay. I'll put someone on that."

Sure he would, Chiren thought as Chase appeared behind Juggernaut, this time in shining black armour. A box in the lower left-hand corner put their speed at 135 mph. Chase moved around to Juggernaut's left and leaped up, spinning so rapidly that he kicked Juggernaut twice before he hit the track again. Juggernaut toppled over, wheels spinning.

Turning sharply, Chase went back to where Juggernaut was lying on his side, tore off one of his arms and began beating him with it.

Paladins swarmed around him, trying to make him stop. One of them, a deceptively delicate-looking woman in bright crimson, distracted Chase long enough for one of the others to get the arm away from him. Chase simply tore off another and began swinging at the other Paladins. Jashugan rolled onto the screen and tried to remonstrate.

In the next moment, all the Paladins were down and Chase was gone.

"Pause," Chiren told the screen.

"What the hell?" Vector said.

"I could play it in extreme slow-mo so you could see all the details, but you wouldn't like it any better. Chase's adrenaline spiked when the other Paladins surrounded him, so he laid them all out."

"Why?" Vector grimaced. "They're all on the same team."

"He felt threatened. He acted too quickly for second thoughts," Chiren said. "It took me two days working around the clock to repair all the damage."

"Can those guys play tomorrow night?" Vector asked.

"Yes, they're all fine. But Chase is gone. He's out there doing God knows what. Picking fights, no doubt. He'll probably end up with a price on his head."

Vector sat back in his chair, took the napkin off his lap and tossed it over his unfinished dinner. "Which some Hunter-Warrior will collect after looting the body. There goes our chip, probably to those northland scumbags. I should've taken out all six of them, but I thought it would look excessive."

"Maybe one of your street rats'll get to the body first," Chiren said. "Then you can buy it back from them."

"This is all *your* fault," Vector said. "You screwed the chip up instead of perfecting it like you said you would."

No, actually, my mistake was letting you talk me into putting a prototype into the cyborg body of a mercurial young man barely out of adolescence, Chiren told him silently. She sighed again.

"*Well?*" he snapped. "How are you going to fix this? What hurts Motorball, hurts me and everyone around me."

Chiren raised one perfect eyebrow. "Am I included in that group?"

"You hurt *yourself* when you screw up," Vector told her. "What are you going to do about it?"

"I could go out and search for him," Chiren said. "Maybe with a big butterfly net."

Vector's eyes narrowed. "For someone who claims to have no sense of humour, you smart off like you think you're funny."

"Would you rather watch more video?" Chiren said. "There's a sequence where he tears off his trainer's cyber-arm and—"

"Don't tell me—he beats him over the head with it," Vector said flatly. "Does he ever do anything else?"

"He's dangerous, but not innovative," Chiren said.

Vector told the screen to shut off. "I'll tell my people on the street to find him. *Discreetly.*"

Chiren's eyebrows went up. He thought his street rats were *discreet*? "Even if you find him in the next fifteen minutes, I doubt he'll be game-worthy by tomorrow night."

"We'll see." Vector nodded at her plate. "If you're done, why don't you go slip into something more comfortable. I have a few calls to make before I join you. I won't be long, so wait up."

"If you want me in the pit tomorrow, I need to get some sleep," Chiren said.

"Fine. Don't wait up. I'll wake you."

Just what she needed—more mediocre sex. Chiren got up and left the room, wishing she didn't know he was watching her ass. Damned stilettos.

Vector called Gamot on voice-only and explained that he wanted a covert search. He'd have preferred to use Soledad, but when he called her, he got a brief recording saying she was unavailable, which hung up on him without inviting him to leave a message. He made a note to look into this and see what was keeping her so content that she could shrug him off. But first he had to get his rogue Paladin put to bed.

Which reminded him.

Afterwards Chiren lay with her back to Vector, pretending to be asleep. Why had he bothered? His heart hadn't been in it.

But then, his heart never was in it. As far as she could tell, he didn't have one, only a mechanism that told him what would pay off and what wasn't worth the salt in his sweat. Not that she'd ever seen him sweat outside the bedroom. The penthouse was like a refrigerator and she could practically see her breath in the limo. Maybe the air had to match the temperature of his blood.

In any case, it didn't last long. Afterwards he got up, put on his silk pyjamas and robe, and went back to the office as if this had been a coffee break. Fine with her.

Hours later Vector stood beside the bed having a nightcap and watching Chiren sleep. She was lucky she was so good at what she did. As long as she kept making winners out of his Paladins, he could put up with her being such a diva. But she had really let him down when she'd lost the Paladin and the chip. He hoped for her sake this wasn't a portent of things to come. The moment she became more trouble than she was worth, he'd toss her down his own garbage chute, and that fall would be a hell of a lot harder than the one from Zalem.

But right now, she was still useful. Her and the kid with the crew—Hugo. For some reason he kept forgetting the kid's name, maybe because he was such a nobody.

At least the kid wasn't a diva. When Hugo screwed up he didn't start going on about this problem or that problem. And even if the kid wasn't a genius, he was smart enough not to make the same mistake twice.

It occurred to him then that he ought to encourage Hugo to hang around Ido's clinic more. Maybe Ido was working on other things he'd like to talk about. The poor guy would be lonely now that his daughter was dead and his wife had traded up. Hugo could act like he wanted to be Ido's protégé. Scientists loved having protégés, didn't they?

Vector went to the window and tapped the control to make it transparent. Nobody else had a view that was so almighty *vast*. He didn't bother looking up at Zalem. At night it was only a darker shadow in the night sky. By contrast, Iron City looked like a spread of glittering jewels.

The flying city was supposed to be so wonderful, a better world full of better people. But if Chiren and Ido were typical of Zalem's supposedly better population, Vector wasn't impressed.

CHAPTER 15

He should have hired a nurse much sooner, Ido thought, watching Gerhad fine-tuning Courage's cyber-arm and gossiping with Spirit. He and Chiren should have hired one when they'd first opened the clinic. It would have taken so much pressure off them. Except he knew Chiren wouldn't have welcomed a ground-level outsider into any part of their lives, not even to help with patients. Working *with* someone born at ground level, as if she were one of them? She might have left him sooner, taking their daughter with her. But then maybe their daughter would still be alive—

Ido shut the thought down hard. He would never know, and he had plenty of real things to worry about. Then he realised Gerhad was looking at him expectantly. "I'm sorry?" he said, a bit embarrassed.

Gerhad traded glances with Spirit. "I was just asking what time you thought you'd be back, and do you want me to wait for you? But if you don't leave, it doesn't matter."

Heat rushed into Ido's face. "I've got a lot on my mind," he said.

"Who doesn't?" Gerhad said. "Think about it while you're out." She made a small shooing motion at him.

Ido nodded, taking a few steps towards the door. "Call me if—"

"I need you." Gerhad made a larger, more vigorous shooing motion. "Go, already, or all the good stuff will be gone before you even get to the market. We need more servos."

"We *always* need more servos," Ido assured her. "Okay, I'm going. For real now."

Ido left by way of the residence so he couldn't stop and talk to patients in the waiting area. He felt a mixture of guilt and relief about leaving, mostly guilt. But Gerhad had assured him she could handle the afternoon's appointments, which were all adjustments, fine-tuning or diagnostics. And she was, after all, an experienced ER nurse. He hadn't left his patients high and dry, and he wasn't dumping his responsibilities on Gerhad so he could goof off. But he did feel guilty about lying to her.

It wasn't a *total* lie—he really *was* going to look for servos. Mainly, however, he was leaving to meet with Ajakutty, who had called him out of the blue to say he had a lead on Chase.

In the last few days rumours had begun to circulate about the super-fast Paladin going AWOL. Vector had denied it, telling people his newest superstar was still in training and when the time was right he'd hit the track and play a game that no one would ever forget. When the other players had asked him what was really going on, however, Vector told them to worry more about themselves.

"It's not like we expect him to be honest with us," Ajakutty said. "Vector lies all the time, about everything."

The two of them were sitting in a small café on the edge of south-town. Ajakutty was practically unrecognisable in mufti, and Ido realised he had never seen him completely out of Paladin gear. Without blades or armour, he looked almost slight to Ido. No one in the place gave either of them a second look.

"Be that as it may," Ido said, looking down at his coffee, "I don't understand why you called me instead of Vector about this."

Ajakutty looked pained. "Well, it's complicated. If I went to Vector and said I knew where the new guy is and what he's been up to, that's me telling him I caught him in a lie. I don't play well enough to get away with that. What do you think he'd do?"

"Nothing good," Ido said sympathetically.

"I'd wake up on the Prefect's doorstep in a box of bicycle parts—and not *my* bicycle either." Ajakutty shook his head. "I know you said you're not coming back, and I respect that. But when I thought about who I could trust—" He shrugged. "I thought about just not saying anything and letting Vector find out on his own. That'd be the safest choice. But the new guy—he hasn't played a single game yet, and all he's ever done in practice is tear everybody's arms off and beat them over the head with them. Nobody wants to be on the same team with him. *I* sure don't, lemme tell you. But he's a Paladin. He's one of us. Vector's acting like there's nothing wrong with him. Except there is, and it's bad. I think it's that new chip."

Ido gazed at the other man, hoping he didn't look as surprised as he felt. That was more than he'd ever heard Ajakutty say in one go. Nor had he ever heard Ajakutty express this kind of concern for anyone, let alone someone he barely knew. But then the only time Ido ever had contact with him was in the pit during a game or a practice. He only knew Ajakutty the Paladin, not Ajakutty the man.

"I'm sorry," Ido said, "but I'm not sure I can do anything. I didn't put the chip in. Chiren did."

"You guys used to work together. I thought maybe you'd know what she did wrong."

There were any number of things Ido could have said to that, but he decided not to burden Ajakutty with any of them. "If I find him, I'll try to talk him into going back to Chiren so she can take care of him."

Ajakutty looked disappointed.

"The problem is, he's not my patient," Ido said. "If I did anything else, Vector could quite rightly claim I was interfering with one of his players."

Ajakutty's disappointed expression intensified. "If you came across him lying in the middle of the street, twitching and buzzing in a pool of cyber-blood after a truck hit him, would you just leave him there so you wouldn't be interfering?"

"It's not the same thing," Ido said as kindly as he could.

"I think it is," said Ajakutty. "Only now I have to get to the stadium and put on my game face and all the stuff that goes with it." He got to his feet, pushed the chair in, and suddenly his expression softened. "I'm sorry, Doc, I shouldn'ta put you on the spot like that. Forget I said anything." He hesitated. "But if you wanna know where he'll be tonight instead of on the Motorball track, I sent the address to your phone. Don't ask me how I got it. Things get going there about midnight."

"Ajakutty, wait," Ido said. The Paladin turned back to him. "If you feel like stopping by the clinic for any reason, you'll be welcome. After hours is best. I'll have more time."

Ido thought for a moment that the Paladin was going to hug him. "Thanks, Doc," Ajakutty said. "And don't worry—I'll be discreet."

Ido watched him leave the café and climb onto a gyro parked out front at the curb. Then he looked at his phone. The address Ajakutty had given him was halfway between the café and the edge of the scrapyard; how convenient.

He had another coffee, telling himself that after he drank it he would go back to the clinic and finish out the day with Gerhad. He definitely would *not* go picking through the south-town edge of the trash pile looking for servos. And even if he did, he would *not* stay there killing time until midnight.

If, on the other hand, he got caught up in what he was doing and somehow later ran into the AWOL Paladin who, for reasons of his own, agreed to give him the chip, that would simply be a lucky break.

The address wasn't as easy to find as he'd thought it would be. He passed the entrance at least twice before he found it, a door in the middle of a narrow passageway between two buildings that might have been erected specifically to be rundown and empty. There were generations of graffiti on the boarded-over windows, tags layered on tags layered on tags.

Inside, glow-in-the-dark arrows on the walls pointed to a stairway leading down. The arrows disappeared after three flights; they were no longer needed. Ido could hear the sound of many voices below. When he finally reached the bottom, Ido estimated he was at least seven storeys underground.

The beefy woman stationed at the foot of the stairs was a head taller than he was. She was wearing a short pleated skirt, an impossibly clean white blouse and a tie in a Windsor knot. Her hair stood straight out from her head in all directions, stiffened into spikes that looked sharp enough to impale flesh. Ido recognised it as some kind of nostalgia fashion trend.

The woman looked down at him as if he were the most uninteresting thing she had seen. "Weapons," she said.

Ido was baffled. "Excuse me?"

"Weapons. Got any weapons?"

"No," he said. "No weapons."

She nodded at the shoulder bag slung across the front of his body. "What's in there?"

"I was trash picking."

"Get anything good," she said languidly.

It took Ido a second to realise it was a question. "Well, just this—" He fished a partial servo out of the bag.

"Cool," she said in the same utterly bored tone. "Hand." She held out her hand and Ido put his in it. She produced a stamp and rolled it over the back of his hand. "That says you got here unarmed. Unarmed's to the left as you go in. Or take your chances on the right. Up to you." She shoved him through a doorway into an enormous dark room.

The warm air was heavy with alcohol and sweat and too many people too far underground. Ido felt as if he couldn't breathe deeply enough. He couldn't do this, he thought. He had to get out before he keeled over—

A gust of cold air suddenly blew down on him from overhead, lasting just long enough for him to take a single breath before it cut off. Maybe if he stayed right where he was, there'd be another one.

"Hey, you," said someone much closer to Ido than he'd have liked. He turned to find himself nose-to-nose with a sweaty male face that looked mildly homicidal. "Move. Don't be an air hog."

Ido gave ground, standing on tiptoe to look over the heads of the crowd for something bar-like. In the centre of the room bright-white spotlights shone on a raised rectangular platform bounded by three rows of ropes on every side. It looked like an old-fashioned boxing ring. Ido had never actually seen one except in Zalem's historical archives.

He kept his eyes on it as he moved slowly through the crowd on the left side of the room. No seats—this would not be a sedate performance for audience applause. He just hoped everyone around him really was unarmed.

Finally, he spotted a bar against the nearest wall. The man behind it was setting out glasses six at a time using expandable hands. Ido recognised him; he had replaced some worn parts in those expander mechanisms.

The man recognised him as well. "Hey, Doc," he said with a smile. "Drink? On me—your money's no good here."

"How long has this been going on?"

"Dunno," the bartender said cheerfully. He opened a small bottle with his left hand and pushed it towards Ido. "On the house. Farm distilled. Won't hurt you."

"Thanks," Ido said and slid a few credits at him.

"I told you, your money's no—"

"One professional to another," Ido said. "Does this always happen here?"

The bartender made the credits disappear. "Nope."

Ido leaned closer and lowered his voice. "This isn't Factory-sponsored, is it?"

"I'm just guessing," the bartender said, sounding careful, "because I'm just a bartender and I don't know anything, but no, it isn't. Otherwise it wouldn't be happening on the same night as a Game."

Ido looked around. There were no screens anywhere. "No one's interested in the outcome of tonight's Game?"

"Just guessing again," the bartender said, "because *I* don't know *anything*—we're clear on that, right?" He waited for Ido to nod before he went on. "It looks like some people want to lay bets without the, uh, *Vectory* taking a chunk."

"So who runs the betting?" Ido asked.

"I keep telling you, Doc, I don't know anything," said the bartender. "I just serve drinks." He nodded at the boxing ring. The bright lights overhead ran through a series of colours from red to purple and back to bright white before two cyborgs dropped down into the ring from overhead. The crowd roared in unison and surged towards the ring.

The cyborg on the left—the unarmed side, Ido remembered—looked like a patchwork quilt of hardware. Every part of him was different, as if someone had cobbled him together from any old random components available. Like the Un-Coupler, Ido thought tensely, hoping he didn't see anything familiar.

The cyborg raised his mismatched arms overhead, acknowledging the crowd—the right one was a telescoping mechanism covered in dirty yellow plastic; the left was some kind of flexible cable that bent in any direction, at any angle. The armour covering his torso seemed to have been thrown on in a hurry; some of the pieces looked broken rather than cut and industrial glue had bubbled out from under the edges. All of it had seen a lot of use—every surface was scarred, scratched or scraped.

The other cyborg had to be Chase. The armour he was sporting was unmistakably Motorball—bright holographic-orange flames on a royal-blue background. He wasn't as large as his opponent—he was compact, streamlined, lithe. Definitely Chiren's work, right down to the guy's narrow face framed in orange flames. She'd intended him to look cunning; to Ido he looked like a cunning twelve-year-old boy.

Having acknowledged the crowd, the cyborgs turned to each other. There was no referee, no announcer, no apparent signal. Ido climbed up on top of the bar to see better. The patchwork cyborg's telescoping arm shot out towards Chase, who was now standing on his left.

Chase swept the other cyborg's legs out from under him. By the time the patchwork cyborg had fallen all the way down, Chase was back at his original position, feigning surprise.

Then he *flickered* and suddenly he was leaning on a corner post, looking at his opponent with innocent confusion. Another flicker and he was in a different corner. The patchwork cyborg lunged for him with an angry yell; Chase appeared behind him and gave him a kick. The other cyborg sprawled on his belly, then scrambled to his feet, or tried to. Chase swept his legs out from under him again.

The patchwork cyborg scuttled forward and tackled Chase clumsily. Ido could see by Chase's expression of irate surprise that this wasn't supposed to happen. The other cyborg gripped Chase by the shoulder and tumbled forward, forcing Chase to roll with him. He ended up kneeling on Chase's back, pulling his arm up behind him. There was a sharp metallic whine and a spinning circular-saw blade began to emerge from the patchwork cyborg's middle.

The crowd was still roaring when the patchwork cyborg lost his balance and tipped over. A moment later, Chase braced one foot against his side, took the flexible arm in both hands and tore it from his shoulder.

The crowd bellowed in collective delight and horror as cyber-blood splattered the ring and more than a few people at ringside. Ido felt sorry for them as they drew back with repelled expressions. Action that was wildly entertaining in the Motorball stadium became unnervingly gruesome when it was scaled down to life size.

The fallen cyborg was clutching his shoulder and grimacing in pain. Ido spotted heart's-blood seeping out between his fingers. He struggled to his feet, and a few people at ringside held the ropes apart so he could climb out of the ring. Chase watched, his expression still enraged. As the cyborg and his friends started to leave, Chase called to them; when they turned, he flung the arm at them. More bright-blue cyber-blood decorated the ring and sprinkled people nearby. Ido winced.

Another cyborg dropped down into the ring from overhead. This one was twice Chase's size and looked like a clumsy imitation of Claymore, but without any of the shine or the fancy weapons. Or the skill—within thirty seconds Chase punched him into a pile of dented metal with no visible effort.

Ido felt a tug on his leg and looked down. "Does it look any better from up there?" asked the bartender.

Ido shook his head. "I can't believe nobody here cares about the Game tonight."

"They're amateurs," the bartender replied. "Motorball isn't low-rent enough for them."

"But *he's* not an amateur," Ido said, exasperated. "He could be on the track *right now*. He's supposed to be, anyway."

"You tell him what he's *supposed* to do," suggested the bartender. "See what happens."

Ido squatted down to talk to him. "What do you know about him?"

In the semi-dark he saw the bartender's eyes narrow slightly. "Told you, Doc, I'm just a bartender. All I know are drinks." He paused. "But I've heard stories—whispers—about Watchers."

"'Watchers'?" Ido was baffled. "Watchers? Where?"

The bartender's gaze was on the ring. "Watchers behind the eyes."

"Watchers behind the—" Ido felt a mix of disbelief and revulsion. "*Whose* eyes? Watching from *where*?"

The bartender's eyes swivelled to him. "Sometimes I don't know when to shut up. Do me a big favour, Doc, and forget I said anything."

"Watchers from *where*?" Ido demanded in a whisper.

"No idea what you're talking about," the bartender told him firmly.

Ido looked at the man's hands, which had contracted to normal size. "Maybe you should come by the clinic so I can make sure your expanders are working right."

"They're fine," the bartender replied. "You're missing the fight."

Chase's new opponent was trying to box him with over-sized fists. He managed to land a few blows before Chase tore both his arms off and tossed them into the crowd on the right side of the room.

Well, it was the *armed* side, Ido thought, wishing that were funny.

More bright-blue cyber-blood splattered the ring and the crowd, many of whom weren't thrilled about it. But Ido could see some of them did enjoy it, far too much. He was familiar with the concept of blood lust but only academically, from historical records. Now he was starting to get an idea of what the real thing was like. This wasn't the cartoon violence of Motorball. This was something a lot more primal, something that made him wonder about the odds of his getting out of this room alive.

Chase's complexion didn't look good; his lips had gone brown. His heart's-blood wasn't circulating quickly enough to keep up with the physical demands he was making on his body. Chiren should have caught this, Ido thought; it wasn't like her to miss something so important—

She wouldn't have, Ido realised, if the cyborg hadn't run off. Because the chip had turned him from a regular person into a loose cannon with no impulse control and a mean streak. And if he were being honest, Ido thought, he should have seen the potential for that himself when he was working on the chip. Everything you did to the body affected the mind. The Law of Unintended Consequences never slept.

Chase was now stomping around the ring, pounding his chest and yelling for a new opponent. He stopped in the centre, looked up and roared a demand. Nothing happened. Cheers turned to boos, although Ido wasn't sure whether they were booing Chase or the fact that no one else wanted to fight him.

The cyborg began pointing at people in the crowd, challenging them. They drew away from the ring, some of them turning their backs on him and averting their faces, moving for the exit. Infuriated, Chase vaulted over the ropes onto the floor. People melted away almost magically, leaving him standing alone with his fists up, looking around for someone to fight.

"Bitch-ass punks," he snarled. "Screw alla you." He headed for the door, and Ido jumped down off the bar to follow him.

The cyborg took the stairs three at a time, stamping his foot so hard on the steps that Ido was sure he heard a few of them crack. As a Hunter-Warrior, Ido was in better shape than most men his age, but after coming out of a badly ventilated room to run *up* seven storeys he was shaky and panting, barely able to call to the cyborg striding up the dark alley, bashing his fists against the buildings on either side, as if he thought he could shove them away and make the narrow space wider.

He was at the end of the alley when the cyborg finally heard him and turned around. "What do *you* want, old man?"

"There's something you need to know," Ido panted, taking a step towards him. "About that speed of yours. Or rather, what gives you that speed."

"What about it? You looking to get some yourself?" Chase sounded amused as well as pissed off. "You couldn't take it." He turned away and kept going up the street.

"*Wait!*" Ido huffed. The cyborg stopped and turned around with a dangerous expression on his face. "The chip," Ido said. "Chip's *faulty.*"

"Nah. Works just *fine,*" the cyborg said in a low snarl.

Ido took another step forward on shaky legs and had to lean on a wall to stay upright. Seven flights of stairs had kicked his ass. "It's black-market tech," Ido said breathlessly. "And if you don't let me remove it, it'll kill you."

"Is that so," the cyborg said.

You tell him what he's supposed to do. See what happens.

Ido looked around. The street was empty. He wasn't in midtown, where life went on around the clock. This was southie, where nobody heard or saw or knew anything.

The cyborg tilted his head to one side. "I should let you remove my chip," the cyborg said quietly. "Or you'll kill me."

"Not *me*—the *chip*," Ido said desperately. "*It* will kill you. You can feel it's not right, can't you? It runs away on you. Or you want to do something and nothing happens—"

"Okay." The cyborg grinned at him. "Tell me if nothing happens."

Ido never saw him flicker.

CHAPTER 16

According to Tanji, it was stupid to live with regret. Hugo thought Tanji was probably right. The problem was, Hugo couldn't seem to stop doing things he regretted; the latest one was telling the Duchess he'd wait on the cathedral's front steps for her.

The Duchess herself was inside with some people she called her enforcers. Hugo hadn't seen them but he'd heard them, or rather he'd heard their effect on the three south-town guys. The Duchess had stationed her enforcers inside the cathedral to wait for the south-town crew to come back for more of her inventory. Now the enforcers were explaining to them in no uncertain, albeit nonverbal, terms how wrong it was to trespass and steal, especially after taking such vigorous exception to parking violations on their own turf.

Hugo wasn't sure how the Duchess had found out about that. He certainly hadn't told her. But drug dealers could find out anything, which was probably how they survived.

The Duchess had survived for quite a while; if she had an ordinary name, no one knew what it was. Hugo suspected that someday he'd be summoned to a limo meeting and find her sitting in the back seat instead of Vector. He had no idea whether this would be an improvement or not. He couldn't picture her running Motorball like Vector did—she seemed too coolly reserved.

The sound of the south-town crew leader begging whoever was hitting him to stop—he'd learned his lesson, *really*—brought Hugo back to the present. He thought about covering his ears, but he was afraid the Duchess would be offended if she saw him like that. Offending the Duchess was the last thing he wanted to do.

As if his thoughts had summoned her, the lady herself came out of the front entrance. Half-remembered manners learned in another life made him start to get up, but she motioned for him to sit as she went down the steps to stand in front of him. She was dressed in her usual outfit: a slim black gown that seemed to be made of dozens of black scarves of various sizes and types. Some were lacy, some diaphanous, some silky; combined, they covered her from neck to ankle, revealing nothing except the slender yet curvy outline of her body and underscoring the grace of her movements. Hugo had noticed, however, that her graceful arms were very subtly well-muscled. Only a fool would mistake grace for weakness.

"Awful, isn't it?" She looked at the dark flat-screen on the buildings across the street. "Too bad it only lights up when it senses three people. Watching it would distract you."

She usually kept her hair covered with another black scarf, with only a few locs trailing down her back. This evening they were all hanging free, and Hugo saw small charms and beads woven into them.

"Even a lady in black likes a little sparkle here and there," she said, amused.

"I'm sorry." Hugo looked down at the steps. "I didn't mean to stare."

"I'm not offended." She was about to say something else when there was a bloodcurdling scream from inside the cathedral that made them both jump. "Excuse me," she said, looking annoyed and went back inside.

Hugo rested his elbows on his knees and cupped his chin in his hands. He told himself to remember lying on the ground while the southie crew punched and kicked the hell out of him, and peeing blood for days after. But that seemed so far away now, over and done. Except for one thing.

He heard the Duchess saying something he couldn't make out; someone answered, just as indistinctly. Probably an enforcer—the voice was unfamiliar. One of the south-town crew spoke, complaining and defensive.

"Oh, boo-*hoo*! Don't be such a big baby!" the Duchess scolded. Maybe she *could* run Motorball, Hugo thought.

There was a loud slap and a southie guy yelled, "Okay! *Okay!*"

There was another slap. A few moments later the Duchess came out again. This time she sat down beside Hugo. "I *swear*," she said, "there's nothing in southie but a bunch of *big babies.* The only reason they're still alive is nobody told them to die."

That jerked a surprised laugh out of Hugo in spite of everything.

"I'm not the only one who says so either," she added. "My Aunt Frida works in the—" She cut off and made a small dismissive gesture with one hand. "Never mind. Instead of gossiping, I should be thanking you— again—for letting me know I was being ripped off. I feel like I should give you more of a reward than this."

She produced the bracelet from somewhere among the scarves and veils, holding it in one hand, looking at the hammered copper and the fake green jewel set into the middle.

"That's okay," Hugo said. "That's all I want." Pause. "Also that those guys never find out I tipped you off."

"It's that important, is it? I mean the bracelet." The Duchess ran a finger over the bracelet, feeling the texture of the hammered metal, then looked at him expectantly.

"It was a very long time ago," Hugo said. "I was just little." He had intended just to tell her that it had belonged to his mother. Instead he found himself giving her a condensed version of the story that included his brother's death, but not the circumstances, and saying only that he'd found the bracelet, *sans* details.

"Ah, family," the Duchess said. "Nothing else could make it so valuable." She pressed it into his hand and Hugo felt his heart leap. "Now it's yours again. Along with my gratitude and friendship. I'm a good friend to have, you know."

"Thank you," Hugo said, feeling awkward and a little anxious.

"I bet you're a good friend too," she went on. "But you've got better things to do than listen to some south-town wimps get what's coming to them." She tilted her head at Hugo's gyro parked at the curb. "Go ahead, get outta here."

Hugo stood up, hoping he didn't look as relieved as he felt. He took a step down, then hesitated and turned back to her. "Hey, you're not gonna—you won't—those guys—" He winced. "They're gonna—you know, go home after this?"

The Duchess laughed as if he'd just told her a joke. "Oh, don't you worry your pretty little head, Hugo. There's no point to taking so much time and trouble with our south-town friends unless they live to regret what they've done. Now get yourself gone while we're all still young."

Hugo got himself gone.

Sitting in the CAFÉ café, Tanji glanced at the bracelet on Hugo's wrist. "Yeah, there it is."

Koyomi gave him a dirty look. "Nice, Tanji. Real nice."

"Oh, for cryin' out loud," Tanji said. "It's jewellery. I'm a guy. What am I supposed to say?"

"What about not ragging on a dead mom?" Koyomi asked.

"I wasn't," Tanji said.

"I think it's beautiful," Koyomi told Hugo. "It really is." She gave Tanji a look.

Tanji let out a heavy put-upon sigh. "Really goes with your outfit, Hugo," he said in a flat voice. "The green brings out your eyes." He turned to Koyomi. "Okay?"

"I got it back," Hugo said. "That's all I care about." He pulled his sleeve down to cover the bracelet, then changed his mind and let it show. "Now let's get back to our unfinished business."

Tanji gave a short, humourless laugh. "Oh, yeah. About that."

"What?" Hugo looked from Tanji to Koyomi, who had a pained expression on her face, and back again.

"We shoulda taken him that night," Tanji said. "Because nobody's seen him since. Dif and Louie've been keeping an eye out, but it's like he disappeared."

Hugo shook his head. "He's somewhere. We just have to find out where. The guy's a show-off. They look anywhere but northland?"

Tanji gave an awkward shrug. "How many more people you want to bring in on this?"

"None. Just Dif and Louie," Hugo said.

"Good," Tanji replied. "The take'll be thin enough split five ways. Any more than that and we might as well not bother."

Hugo nodded; he'd been thinking the same thing. He might have tried doing the job with just the three of them anyway, except his tailbone and his armpits still hurt, as if to remind him how much he wanted payback.

The key to going down steps after every part of your body had been bruised, pounded and pulped to within an inch of your life, Ido discovered, was to make no sudden movements. Patience, concentration, precision— it was like surgery. As long as he concentrated, going downstairs hurt less than getting dressed.

The sound of Gerhad chatting away to a patient made him smile, although even that hurt a little. Once again, he could thank whatever gods or forces he didn't believe in that he'd had the good judgment to hire a nurse who could cover for him when he'd had the bad judgment to confront a rogue cyborg whose anger management was as non-existent as his impulse control.

When Ido finally reached the bottom of the stairs, he went to the hook where he usually hung his lab coat only to find it wasn't there.

"Jeez, Doc, I hope you got the number of the ass-kicking machine that ran you down," said the patient. That was Corky—agriculture and produce. His job had him working sometimes out at the orchards and sometimes at a predistribution and quality-control centre, picking through all the best orchard fruits to be sent up to Zalem. The Factory put a lot of demands on his specialised arms but were lousy when it came to maintenance.

If he could remember that much, Ido thought, he hadn't suffered a traumatic brain injury. A mild concussion, certainly, but that came with the territory.

"Pardon me a second," Gerhad said to the patient and helped Ido to the other chair, adjusting it so he was sitting straight up with extra lumbar support. "Am I gonna have to strap you in here, or are you gonna be a good boy and sit quietly while I finish with Corky?" she asked Ido.

"Hi, Corky," Ido said, trying to sound hale and hearty. "How's it going?"

"Better for me than you, Doc. You got two black eyes. *Two!*"

"That's what happens when you break your nose," Ido told him matter-of-factly.

"No kiddin'," Corky said. "Man, whoever mugged you was a real *pendejo.*"

Good cover story, Ido thought; very mundane, totally believable. He was about to say something else when he felt a sting in his arm.

The next time he opened his eyes, late-afternoon sunlight was slanting through the windows, and Gerhad was seeing a different patient to the door.

Ido tried to get out of the chair and discovered he was belted in. Maybe if he turned the chair upside down, he could slide out like Hugo had, only he couldn't find the control pad.

Gerhad swivelled the chair around. "Doctors always make the worst patients," she said, shining a bright light into each eye then pinching his nose shut so he would open his mouth. "But you're in a class by yourself."

"It's bad to just lie in bed," Ido said, trying to sound reasonable rather than defensive. "Blood clots."

"It's worse to get up and wander around before all your pressure dressings are applied," Gerhad scolded.

"Pressure dressings?" Ido blinked at her in bewildered surprise. He was less woozy, but her face was still shifting position. So was the rest of the world. "Aren't they already on?"

"Tissue swelling has to go down first, Dr Genius, remember?" Gerhad chuckled. "You're almost there. Or you should have been. Getting up and running around may have undone all the anti-inflammatories' good work."

"I wasn't *running around*," Ido said. "And I don't feel swollen."

"Who's the nurse, you or me?" Gerhad said. "I outrank you on this case. Wait here. I'm gonna bring you something you'll like."

Wait here? What a joker. He heard someone moving around in the kitchen. Then Gerhad was back, sitting him up straighter.

"Open up," she said. A spoon with something cold and tasty slipped between his lips.

"Gazpacho!" Ido was delighted. "How did you know?"

Gerhad laughed. "There's always at least a quart in the refrigerator and you keep copies of the recipe with your prescription pads."

"Oh, right," he said, feeling a bit silly. "You don't have to feed me."

"Yeah, I do," Gerhad told him firmly. "Until I get the pressure glove on you, anyway."

"How many bones did I break?" Ido asked, startled. Suddenly he felt much more alert, almost wide awake.

"Not as many as I thought," Gerhad replied, "and they're all hairline fractures. Pressure dressings will take care of them."

As Gerhad continued feeding him, Ido tried to remember what had happened. His last clear memory was of standing on a bar in a badly ventilated sub-sub-sub-basement, watching a cyborg in blue-and-orange armour tear another cyborg's arm off. Everything after that was patchy.

"You've got excellent bones, Doc," Gerhad said. "Well above average for Iron City. I don't know where you grew up, but it wasn't here."

Ido said nothing.

Gerhad went on feeding him in silence for a minute or two. "Scanner showed you've sustained a whole lot of previous injuries," she said finally. "More than a lot of people I saw in the emergency room. I know you're not playing in an amateur Motorball league on the weekends. These aren't consistent with Motorball anyway. They're more like martial arts injuries, but not from sparring. These are what you'd get if someone had tried to kill you." Pause. "Or vice versa."

Ido remained silent for a few moments. "The gazpacho recipe is actually from the taqueria across the way," he said. "I like having chunks of vegetables. Tastier than just liquefying everything."

"I'm not trying to pry into your private business," Gerhad said, putting the bowl down on the tray-table beside her. "You don't want to tell me you're one of those fight club weirdos that needs to get your butt kicked once or twice a month in south-town, that's fine. I'd just like to point out that you built up a practice here. People depend on you—"

"That's not it," Ido said.

"Thank God for that," Gerhad said, picking the bowl up again. "Some people say you should try not to judge, but they don't work in an emergency room."

"I'm a Hunter-Warrior," Ido said.

Gerhad put the bowl down again and folded her arms. "Which is the other stupid thing you could be."

"I have my reasons," Ido said.

"Everybody's got their reasons for everything." Gerhad sighed. "So that's what you were doing that I had to scrape you up off a south-town alley?"

"No," Ido said. "But I should've been. I won't make the same mistake again."

"That doesn't sound promising," Gerhad said glumly. "Did you miss my saying you have patients counting on you?"

"That's why we should get those pressure dressings on right away," Ido said.

Gerhad blew out an exasperated breath. "I oughta dope you up and strap you to this chair."

"If you do, worse things will happen," Ido told her. "And not just in south-town."

"I didn't say I *would*," Gerhad replied.

CHAPTER 17

The sun was setting when Tanji found Hugo sitting on a cement barrier at the edge of the broken causeway, a couple of blocks from where the main road curved away from the dead remnants of a highway system no one understood any more. Farther out, more broken pieces of road sat atop tall supports of weathered concrete. Here and there chunks had been blown out of the supports, showing a metal framework inside; Hugo thought of them as Iron City's secret skeletons.

"What are you doing out here?" Tanji asked him, parking his gyro behind Hugo's before sitting down beside him. "Koyomi's probably got a candle in the front window at CAFÉ café by now."

"I needed thinking space," Hugo said.

"Did you think up anything good? Like how we're going to deliver on time to the big man?"

"Vector," Hugo said, suppressing a strong urge to say he wasn't the big man.

Tanji looked down at the bracelet on Hugo's wrist. "Is that giving you inspiration?"

"It's a good luck charm," Hugo said. "Or it was. But you found me anyway."

Tanji clutched his chest. "Ow, ya got me. But I think I'll live," he added, looking down at himself. "Seriously, what's your damage? Are we gonna take this guy tonight or what?"

"Unless you have a better plan," Hugo replied, a bit testily.

"Not me." Tanji looked over his shoulder, down at the weedy area that marked the edge of the lower-level streets. "You didn't come here to scout real estate down there, did you?"

Hugo followed his gaze. The street on the lower level dead-ended at the same point where the upper street curved. You had to go much farther out, into the wild grass and weeds before you found any more fragments of road; no one ever did. There were weird, ugly biting insects in grass that had edges sharp enough to slice skin. The only people down there were no-hopers, those who had fallen so far that the upper level of Iron City had become their Zalem. They sheltered directly under the causeway and survived by raiding dumpsters for food.

The Factory had a number of operations on the lower level; no one seemed to know what they were, as the buildings had no windows. A panhandler had told Hugo that they were where the Factory manufactured defective robots, which they slipped in among the population. It was a paranoid fairy tale, the sort of thing that sounded reasonable to anyone off their meds. At the same time, however, Hugo didn't think it sounded any crazier than the idea of living in a city that had two basic purposes: A) to support Zalem, and B) to be Zalem's trashcan. Sometimes Hugo wondered what it would have been like to live in a world that made sense.

Tanji gave him a hard nudge. "What is *with* you? You act like you don't care whether we get this guy or not."

"I care," Hugo said. "And we'll get him. I got a message from Dif earlier. He and Louie know right where he is."

Tanji blinked at him. "And you didn't feel like that information was important enough to share with me and Koyomi?"

Hugo made a face. "He's in the Velvet Orchid."

Now Tanji let out a hearty laugh. "They cater to everybody, I guess. Although I never understood why a TR would go to a place like that."

"Well, number one, TRs have senses like anybody else. Their bodies have feeling in them; they aren't just numb from the neck down. And, number two, he's not a customer."

"If he's not a customer, what—oh." Tanji looked revolted. "Maybe we'd better bring a couple of gallons of disinfectant to dunk him in before we disconnect his cyber-core." He gave a small shudder. "Dammit, now I don't even want to touch him with gloves on."

"I had no idea you were such a prude," Hugo said, amused in spite of everything.

"I'm *not*," Tanji said defensively. "I'm just—" He gave a small shudder.

Hugo waited for Tanji to go on, then said, "Okay, you're not a prude. You're just *kind* of a prude. What're you gonna be when you grow up, the guardian of public morals?" He paused, thinking of Koyomi in Widow Shins. "The Velvet Orchid is probably pretty tame compared to some places."

"What places?" Tanji asked. "Gimme a for instance."

"How should I know? I don't go to any of them." Hugo shrugged. "Use your imagination."

Tanji gave a brief shudder. "No, thanks—I don't want crap like that in my head. So how're we supposed to get him? Go in, get naked, give him a few jolts, then toss him out a window?"

Hugo shook his head. "Dif and Louie said most nights he comes out about three A.M. and goes to an all-night one-stop for candy bars."

"'*Most* nights'?" Tanji's frown was sceptical. "What if tonight isn't 'most nights'?"

"I don't know," Hugo replied, annoyed. "Phone and ask him to make a house call. Pull a fire alarm. Stop fretting. You're like a little old lady. We'll get him."

"We better," Tanji said. "If we mess this one up, Vector'll drop us. Then we're screwed."

"I know. I *know*," Hugo snapped. He shifted position on the barrier and his tailbone gave an intense twinge, making him stand up.

Tanji followed suit. "I'm going back to CAFÉ café. You coming, or do you want to stick around and listen to them whispering down there?"

"You hear whispering?" Hugo asked him. "How long has *that* been going on?"

"Shut up," Tanji said, starting his gyro.

Koyomi was waiting for them at their usual spot by the window. "I was starting to think you guys were no-shows," she complained.

"Not you too." Hugo sighed.

"What's *that* supposed to mean?" she said, frowning.

"Tanji's pissing and moaning about how tonight's our last chance," Hugo said.

"Well, it is, isn't it?" Koyomi replied. "If we're late again, we lose our whole gig with Vector."

"Hey, it took a few days for Dif and Louie to find him." Hugo told her where the cyborg was and how they were going to take him down.

"That's... really weird," she said when Hugo finished.

"'Weird' is one way to put it," said Tanji. "I'll be double-gloving tonight. And bringing spares, just in case."

"I don't understand," Koyomi said.

"You don't understand why I'd wear two pairs of gloves?" Tanji asked, baffled.

"No, I get *that*," Koyomi said. "Everybody knows what a prude you are. I don't understand why someone with all those enhancements would just be a fancy man-whore. It doesn't make sense."

Because the world doesn't make sense, Hugo replied silently while Tanji and Koyomi argued over whether Tanji was a prude.

"You're not from around here," said the woman sitting across from Ido at the small table in the west-side marketplace. She had sent him a text telling him she had a line on a certain rather speedy cyborg, and if he came here at one A.M. she'd share it with him. It was now one-fifteen and she had yet to share anything substantial; meanwhile his analgesics were fading. Ido had plenty in his coat pockets and more in the Rocket Hammer case standing like a sentinel beside him, but he didn't want to take them in front of this woman for no good reason he could think of. If he didn't top up soon, however, he was going to have a hard time getting up from the chair, and he didn't want her seeing that either.

The problems of the modern Hunter-Warrior: going out to bag a mark before you were completely healed up from your last beating. It was an occupational hazard. That, and the occasional anonymous tip that sent you down a blind alley to a fortune teller. If Gerhad knew what he was doing, she'd kill him.

"I've been here for years," Ido said. "Most of the cyborgs in Iron City have come through my clinic at one time or another. I just might see them all before I'm done."

"Yes, but you didn't spring up out of the rain and the rust and dust of Iron City like they did," she said.

"Who knows where *anyone* sprang up?" Ido had a strong urge to tell her she didn't look much like an Iron City native either. There was something about her face that was—well, not exactly wrong, but not quite right either. She wasn't unattractive—quite the opposite. But Ido couldn't shake the idea this wasn't her natural face, that she had undergone extensive reconstruction, and while the surgeon had been very skilled at putting everything back together, it was all ever so slightly out of true somehow.

But it was really her eyes that made her look so uncanny. The fortune teller was the first and only case of complete heterochromia Ido had ever seen in Iron City: her right eye was a dark golden-brown and her left was green. If those were contact lenses, they were far too good for Iron City, more like something slipped out of a shipment headed for Zalem. Only Vector could get away with skimming—

But if she were that well-connected, why was she telling fortunes in an all-night marketplace? It couldn't have been to gather information and report whatever she saw or heard to Vector; there were easier ways to spy on people. And Vector certainly didn't need to hire anyone to spy on Ido; Chiren would tell him anything he wanted to know, right down to the combination to the safe in the cellar.

The thought came unbidden: maybe she was working for someone higher than Vector.

Ido glanced up at Zalem, a circle of starless black in the night sky. Zalem took anything and everything worth having from Iron City and didn't communicate with anyone except Vector. There was no way for them to make contact with anyone else at ground level—

Unless the whispered stories about the Factory putting chips in people's heads so that those on high could ride them really were true. Ido hadn't believed it. It sounded like classic folklore from the land of the clinically paranoid. None of the alleged joyride chips scanned as anything more than standard internal ID registration. Why would anyone from Zalem want to ride someone at ground level? There was nothing down here that any of them would want to see.

Only now that he was thinking of it, he knew one person who would have enjoyed being a misery tourist. Ido reflexively touched the back of his neck, where the cyborg ID chips were located. Not being a cyborg, he didn't have one himself. Chiren hadn't either. He looked up at Zalem again, then suddenly realised the woman had spoken to him.

"Uh, excuse me?" he said, feeling his face grow warm.

She leaned her elbows on the table as she studied him. "I said, you look like you think someone's gonna hit you."

Ido shrugged; the sharp pain in his ribs made him regret it immediately.

"Probably because someone already did," she added. "Your glasses hide the black eyes pretty well. Don't worry; most people won't notice."

"I'm not worried," Ido said.

"Not about that. You're worried that maybe it's a little soon to go looking for trouble." She picked up the deck of cards sitting to her left on the table and shuffled them. They were a bit over-sized but she handled them easily. "Let's see what the cards say."

Ido gave up and took a couple of analgesics from a box in his pocket, washing them down with some bottled water. "Shouldn't I shuffle?" he asked. "I thought that was how it worked."

"The cards know you're here." She laid out three cards face down, starting on his left. "Whenever you're ready, you can turn the first one over.

Use your left hand," she added as he started to reach for it with his right.

The image on the card was a skull and crossbones. Ido stared; it was all bullshit, but his heart thumped anyway.

"Don't see a whole lot of people pull Death first," the woman said cheerfully.

Ido gave a short, humourless laugh. "I suppose that means I'm going to die tonight."

"No, it means you're already dead." She smiled at him even more cheerfully. "You've had a moment of definitive conclusion in your recent past. Something came to an end permanently."

"That's probably true of most people," Ido said, trying not to think of his daughter or Chiren.

"All good things come to an end," the woman replied. "But yours had an exceptional end. You lost your life. Next card, either hand."

"I'm still alive," Ido said a bit defensively, using his left hand again. His heart gave another thump. The image on this card was the ruined cathedral, at an angle that showed the screen on the building across the street in the background as well as a supply tube arching over the single intact spire. Zalem wasn't in the picture.

"Traditional tarot has the Tower. Iron City tarot has the Temple in Ruins," the woman told him. "This is your here-and-now."

"That's everyone's here-and-now," Ido said, not bothering to hide his disdain. He took some more analgesics.

"But it's yours in particular," the woman insisted. "Last card. Right hand this time."

"I figured," Ido said, turning the card over. The picture on this one showed a man hanging upside down by one foot from a structure in the trash pile. A small portion of Zalem's trash chute showed in the upper left-hand corner. "So, what—are they gonna hang me for my crimes?"

"Not hanging; suspended." The woman smiled at him. "Taking time to think."

"Thanks. This has all been very informative." Ido leaned on the Rocket Hammer case to push himself to his feet. "But I have to go do some real things in the real world."

"Look at the cards," the woman ordered him, her voice suddenly hard and impatient, as if *he* had been wasting *her* time.

"All right, I'm looking," Ido said. "They haven't changed."

"No, they haven't." She covered the first card with one hand. She tapped the centre card, the one picturing the ruined cathedral. "Don't live in the past; it's gone. And you're not in the future yet. Tomorrow isn't real." She covered the third card with her other hand. "You need to be right here in the present."

Ido sighed, feeling a little stupid that it had taken him that long to get it. Although why she had felt the need to go through a silly charade just to tell him the cyborg was hiding out in the cathedral was beyond him. She could have simply whispered it in his ear. Or sent an anonymous message.

"You never know who's watching," she added. "Or from behind whose eyes they're watching." She tilted her head to one side. "Except you. Your eyes are always your own, aren't they?"

"That's a different conversation for a different time. I have to go," Ido said, remembering the bartender's words and wondering if he'd ever see him again. He put a few credits on the table, then added some more. It was a generous amount and she made it disappear quickly.

"Thank you," she said. "As our ancestors used to say, have fun rocking the casbah."

Ido wasn't sure that was quite right, but he put another credit on the table before he left anyway.

All right, I did what you asked. I sent him there, just like you wanted, she thought at the shadow in the sky.

High above her, the man with the chrome optics leaned on the railing and smiled as he looked down. This was going to be good.

The cathedral was as deserted as Ido had ever seen it, but that didn't mean anything. Legend had it that drug dealers hid their various goods here, but Ido was pretty sure that wasn't true. It seemed a bit too obvious for one thing, and not terribly convenient for another. Plus, having been a psycho cyborg's killing ground hadn't done much for the ambience.

So maybe it *was* a good hiding place for drug dealers to keep their inventory.

Ido shook his head. He was over-thinking worse than when he'd first landed on the ground, uncertain but determined to make the best of a bad situation, without the faintest idea there could be worse things waiting.

And now here he was, an experienced survivor of catastrophe. He dragged the Rocket Hammer case up the cathedral's cracked and broken front steps.

The debris seemed to have increased several times since he'd last been inside. But then, he didn't usually go inside—it was more convenient to assemble the Rocket Hammer outside in the shadows. Not tonight, though; he wanted the case close at hand, so the analgesics were in easy reach.

Ido moved along the wall to his left. Here the empty arched windows were high up and the structure was still pretty solid. There wasn't as much large wreckage there, so it was easier to manoeuvre the case.

Finally, he found a spot behind a pile of large broken stones and chunks of splintered, mouldy wood where he could lay the case down and open it. Before he did anything else, he topped up all the analgesics.

He was definitely overdoing some of the meds, but he decided he would be okay as long as he didn't make a practice of hunting while still wounded from his previous misadventure. The thought replayed itself in his mind and he almost laughed aloud. "Misadventure"—as if he were a character in a novel doing something brave but foolish, and not quite legal.

Whether it was brave or foolish was debatable, but it certainly wasn't quite legal. If there was no mark out on the cyborg, no price on his head, then by the letter of the law Ido had no business hunting him, even if he had absolutely no intention of killing him, none whatsoever. He simply had to pull that chip out of him. Without the chip, the cyborg would no longer have episodes of uncontrollable, violent rage.

No, Ido thought sadly, he was almost certainly wrong about that. The cyborg would never be the same. After being repeatedly taken over by anger and fury, the man was almost certainly a rageaholic now. And he didn't have to be fast to be dangerous. He was as ruined as this cathedral. Vector wouldn't want him any more, and he wasn't fit for anything apart from illegal fights in south-town.

Ido had just finished assembling the Rocket Hammer when he heard a voice say, "I know you're here, old man."

Ido froze, kneeling behind the pile of broken stones.

"Thought you woulda had enough the other night," the cyborg said. "I coulda killed you then, you know. Coulda just squeezed your head between my hands till it was nothing but bad meat in a basket of broken bone, or just tore it off your neck and drop-kicked it into the trash pile. Pounded you into the street till there was nothing left but a stain. Lotta ways I coulda killed you. But I let you go because I thought you were just a sad old man playing hero. I even called your ride home for you."

Ido suppressed a sigh. This was Iron City; what did he expect? The fortune teller hadn't promised not to give the cyborg a heads-up. It was a hard world, and if he got the worst of it again tonight, he had only himself to blame. He'd come here knowing damned well he wasn't ready for a fight.

"Are you just gonna hide in the dark, old man?" the cyborg asked. "Did you lose your nerve? You gonna make me come and find you?"

Holding the Rocket Hammer, Ido rose to his feet, ignoring the muffled pain in his ribs and back. His eyes had adjusted to the darkness so that he could see the cyborg fairly well. "No, I'm right here." His voice echoed and he felt a tiny bit of gratification when the cyborg looked around, obviously unable to figure the direction it was coming from. Maybe the cyborg's built-in night-vision wasn't very good. "But tonight, I'm not just some old man you can beat with one hand tied behind your back."

The cyborg spotted Ido as he approached and burst out laughing. "What kind of an outfit is *that*?"

"An old-man outfit," Ido said.

"And you brought a toy!" The cyborg lunged for the Rocket Hammer.

Ido slammed the blunt end into the cyborg's midsection. The blow sent him flying backwards to land on his back on a small pile of rocks, looking surprised.

"Okay, *now* it's a party!" The cyborg flipped up to his feet, wavered as he almost lost his balance and then dropped into a fighter's crouch, hands up and ready.

A brief but intense wave of déjà-vu swept over Ido; he shrugged it off as he moved around to the cyborg's left. The cyborg tracked him. "You think you're some kind of Hunter-Warrior? There's no bounty out on me, old man. I've committed no crime. You can't attack me. That's against the law and against the Hunter's Code."

"What would you know about the law or the Hunter's Code?" Ido said, unable to help himself.

"I know all kinds of things, thanks to the *Watcher.*" The cyborg actually sounded smug. "You don't know about him, do ya? Course not. He won't speak to *you*—you're just an old meat-bag and that's all you'll ever be. *I've* been chosen."

"For what?" Ido asked. If he could keep the guy talking, he'd be too distracted to think about making any super-fast moves, which might allow Ido to take out a knee. It was hard to make any moves, super-fast or otherwise, with only one good leg.

"Enhancements!" the cyborg crowed.

"Good for you." Ido feinted high with the Hammer and the cyborg raised his arms to counter. Ido twisted the weapon as he dipped and added propulsion to the pointy side. It made a direct hit on the cyborg's left knee and took the lower part of the leg off completely. The cyborg bellowed in rage as he toppled over, blue cyber-blood spurting from his thigh.

Ido was shocked. He had expected the joint to break, not break off. Chiren would never have done such shoddy work that one blow could amputate a leg—

She hadn't. The cyborg had been AWOL for over a week, which meant he hadn't had any maintenance. He'd been out picking fights and tearing arms off other cyborgs as if nothing could hurt him, as if he weren't subject to wear and tear himself. Now he was probably on the verge of falling to pieces, and this "Watcher", whoever or whatever that was, hadn't thought to mention the need for maintenance along with the Hunter's Code.

The cyborg was trying to get back up on his good leg. "Okay, old man, you *want* a fight, you *got* a fight. I was holding back before. Now I'm gonna *kill* you." He managed to get to one knee, propping himself up on the stump of his left thigh. "You think I can't fight you like this?"

"You haven't laid a hand on me," Ido pointed out. "Listen, you're very close to complete system failure. You need maintenance—"

"I handle that myself," the cyborg said scornfully. "And I never felt better. Come on, you think you can fight me? Then fight me!"

Ido sighed and raised the Rocket Hammer over his head, aiming for the place where the cyborg's arm connected to his shoulder. The cyborg smiled and Ido felt a surge of guilt mixed with pity for him.

Then the cyborg flickered.

When Ido came to, the cyborg was shaking him like a dog with a chew toy and his body was screaming with every different kind of pain there was.

"Wake up, you old bastard! C'mon, I wanna see you give it up!" The cyborg had both hands around his neck. "This ain't gonna be quick for you, old man. You don't get off that easy!"

Ido's hands were empty. Where was the Rocket Hammer? How long had he been unconscious? He was trying to look around when everything suddenly went black again.

This time, it was the impact of the back of his head on a cement floor that jarred Ido awake. His ribcage was on fire as he started dragging himself away from the cyborg's mocking laughter. How the hell had he managed that *flicker* move with only one leg, Ido wondered; how had—

Something like a steel vice caught him by the ankle and squeezed. The sound of his bones breaking made Ido's stomach lurch violently; the taste of bile and dirt made him vomit again.

"Shouldn'ta eaten a big dinner!" the cyborg said, laughing even harder as he dragged Ido through the dirt and rubble on the cement floor by his ankle. Ido grabbed desperately for something, anything he could use as a weapon. His right hand closed on a rough chunk of stone or concrete.

"Now, where were we?" the cyborg said in a chatty tone, pulling him close and reaching for his neck. Ido brought his right hand up and slammed the chunk of rock into the cyborg's face as hard as he could.

Everything stopped.

At first Ido didn't dare move. But time stretched and the cyborg didn't even twitch. Ido manoeuvred himself out of his grasp and scuttled backwards, vaguely aware that his ankle was swelling rapidly.

The cyborg sat upright, still not moving. The broken chunk of rock was still stuck to the spot where Ido had hit him, defying gravity and all sense.

"I must be dead," Ido said aloud, just to find out if he could speak. He dragged himself over to the cyborg's left side, wondering what was keeping the rock stuck there. But he couldn't see anything.

It took him a few seconds to work up enough nerve to touch the rock. To his surprise, it still wouldn't move. He pulled on it and it came away with a sickening wet sound. Finally, he saw there was a short length of iron bar protruding from it that had stuck in the cyborg's eye. Horrified, Ido hurled the chunk away; at the same moment the cyborg toppled over backwards.

Ido waited a few moments; when the cyborg didn't move, Ido rolled him over and took a jackknife out of his coat pocket. The pain in his ankle was intensifying but he had to get this done before it got bad enough to incapacitate him. The chip would be at the top of the spine, just below the medulla. He touched the blade to the artificial skin.

"I'd rather you *didn't* do that," said the cyborg.

Ido jumped back from him with a yelp. The cyborg rolled onto his back again. "He's pretty much dead, but I'd prefer if you left the chip. I'm not done having fun with it."

The voice was the cyborg's, but it sounded like someone else was using it. Ido tasted bile as his stomach threatened to lurch again.

"I didn't want to kill you—him," Ido said.

"You actually surprised me, Ido. I never thought you had it in you. I'm going to have to rethink some things. But don't worry, I'll be seeing you. I see *everything*."

Ido waited but there was nothing else. After a moment, Ido rolled him over again and removed the chip. The extraction was more the work of a slasher than a surgeon; his hands were shaking and his eyes were watering from dust and mould as well as from the pain of his broken ankle. Once he got the chip out, he braced himself for another surprise pronouncement but apparently the cyborg had breathed his last. Ido would have wondered more about what had just happened but his ankle was now screaming so much, he was no longer sure he hadn't imagined everything.

He called Gerhad, knowing she wasn't going to take this well. In fact, she would probably kill him. He hoped so anyway.

CHAPTER 18

Sometime after Dyson Ido heard his ankle bones crack, Hugo was peering down into the darkness of an open manhole in an east-side alley and trying to decide if the job was really worth climbing down into it.

"It's not the *actual* sewer," Dif said for what seemed like the hundredth time. "It's an access tunnel the maintenance guys use to get around. Access tunnels run all over the place—they're like invisible streets underground. You can climb down here and come out anywhere in Iron City."

"If you know where you're going, anyway," Louie added.

"You got a map?" Hugo asked him.

Louie and Dif exchanged glances. "Not for the whole city," Dif said. "But I know how to get from here to the Velvet Orchid. And I know this is where our guy comes out."

"The Velvet Orchid isn't directly above the sewer," Koyomi said. "If it were, they wouldn't do any business."

"No, but they're practically on top of a main access point," said Dif. "Makes it convenient for people to get in and out of the place without anyone seeing."

Hugo sniffed. "Like their clients would rather use the sewer than the back door. You guys are nuts."

"Married people would," Dif said, a bit defensively.

"That I *can* believe," Koyomi said, nodding.

"Not me," Tanji said.

"Only because you're such a prude," Dif said matter-of-factly.

"See?" Koyomi said to Tanji. "Told you—everybody knows."

"Would everybody please shut up for a minute?" Hugo said, exasperated. "I can't hear myself think." He went over to the truck and leaned against it. After a moment Koyomi joined him, leaving the other three to linger around the open manhole.

"I'm not crazy about the idea either," she said, "but we can take him down out of sight—no witnesses."

Hugo made a face. "How big is the tunnel?" he asked.

Dif and Louie glanced at each other. "Well, it's higher and wider than I can reach," Louie said, demonstrating.

"How much higher and wider?" Hugo asked with a sigh.

"We didn't have a ruler," Dif huffed. "Our guy's pretty big and he can walk through them okay. So it's at least ten feet high. And at least ten feet wide too. I guess."

Hugo sighed again. "That doesn't give us much room to manoeuvre."

"Gives him even less," Louie pointed out.

"That's not necessarily an advantage," Hugo said.

"I don't like it," Tanji said. "There's all kinds of things down there. I heard Grewishka's down there."

"Really?" Koyomi's eyes widened.

"It's just a rumour," Louie said. "But even if it's true, he'd be in the *sewer*, not the access tunnels."

"How do *you* know?" Tanji asked evenly.

"Hey, we're not gonna *live* down there, just jack this *one* cyborg *one* time," said Dif. "It won't take long—we're in, we're out. What's the big deal?"

"It *smells*," Hugo said.

"You'll hardly notice it," Louie said. "And it's not as bad as the sewer."

"That's not saying much," Tanji said.

"Okay, okay!" Hugo made an impatient shushing gesture with both arms and they all shut up. "It's gotta be fast, no screwing around. He has to go down in sixty seconds, ninety at most. If we screw up, we won't get another chance. Or another job from Vector. Koyomi, you move the truck so it's over the manhole—"

"Maybe we should put a sticky-net over it too," Tanji said. "Just in case he gives us the slip and makes a break for it.

"Good idea," Hugo said.

"Not bad for a prude," added Koyomi, giving him a soft punch on the arm.

Tanji looked over her head at Hugo. "Thanks, but you don't have to sound so surprised."

"Gear up," Hugo told the crew. "Except no fire-bottles."

"Why not?" asked Dif.

"Because that smell is sewer gas, and sewer gas is methane and a bunch of other stuff, all of it flammable." He turned to Dif. "When you were scouting it out, did you happen to feel any breezes or drafts or anything?"

Dif frowned at him incredulously. "Are you kidding?"

"No ventilation," Hugo replied. "Fire burns oxygen. If a fire-bottle goes off down there, we'll have a hard time breathing. You can't fight if you can't breathe."

Louie looked at Hugo with something like wonder. "How do you know all that?"

Hugo shrugged. "Just stuff I picked up," he said. In truth, he wasn't sure himself. "You want to talk about it later, we can as long as you take my word for it right now. If I see a fire-bottle in the tunnel, you're off the crew even if we *don't* die."

Once they were down in the tunnel, Hugo almost called it off. There was more light than he'd expected—Dif actually hadn't exaggerated how bright the long overhead rods were, and they had come on while they were still climbing down the ladder. But that much light made Hugo think there had to be surveillance cameras, although he couldn't find anything that looked like it had a lens.

The space, however, seemed smaller than Dif had described. Small enclosed spaces had never bothered Hugo, but with his hood up, goggles on and a bandanna over his nose and mouth, he felt like he was being smothered. Worse, the bandanna did little to block the smell, which was more pungent than Dif had led him to believe. Hugo was sorry he hadn't made them stick to the original plan of ambushing the cyborg as he came up out of the manhole.

Why the hell was the cyborg using underground tunnels to move around anyway? He probably had to be hosed down several times a day to get rid of the smell, which seemed almost as solid as the tunnel itself.

Dif showed them two junctions—one where a tunnel branched off to the right, and another farther on that went off to the left. Dif and Louie took the latter and Hugo, Tanji and Koyomi hid in the former. The plan was simple—he, Tanji and Koyomi would jump out and confront the cyborg, while Dif and Louie came up behind him with a net. They'd throw the net over him, then everyone would hit him all at once with paralyser bolts. A shock to the back of the neck was usually enough to take a cyborg down, but Hugo wanted to hit him in the shoulders, elbows and knees, just to be sure everything was immobilised.

Twenty minutes after they took their positions, the lights went out. Tanji and Koyomi both jumped; Hugo hoped they didn't notice he had as well. "It's just the motion sensors," he whispered to Koyomi. "They'll go on again when we move."

Koyomi yanked down the scarf covering the lower part of her face. "I *know* that," she snapped.

"Scarf up," he ordered.

She made a face as she obeyed. "I can hardly breathe."

"Breathe later, shut up now," Tanji whispered. "I think I hear something."

Hugo heard it too: the sound of distant voices. He couldn't make out any words but they had a metallic quality, like they were coming from the bottom of a big empty basin.

What if the cyborg wasn't alone?

That should have occurred to him before now, Hugo thought, wincing. Just because he'd always been alone when Dif and Louie had been tracking him didn't guarantee the cyborg would be alone tonight. Hugo wanted to pound his head against the wall. If he had another TR cyborg with him, they were going to have their work cut out for them. Could the five of them take down two big cyborgs in this confined space?

Hugo could see it going either way. If both cyborgs were tangled up in the net, all they had to do was keep hitting them with paralysers until they stopped moving. Would Vector pay for the extra cyborg body, or would he expect them to throw it in for free? They should talk it over before they delivered, Hugo thought.

What if there were *three*?

Abruptly, Hugo realised the voices had stopped. Farther down the tunnel, lights went on as the cyborg moved towards them. Hugo's phone vibrated with a text from Dif: *He's coming.*

Is he alone? Hugo texted back and received a thumb's-up in reply. But he could hear the footsteps now—just one person—and he almost went limp with relief. He had to plan a lot better next time, Hugo thought, and not let himself get talked into anything, especially when the person doing the talking wasn't the sharpest knife in the drawer.

More lights were going on now. The sewer smell was also getting stronger. By the time the lights in their part of the tunnel went on, Hugo was breathing through his mouth, although it didn't help much. Was the cyborg bringing a load of raw sewage with him?

Hugo's phone lit up with another message from Dif: *NOW.*

He jumped out in front of the cyborg with Koyomi and Tanji following. The smell hit him in the face with renewed force and he heard Koyomi make a disgusted noise.

"And what would you little bugs want?" the cyborg said, laughing. There was a dark smear on his cheek below his right eye and stains on his metal arms, but most of the smell seemed to be coming from whatever was caked on his feet. "Better not run around in here or the exterminator'll come for you!"

Dif and Louie were creeping up behind him. Why didn't they just throw the net over him already? What were they waiting for?

All at once the cyborg gave a shudder and his face lost all expression. "The underworld is where my children live," he said in a low voice that made Hugo's skin crawl. "You have no business here."

Agree totally, Hugo thought and looked past him at Dif and Louie. "Net him already!"

But the cyborg had turned around. Before Dif and Louie could even raise the net, he grabbed them and banged their heads together, taking the net away from them as they fell. The cyborg pivoted and tossed the net at Hugo. Hugo dived between his legs, getting another faceful of stink, while Tanji dodged to one side. The net went over Koyomi and the cyborg pulled her close, saying something else about their not belonging there. Hugo bounced to his feet behind him and stuck his paralyser in the back of the cyborg's neck.

Koyomi let out a scream that gave Hugo an instant and complete understanding of the term "blood-curdling". He heard her banging on the cyborg's metal chest with her fist and saw the smaller, framework arms thrust outward. A long moment later, Koyomi fell to the floor of the tunnel and scuttled away, sobbing and retching as she disentangled herself from the net using one hand and keeping the other arm close to her chest. Hugo hit the cyborg in the back of the neck again and he fell forward on his face, the extra arms thrusting straight out.

Tanji appeared beside him as if by magic and stuck the cyborg at the base of his spine. Not his tailbone, but close enough to give Hugo a brief surge of spiteful satisfaction. The back of the cyborg's thigh sprang open and a cable snaked out to wrap itself tightly around Tanji's legs.

"*Oh, gross!*" Tanji hollered, falling over almost on top of the cyborg. "Get it off, *get it off!*"

Hugo vaulted over the cyborg, grabbed the net and threw it over him, giving him another shot to the base of his skull with the paralyser.

The cyborg's torso lifted, all of his arms contracting. Tanji was yelling for him not to do that, it made the cable squeeze *harder. Get it off, get it off!* Dif stumbled over and stuck his paralyser at the place where the cyborg's leg joined his torso. There was a sharp crack and the cable around Tanji's thigh went limp.

Tanji staggered away, picked up his paralyser bolt and hit the cyborg in the same spot on the other leg. "Just in case," he said grimly. "*Bastard.*

I'll have to shower for a *month* to get rid of the stink."

The cyborg began to laugh. The sound made Hugo draw back with revulsion, but Dif, Tanji and Louie all sprang forward and jabbed their paralysers into the base of his neck. The laughter cut off.

"I never want to hear anything that creepy ever again," Hugo blurted.

"Guy's obviously some kind of nutcase," Tanji said. "One minute he's calling us bugs, the next he's talking about his children? What the hell was *that* about?"

"Multiple personalities," Dif said knowingly. "Some people have, like, a hundred."

"I don't care," Hugo said. "Let's just get him disconnected before he wakes up—"

"Yeah, about that," Louie said, giving Dif a significant look. "You forgot to tell them."

"*We* forgot," Dif corrected him.

"*What?*" Hugo yelled.

Dif looked sheepish. "Well, that buzzing you hear?"

Hugo was about to say he didn't hear anything when he realised he did.

"It's more of a humming," Louie said.

"It's the exterminator," Dif said quickly. "All the movement and thrashing around triggered it. It thinks there's rats or something it has to exterminate."

"Wrap him in the net so we can get him up the ladder," Hugo ordered them, and turned to see Koyomi, still holding her arm protectively to her chest.

"I can't climb," she said in a small voice. "He broke my arm." She started to cry. "*Bastard.*"

Hugo got them to drag the cyborg all the way to the ladder, then told

Koyomi to get on top of the cyborg and loop her good arm through the net.

"No," she said. "I hate you just for suggesting it."

Tanji bent down with his back to her. "Can you hold onto me, then?" She climbed on and he carried her up the ladder piggyback-style. Hugo, Dif and Louie were about to pull the netted, unconscious cyborg up the ladder when the exterminator appeared at the far end of the tunnel.

"*That's* an exterminator?" Hugo said. It was a metal dome four feet high wearing a skirt of constantly moving knives.

"Nasty, isn't it?" Louie said as they struggled up the ladder with the cyborg.

Hugo grunted; a lot of things in Iron City were nasty. At least this one couldn't climb.

"What do you want?" said Vector without looking away from the wall screen. "And why in God's name do you *stink*?"

Hugo was at a loss for words. He looked at the cyborg body lying near the door of the laboratory. After he'd dropped Koyomi and Tanji at the emergency room, he and Dif and Louie had wrapped the thing in several garbage bags. Louie had suggested adding baking soda to get rid of the smell, but they didn't have any and none of them knew where to get some at stupid o'clock in the morning. Now Hugo was glad he'd told Dif and Louie to wait outside after they'd helped him bring the body into the lab.

"I'm delivering your order," Hugo said. "The cyborg body with all the extras. That's what you're smelling." *Please believe that*, he prayed in silent desperation.

Vector turned his head and looked at him with the expression of a man who was fed up with being fed up and wanted someone to take it out on.

"You want to explain yourself? And this better be good, because I *know* I never asked for anything smelling like *that*."

Hugo hesitated. Down at the other end of the room, Chiren was moving from examination tables to cabinets to shelves, picking things up and banging them down or slamming cabinet doors, all the while muttering under her breath. She was pretending she was busy, Hugo realised, and Vector was pretending she wasn't shredding his last nerve.

"We found your order in the sewer," Hugo said finally.

"I did *not* order *anything* from the *sewer*." Vector sat up straighter in the chair, frowning at Hugo. "What is it with you? First south-town; now the sewer? You can't go any lower, kid. Not in *this* life."

"We thought he was in the Velvet Orchid," Hugo said unhappily, trying to make his face a neutral mask.

"How the *hell* do you get from the Velvet Orchid to the sewer?" Vector demanded.

Practice, Vector, practice. Hugo had to bite his lips together so he wouldn't say it out loud. "By an access tunnel," he said finally. "That's where we grabbed him after he came up out of the sewer."

Vector frowned at him for a couple of seconds longer and then started to laugh. "Seriously? You found him in the *sewer*? Damn, kid, that's perfect. You have no idea how perfect it is." He twisted around to look at Chiren, who was rattling the glassware in one of the cabinets as she searched for nothing.

"Hey, Chiren!" Vector called to her.

Chiren kept looking through the cabinet, giving no indication that she'd heard him.

"Hey, baby, got some good news for you!" Vector went on. When she still didn't respond, he added, "Stop that and pay attention when I'm talking to you or I'll come over and make you."

He hadn't raised his voice. If anything, he'd lowered it, but it made Chiren freeze. Then she slowly closed the cabinet and turned around to look at Vector. Hugo tried to keep his face neutral. He hadn't thought anyone could be so pale. Her blue eyes had gone from icy and intense to watery and faded. Whatever had happened tonight had been really bad, and Vector blamed her, whether it had been her fault or not. Hugo tried to think of some way to get out of there and come back later. No one was supposed to see Vector like this, especially not him.

"Our friend Hugo here has just delivered our special order," Vector was telling Chiren. "You know, the cyborg body with all those great enhancements, arms within arms, an extra lung and all that fancy shit? Well, you know where the kid found him? You'll *never* guess—in the *sewer*!" Vector gestured at Hugo like a game show host presenting the grand prize. "That's right, baby, our *Next Big Thing* was gettin' down and dirty with our *Last* Big Thing! Who shoulda been our *Next-To-Last* Big Thing but shit happens, and not just in the sewer."

Vector suddenly turned back to Hugo with a big fake smile that Hugo thought was the most hideous thing he'd ever seen. "Hey, kid, you didn't happen to see Grewishka too, did you?"

Hugo blinked at him, utterly baffled. What did *Grewishka* have to do with anything?

"No? How about our chances for a Motorball championship?" Vector asked. "Surely you saw those, seeing as how *they all got flushed down the toilet*!"

Someone touched Hugo's shoulder and he jumped; one of Vector's bodyguards was looming over him. It was all he could do not to turn and run.

But the man spoke to him in a low voice, barely above a whisper. "It's been a lousy night. Somebody killed the new guy and ran off with the speed chip."

Chase was dead? Hugo was shocked, partly by the fact that someone had actually been able to kill him and partly that anyone had dared to even try it, given that the cyborg was one of Vector's stable. And if that wasn't enough, they'd stolen the super-chip. But who besides Chiren would know how to remove it and who could have been that crazy—

Hugo caught his breath. Ido. Only Ido.

"You come back tomorrow afternoon," the bodyguard whispered. "Sometime after two." He started to usher Hugo towards the door and Hugo let him.

"Hold it right there, kid!" Vector hollered. Hugo cringed, waiting for Vector to shoot him. "I gotta pay you! This is a *professional* operation!" He beckoned impatiently. Hugo went to him. Vector jumped up with an even bigger fake smile and pulled him over to a nearby cabinet with a keypad. It took him three tries to get it open; Hugo pretended to be engrossed in something on his phone.

"There, third time's the winner!" Vector announced, with fake cheer that sounded closer to hysteria. He threw the cabinet door open so widely it bounced back. Vector stilled it with one hand as he reached inside and yanked a package of credits off a shelf. "Good job. Thanks a lot," he said, shoving the credits at Hugo with an even bigger fake smile. "Don't spend it all in one place."

"I, uh, I'll try not to, sir." Hugo couldn't help thinking that wouldn't be easy, given how small one-fifth of the take was. But he wasn't going to short anybody. When he'd formed the crew, Hugo had promised equal shares. He wasn't going back on that, now or ever.

"Great. Glad you were on time, kid. I always appreciate that. But the way things worked out, you coulda taken another week." Vector's grin looked totally demented as he gave Hugo a clap on the shoulder, shoving him towards the exit. Then he raised his voice to address the whole room. "Now, somebody—I don't care who—" Vector looked pointedly at the bodyguard. "Take that stinking thing outside and turn a power hose on it. *Now!*"

Go, the bodyguard mouthed at Hugo, and Hugo went.

At least Dif and Louis had the good grace not to comment on the small size of their shares. Hugo took them to the CAFÉ café to pick up their gyros, then drove to the hospital to check on Koyomi.

He found Tanji alone in a nearly empty waiting room. He'd taken off his hoodie and stuffed it into a plastic bag. "Yay, hooray," Tanji said in a flat voice as Hugo gave him his share. "So how overjoyed was Vector that we delivered on time?"

Thank God he'd made Tanji stay with Koyomi, Hugo thought. "He'd have danced and shouted Hallelujah but they were having a weird night."

"Did he at least say thank you?" Tanji asked.

"Only in words."

Tanji made a sour face. "I think we're gonna have to raise the going rate," he said. "We should figure the headcount into the charge."

"You think we could've done it with just us three?"

Tanji shook his head. "We'd've probably still been fighting him when the exterminator showed up. And he might've broken *all* our arms." He pulled up the neck of his t-shirt and sniffed it. "I think my hoodie caught most of the smell."

Hugo took off his own hoodie and sniffed his own shirt. "I can't tell," he said. "As far as I'm concerned, the whole night stinks. Where'd you get the bag?"

Tanji nodded at the reception desk where a man in a blue-and-white uniform was sitting with his face cupped in his palm and his eyes closed. "Just ask the nurse. He'll give you one."

Hugo hadn't quite reached the desk when the man produced a plastic bag and shoved it across the desk at him, without changing position or even opening his eyes. Hugo thanked him and put his hoodie into it. Tanji had been right—the smell lessened right away.

It was another hour before Koyomi finally emerged, sporting a hot-pink cast on her right forearm. She was dressed in disposable blue hospital scrubs and carrying a small plastic bag with the few things she'd had in her pockets, but nothing else. Her braids were undone and her loose hair was damp.

"They made me take a shower," she said. "I didn't think I was as bad as you guys, but I guess I was bad enough. They told me they burned my clothes and gave me this to wear home. Do I look like Dr Koyomi?"

"You look like an operator," Tanji said. "But that's how you always look." She laughed as Hugo put her share of Vector's payment in the bag she was carrying, then paused to look at it dubiously.

"I'm not so sure I should take this," she said after a few moments.

"Why not?" Hugo and Tanji said in surprised unison.

"All I did was get my arm broken." She looked pained. "I couldn't even climb up the ladder."

"Hey, you earned that," Hugo said, nodding at the bag.

"Besides, if you hadn't got your arm broken, someone else woulda," Tanji added. "Maybe me—and that would've been *really* bad because I'm a lot more important than you are."

Koyomi sighed. "I'd test that out but I'm too tired and too whacked out on pain drugs."

As she started for the exit, Hugo caught her good arm. "Wait, I want to give you something." He slipped the copper band onto her wrist next to the cast.

"Hugo, you can't!" Koyomi said, shocked. "Not your mother's bracelet—not after all you went through—"

"You need it more than I do," he said. "Copper's got healing properties. It's good for your bones."

"How does that work?" asked Koyomi, looking from him to the band on her wrist and back again.

"I dunno," Hugo said. "I'm not a scientist or a doctor. It just does."

"Did Doc Ido tell you that?" Tanji asked him.

"Yeah," Hugo lied. "He gave me this long lecture about it but I didn't understand a word."

"Well, if the Doc says it works, I won't argue," Koyomi said. "But—" She looked pained. "Are you *sure*?"

"Surer than anything," Hugo said. "Besides, it doesn't go with my outfit."

"It doesn't exactly go with mine either," Koyomi said.

"Yeah, but you're a girl," Tanji said, looking at Hugo with genuine respect. "You can get away with it. Nobody looks at you anyway."

"I hate you," Koyomi told him and looped her good arm around Hugo's as they headed for the exit.

"I thought you hated me too," Hugo said.

"Right now, not so much," Koyomi replied. "Maybe later."

Hugo dropped her off in front of her apartment building on the way to the loading dock where he and Tanji had left their gyros. Tanji helped him with the tarp, then took off. Hugo considered just curling up in the cab, then decided he didn't want to prolong the truck's exposure to his jeans. Which reminded him that he was going to have to air out the back and fumigate it. And while he was at it, maybe he should burn his clothes too, or at least throw them away *before* he went into his apartment.

As he was about to start the gyro, his gaze fell on the cathedral, a jagged black silhouette against the dawn sky. He looked from the platform around the single intact spire to Zalem and wished he weren't too tired to climb up there. Zalem was beautiful at sunrise.

Someday his gazing up at Zalem from down here would be the past that he could look back on while living in the contented present up there. No more jacking cyborgs, no more sewers or access tunnels, no more friends breaking bones for a few lousy credits. Someday he'd actually be above it all. That was his future; it had been promised to him and nothing would keep him from it.

CHAPTER 19

It seemed to Chiren that she rebuilt Claymore's joints once a month.

This time it was his shoulders and knees. Next time it would be his wrists and hips, and then his elbows and ankles. After that she might have to rebuild them all completely.

When she wasn't working on him, she had to keep Juggernaut up and running; Juggernaut and his three wheels and four arms. Sometimes there was so much work to do on Juggernaut that she had to delegate Claymore's maintenance (although she always inspected everything personally). If she didn't stay on top of Juggernaut's condition every second, that big old front wheel might come right the hell off. She did everything she could to make sure the wheel had the full range of motion on the track.

Try as she might, though, she couldn't improve the shocks. She just had to make sure she replaced them when they lost their firmness. And of course, any time the shocks changed, everything adjacent to them had to be adjusted and the rear wheels had to be re-stabilised and re-aligned.

Then she'd have to shift to Juggernaut's other end and repair his shoulders. Two arms per shoulder added up to sixteen times the work, she was sure of it. It wasn't just the joints and the range of movement— the arms had to be properly weighted too. Everything had to balance. Without balance, Juggernaut became Doorstop. Fortunately, balance was something she had a genuine instinct for; all she had to do was look at Paladins to know if they were properly balanced.

Vector had seen her demonstrate that instinct many times but, as he wasn't a scientist or even a technician, he didn't understand how remarkable it was. He must have heard the pit crews talking about how they'd never worked with a better Tuner. And she knew for sure that they hadn't. And neither had the Paladins.

In fact she had been working on a redesign on Juggernaut, making sketches, doing calculations. If he let her rebuild his lower body, she could make him into a genuine contender. There hadn't been a non-biped First Champion for years. If Juggernaut let her go ahead with the rebuild, he'd leave the rest of them in the dust, even Jashugan.

Jashugan was emerging as everyone's favourite for First Champion, even though he wasn't heavily equipped with weapons. The rotating grinders on his forearms were all he had to fight with, and he didn't spend a whole lot of time fighting. Most times he managed to avoid the on-track pile-ups that sent the fans into screaming ecstasy. Despite that, he was becoming a fan favourite.

Personally Chiren thought Claymore or a redesigned Juggernaut looked like better bets for Final Champion. But when all the Paladins were together on the track, either as a team or in a game of Cut-Throat, which was every man for himself, Jashugan in his black-and-gold armour drew everyone's eye. It was something about the way he carried himself, the way he could play as hard and as relentlessly as anyone else and never lose control.

For Jashugan, Motorball was as much mental as it was physical. Juggernaut's approach was to throw himself into the game and what would be, would be. Ajakutty kept telling himself he was going to win; sometimes he did. Claymore went onto the track prepared for everything, hoping for the best. Crimson Wind was the only female Paladin in Vector's stable at the moment; she tried out a new weapon for every game, but she hadn't found anything she wanted to stick with, so her game was mostly defensive. Her main strategy was simply to be faster than everyone else—too fast to catch, too fast to fight, too fast to beat. She had won two games since joining the team last year and both times she had looked just as surprised as everyone else on the track.

As time passed Chiren understood that Crimson Wind was actually modelling herself on Jashugan. It wasn't a bad idea. When Jashugan was on the track, he owned it. Off the track, he owned himself. He was the only Paladin in charge of his own repairs and maintenance now that Ido was gone.

Ido had been Jashugan's pet. Chiren had often found the two of them with their heads together, two serious-minded men who might have been discussing the fate of the world. Even then, Jashugan had been telling Ido what needed attention and Ido had been happy to take instruction from him. No doubt this had added to Jashugan's utter self-possession. Jashugan could have been in pieces strewn all over the pit and he'd still have an air of dignity.

But Chiren was certain he had weak moments. Everybody did. There had to be times when Jashugan wasn't composed, when he was a heap of wreckage. No one was always so composed and able, not in Motorball or anything else. Well, no one except Ido.

Chiren had met Ido when they were both in medical training and she had mistaken him for one of the instructors. The mistake made her angry because it wasn't fair that someone who was supposed to be a student—a supplicant, essentially—should have the dignified equanimity of an expert.

But this was no time to reminisce. She was a seasoned professional now, the authority to whom everyone else had to defer, not Ido. Ido had quit, walked off and abandoned the Paladins—she hadn't. Some of them, like Ajakutty, still talked about how they missed Ido, and that galled her, even if she didn't like to admit that to herself. But Motorball players were like children; when you made a living by playing a game, childishness was a given.

She had tried to show Ajakutty that he had no reason to miss Ido. Not by talking to him—what could she possibly have to talk about with someone who had knife blades running up and down his arms? Instead, she had provided superior maintenance, repairing things for him before they had a chance to break.

Not that he appreciated this as much as he should have, but she didn't hold that against him, not really. Ajakutty simply didn't know better; he was just about smart enough to breathe without someone reminding him to inhale.

Chiren had tweaked the blade arrangement on his arms to make them more like protruding shark teeth. It was an idea she'd had the first time she'd seen him on the track. Ajakutty hadn't even known what a shark was. (God, what did they teach in Iron City schools—unassisted breathing?) She had considered showing him a photo, then decided the scary pictures might give him nightmares. Motorball Paladins—children, all of them.

Jashugan too, no matter how self-possessed he always seemed to be. Sooner or later she was going to catch him in a weak moment. It was just a matter of probability—he was going to fall apart and she would have a front row seat. Then she could pick up the pieces and reassemble them in an improved arrangement. After that, he might look as composed as he ever had but he'd lean on her. And she would always be there to prop him up, the way she had for Ido.

It hadn't been easy, getting through Dyson Ido's defences. She'd had to lay siege to him. A lesser person would have given up—she supposed lesser persons had, which was why he was so alone and untouched. But she'd defeated all the barriers he'd erected between himself and the world; she'd got all the way through to the real Dyson Ido and put her mark on him, showed him how being strong meant sometimes letting yourself be vulnerable, even weak. Quite an accomplishment, if she did say so herself.

And here she was, still thinking about Ido even though he was irrelevant and a screw-up. Ido and his famous strength—when Nova had told them they had to leave Zalem, he buckled without a fight. They were probably lucky Ido had had enough nerve to ask for the pod so they could survive the fall.

Thank heaven Vector was so much stronger. But then it took a strong man to run Iron City. She would never be madly in love with him, or vice versa, and that suited her just fine. They both knew what they were getting: he got the best Tuner in the world and a beautiful woman to look great beside him, and she was getting a ticket home. No misunderstandings there.

Dyson Ido, with all his genius and wisdom and perception and sensitivity, hadn't even been able to keep them in their rightful home. While this poorly educated but canny, intelligent and resourceful man born at ground level—in the dirt—had the power to send her home. So who needed love?

Only a fool. She'd been a fool once, but she wasn't any more.

"You're here early. The players haven't even started coming in yet," said a woman's voice behind Chiren.

The voice was almost familiar; Chiren had heard it before, but not in the pit. "Paladins," she replied, still leaning over the drawer of parts she had been inventorying. For once there were enough servos and gaskets to last all night, unless everybody burst into flames. "The pros are Paladins, not players." Chiren finished re-counting the medium-sized gaskets before turning around.

The woman perched on the edge of one of the Paladin maintenance thrones wasn't someone she recognised but she didn't seem to be a total stranger either. Like most women, she was shorter than Chiren, dressed in a faded blue work-shirt over a black sleeveless t-shirt, jeans and black boots with a lot of mileage. On the floor by her feet was an overnight bag with a dark-brown hat on top of it.

"Do I know you?" Chiren asked.

"I know you," the woman replied, smiling. The smile made her seem even more familiar but Chiren still couldn't place her. "I worked around the Factory for a while."

"'*Around* the Factory'?" Chiren frowned. "How do you do that? People work *in* the Factory or *out* at the Farms. *In* the distribution centres or *for* dispatch stations. But I've never heard anyone say they worked *around* anything."

"I did odd jobs around the main building," said the woman. "For Vector."

"I see." Chiren straightened up to her full height, plus the four inches her heels gave her. This was one of the few times she was glad Vector insisted she wear stilettos in the pit. "You mean you're one of our, ah, less formal employees, hired to—" But whatever else she meant to say evaporated. Something was happening to the woman's face.

As Chiren watched, the woman's cheekbones rose slightly up and out from each other; her chin became more pointed and the upper part of the bridge of her nose sank into her face. Her eyes were no longer as deep-set and their shape had changed, although Chiren wasn't exactly sure how. But this face she recognised.

"You're the janitor," Chiren blurted, unable to hide her amazement. "Facial morphing's illegal. Why aren't you in custody?"

"I'm useful," the woman said with a small laugh.

"To Vector?"

"To the Factory."

"As far as Iron City is concerned, Vector and the Factory are one and the same," Chiren said, bristling a little.

"I got assignments from Vector," the woman told her. "But I work for the Factory. The distinction was made clear to me when I took the job."

"What's your name?" Chiren asked.

"Soledad." Pause. "Most of the time."

"And I guess you know who I am, all the time," Chiren said. "So are you here on assignment?"

"No." The woman's smile faded slightly. "I came to say goodbye."

Chiren tilted her head. "You never said hello."

The woman shrugged. "My life is odd that way."

"Where are you going?" Chiren tensed. "Is Vector sending you—" She hesitated. "Somewhere?"

"He doesn't even know I'm leaving. Relax. I'm not stealing your ride to—" She looked up briefly.

"How do *you* know about that?" Chiren took a step towards her.

The woman was unfazed. "Working around the Factory, I pick up all kinds of things. Don't worry, I didn't tell anyone. If it got out that Vector had that kind of voltage, the whole of Iron City would be banging down his door, wanting to go too. He'd turn the Centurians on them, and I don't want *that* on my conscience." The woman seemed about to continue, then shook her head.

She stood up and Chiren saw she was even shorter than she'd thought. "No, I'm just leaving," she said as she put on the hat. It was large and floppy; she tucked her dark hair up into it, leaving a few strands on either side of her face. "I'm getting as far away from here as I possibly can. So far away I can't see Zalem even with binoculars."

"Not afraid of contamination?" Chiren asked. "Even three hundred years after the War, soil samples from the so-called Badlands still test positive for weaponised microorganisms and heavy metals."

"It's a big world," the woman said. "Not every part of the planet was within sight of a flying city, even when all twelve were aloft. Places where people see birds every day but never saw a floating city except in pictures, instead of the other way round, like it is here."

Chiren shrugged. "That's a long way to go just to see birds."

"People used to travel a long way just to see things all the time before the War," said the woman, still chuckling a little. "In flying machines, with no defences shooting them down. Or so I've heard."

"There are lots of fables about the past," Chiren said. "Stories about a race of giant lizards wiped out by a falling star, fish that grew legs and walked out of the water onto the land and turned into people. A worldwide flood that made some of them change their minds and go back to live in the oceans. The human imagination knows no bounds."

"While human reality knows nothing *but* bounds." The woman picked up the bag and slung the strap crosswise. Chiren found she was intensely curious as to what was in it; whatever it was didn't seem to be very heavy.

She thought the woman was about to leave but she lingered, gazing at Chiren thoughtfully.

"Is there something else?" Chiren asked her. "Or is the idea of actually leaving giving you second thoughts? Third thoughts?"

"You're the one who should have second thoughts," the woman said.

Chiren bristled again. Damn it, she had almost started to like this woman. "About what?"

"I think you know," the woman replied.

"Tell me anyway…" What was her name? Chiren had to think for a second: Soledad.

"Everything," the woman was saying. "Your whole life, present and future."

Chiren gave a single bitter laugh. "I could say the same thing to you. You're going off into God knows what for no special reason except to be far away from Zalem. Whereas my present is to do meaningful work I'm extremely good at for the sake of something better—*my* future."

"There's a lot you don't know about your future," the woman said.

"I know where I'll be and what I'll be doing," Chiren said evenly. "Do you?"

The woman nodded. "You've got a point…"

"But?" Chiren prompted. The woman frowned at her, puzzled. "It sounded like there was a 'but' coming."

The woman smiled briefly. "There's a 'but' coming for all of us. The conditions in the fine print, the catch in the deal, or in the throat; the string attached that's really a tripwire. You'll know yours when you see it. In the meantime, have a good game tonight."

Chiren stared after her as she strolled out of the pit with an air that was practically jaunty. Maybe it was the hat. Or just that she was walking away from all her previous responsibilities. Running away was always so much easier than facing whatever you had to face.

When *she* left she wouldn't be running away from anything, Chiren thought; she would be going *to* something. She'd be going *home.*

Until that time, however, she had a lot to do. There were Paladins to upgrade, maintain, repair, and rebuild when necessary so they could win games and take championships. She had to get back to work, make sure inventory had everything they could possibly need. She had to do everything, and she had to do it right.

Vector showed up just as she finished with Claymore. Claymore gave him a big smile and a warm, friendly hello. Vector greeted him just as heartily, grinning from ear to ear as if he had every reason to expect this would be the best game ever, the best night of all their lives.

Once Claymore had rolled out of the pit, however, Vector's eyes went dead and his face went stony. "We set for tonight?"

"I've been here all afternoon making sure," she told him. "We're ready for anything."

"We *better* be."

The pit crew began coming in then, laughing and joking around. Vector had a big smile for all of them. He patted a few backs, bumped a few fists, and gave everyone two thumbs-up before he swaggered off to watch the game from his box. He only did that when he had special guests or when he was pissed off about something, and Chiren knew there were no special guests tonight. She wasn't sure what he was more pissed off about—losing Chase or the chip. Or the fact that she hadn't been able to build another chip from memory. As if that was her fault.

If he'd made more of an effort to find the cyborg—if he'd told that bunch he called his street rats to make finding the cyborg a priority—things would have turned out differently. She'd have been able to yank the chip and try it out in the more sophisticated cyborg body. But it had all gone wrong, and now he was up in his box sulking like a five-year-old.

Vector wouldn't be able to stay up there for the whole game—he never could. Before the Paladins had gone once around the track, he'd be back down in the pit, breathing down her neck, barking orders, demanding results. Which was pretty much what he did all the time, no matter what kind of mood he started the evening in.

She simply had to show him it wasn't all about chips. It was all about what *she* could do. She could build him Champions. Then he'd understand he didn't have to have his nose out of joint over some piece of hardware that hadn't worked right to begin with. He'd see she was living up to her part of the bargain, and when the time came, he'd live up to his and send her back to Zalem.

It wasn't ideal, but if this was the only way to get home, she could stand it. She could stand it. She could stand it.

She could. She could.

CHAPTER 20

"I can't stand it," Gerhad said. "If this is gonna be the norm with you, I quit."

"Okay," Ido replied.

"Okay, what?" Gerhad fixed him with a glare worthy of an interrogator. "Okay: you're gonna stop trying to get killed. Or, okay: it was nice working with me and you'll give me a recommendation?"

They were sitting at the kitchen table together while Ido nibbled at some quesadillas from the taqueria across the street, his first solid food since that night in the cathedral. Gerhad had been staying in the spare bedroom to look after him. She had also taken it upon herself to close the clinic to all but emergency patients. Ido might have argued that all his patients were emergencies of one kind or another. They were all urgent, certainly—they had jobs, families to take care of, promises to keep. He'd been too incapacitated to argue. But God help him, he was glad Gerhad had closed the clinic, because he'd had nothing to give.

Gerhad was staring at him. Still waiting for an answer, Ido realised. He grinned sheepishly and held up his cup for a refill. "Are you kidding?

Your coffee's a hundred times better than mine. If you think I'd jeopardise that, you're crazy."

"No, *you're* crazy," she said, pouring for him.

"You're probably right," he said good-naturedly.

"Don't humour me." Gerhad wasn't smiling. "I'm gonna take a moment to point out that I have shown great consideration in not raising these issues with you until now, so as not to stress you too early in your recovery."

"I noticed," Ido said truthfully. "My body and I thank you. I also thank you for understanding my fondness for quesadillas for breakfast."

"That I *don't* understand," Gerhad replied. "I'm just going along with it. I can make a list of things I'll just go along with. Be warned—it's not a long one."

Ido grimaced apologetically. "I told you I'm a licensed Hunter-Warrior. The bounties keep the clinic open and pay your salary. If you can't go along with that, I'm sorry for both of us."

"I didn't say I wouldn't go along with that," Gerhad said, still not smiling. "What I won't stand for is your hunting when you haven't healed from the previous beating. What the *hell* were you thinking?"

"That if I didn't put a stop to him, he'd kill someone," Ido said.

"And that someone was almost *you*," Gerhad snapped. "And for what? There was no bounty to collect."

Ido nibbled some more of the quesadilla. It wasn't as spicy as he would have liked. No doubt Gerhad had ordered them mild for the invalid. "It was a special case."

"I guess so, seeing as how this was all you came home with." Gerhad dug in her pocket and put the chip on the table between them.

Ido sighed with relief. "Thank God. I couldn't remember what I'd done with it."

"You didn't *do* anything. I had to pry it out of your hand. Is this the super-chip you've been making noises about?"

"What did I say?" Ido asked, slightly alarmed.

"A lot." Gerhad chuckled. "Someone got in and stole it, and you don't know how or who, but you're sure Vector and your ex-wife Chiren were behind it. They put it in one of their players to make him fast and it didn't work right. The player went crazy and it's all your fault." Pause. "I pieced that together from several delirious rants, so I might not have it right."

"No, that's pretty much it," Ido said. "I was working on a way to make the physical experience of Total Replacement cyborgs seamless and natural at all levels. I figured if I could do that, it would also improve things for people with only one or two replacements."

Gerhad put her left elbow on the table and raised her forearm, turning it one way and then the other. She was wearing the hand rather than any of the surgical instruments. "I've got no complaints."

"Does it feel exactly like your organic arm?" Ido asked.

"No, but I didn't expect it to. You told me it wouldn't and I'd have to get used to it. News flash, Doc—it's easier to get used to having an arm that feels kinda funny than it is to get used to not having an arm at all."

Ido took a sip of coffee, holding the cup with both hands to keep it steady. "Any phantom limb sensations?"

"None that I've noticed," Gerhad said. "Does that happen much?"

"More often with traumatic amputations like yours than with elective replacements," Ido told her. "Sometimes the homunculus in the brain will fight a prosthesis as an intruder or a usurper."

"'Prosthesis.'" Gerhad gave a small laugh. "I never thought of it as a prosthesis, just an arm. *My* arm."

"We put it in pretty quickly. Your brain didn't have much time to register the absence of your organic arm."

Gerhad chuckled. "Maybe I'm just that adaptable. I've never felt any drop-out or loss of sensation."

"You don't put any extraordinary demands on your arm, do you?"

Gerhad frowned at him. "What would you call 'extraordinary'?"

"I'm really not sure." Ido shrugged and regretted it. His upper body still objected to even small movements. "I built in a capability for extremely rapid suturing. Maybe if you had to use that several times a day, every day, you might start getting some hesitation."

"There's a little of that when I first wake up in the morning," Gerhad said. "But the rest of me isn't hitting on all cylinders either."

"Keep track of that," Ido said. "I mean, log every occurrence and let me know if it increases or decreases."

"Okay, just because you asked me to," Gerhad said. "But I'm not sure it's really all that important."

"Why not?" Ido asked, surprised.

"It's an artificial limb interfacing with an organic brain. But even organic limbs don't work exactly the way they're supposed to all the time." Gerhad nodded at the chip on the table. "I think you're chasing perfection with that, Doc, and that's futile." She put her hand gently on his arm. "We are all of us imperfect vessels, Dyson. We don't need perfection; we need something that works."

Ido shifted slightly in his seat, ignoring the pain in his ribs. He had spent his whole life striving for perfection, knowing even as he did that he would always fall short somehow. Nonetheless, perfection always had to be the goal.

But then, perfection was much more clearly defined in Zalem; it was easier to conceive of. It was more obvious, because in Zalem, it was closer—or so he'd thought. When Nova had exiled him and his family

284

because of his daughter's so-called imperfection, he'd learned just how far from perfect Zalem was.

Iron City wasn't really any further—it was just at ground level.

Gerhad got up from the table. "I'm gonna check for emergency messages," she told him. "You finish that quesadilla. You need it."

"It's kind of bland," Ido said, half-joking.

"You don't get anything spicier till you finish what you've got."

Ido stared after her. He wanted to follow her into the clinic, but he just couldn't get up from the chair.

Later in the afternoon Gerhad decided Ido was rested enough to spend some time at his workbench.

"But only puttering," she told him firmly. "Read notes, make more notes, think complicated thoughts, stare into space."

"I left an arm here—" Ido said, looking around as Gerhad helped him lower himself into the chair.

"I finished that for you," Gerhad said. "Patient wore it home, says everything's fine."

Ido looked up at her wide-eyed. "You finished Gladys-Jean's elbow?"

"Actually, you did," Gerhad chuckled. "I just closed the housing and re-attached the arm. She's the only non-emergency I took, and only because her arm was pretty much ready so there was no need to make her wait."

"That was a good thing," Ido said. "Thank you."

"*De nada*. You sure you don't want to take a nap instead?"

"No, I'll putter," he said, flipping on one of the two monitors.

What he wanted to do was read through the notes on the super-chip, which was now sitting in a small receptacle on the workbench. But he could read only marginally better than he did anything else. He couldn't seem to retain anything. That would be the pain meds, of course. He should look into developing pain relief that didn't make a person too high to function, he thought.

On the other hand, said a small voice in his mind, *if you need that much pain medication, maybe you* shouldn't *function. You might forget how injured you are.*

Ido frowned. That didn't sound like him… but it was a good point. Concentrating his practice on cyborgs had given him a tendency to think of recovery from illness or injury more in terms of the physical. Cyber-medicine was making him into a raving dualist, treating body and mind as separate and distinct. Perhaps that was where humanity was going now—brains in boxes, ghosts in machines.

And brains in boxes would still like getting high.

Even so, if there was some way to remove the euphoric effects of the drugs Paladins had to take to help align their brain function with their bodies, it would solve the problem of addicted ex-players selling off their parts, doing anything for a fix—like, say, breaking into clinics and killing innocent bystanders. Ex-players could gradually downshift the dosage to a level adequate for life without the extraordinary physical demands of Motorball. They'd have a chance at a normal existence.

The problem was, a normal existence wasn't really what they wanted. They wanted to not have been cut from the team, to not be an ex-player. The high that came from the screaming stadium crowds was as addictive as anything else, and no one had ever developed a detox for that.

Ido's gaze fell on the chip and he remembered he'd meant to look up his notes on it. He woke the screen and found them. The hard data—materials, circuits, the time it had taken for construction—was thorough, but he couldn't make sense of it for longer than a minute, if that. And there was so much of it, including all the information he had recorded when he had still been working in the crew pit with Chiren: entries on all the various glitches—dropout, hesitation, stutter, blockage, rebound and resistance. There were copies of Chiren's notes as well.

Reading everything over now, Ido realised it said a lot about physical performance—how well the Paladins played, or how poorly—but very little about their state of mind unless it involved some kind of cognitive impairment or a change in consciousness. And nothing about their emotions.

Because he'd been pursuing a goal of perfect performance. That was, after all, what Vector had paid him and Chiren to do. Make his Paladins perfect; make them winners.

He punched Chiren's number into his phone before he could think better of it.

"What do you want, Ido?" Chiren asked impatiently. "I'm busy preparing for the game tomorrow."

"I know what you did," he said. "I know you broke into the clinic and stole the chip."

"And I know you killed the man who was going to be our top player and stole it back," Chiren replied evenly. "Anything else you want to get off your chest?"

Ido felt the universe split in two. In one, he said: *Come home now. We got lost and now each of us is living a life neither of us wants. Come home; we can find our way to something better together.*

In the other, he said: *I'm done. I've actually been done for a while but now I know it. I'm not happy about it; it doesn't feel good and I don't like it. But I accept it now, and I'll live.*

But apparently the universe had actually split into *three*, because what he heard himself say was, "No. You?"

There was a long moment of silence. Finally: "I'm afraid not. We have nothing to say to each other that we both don't already know."

"Why are you afraid?" Ido asked.

"I don't have time for your mind games, Dyson." She broke the connection.

"That's not an answer," he said. He felt slightly ashamed of the smug note in his voice even though Chiren hadn't heard it.

Ido looked down and saw the chip was now on the desk in front of him. At some point, he had taken it out of the receptacle and broken it in two. One piece for each universe he didn't live in. Perhaps that was why he didn't remember doing it.

He became aware then that his ankle and his ribs were throbbing. The sight of Gerhad coming towards him with a syringe made him want to weep with joy.

Hugo had come to enjoy riding his gyro through Iron City before dawn. That was why he did it, he told himself, not because he seldom got as much as four hours sleep every night and always woke before dawn, feeling too restless to stay in bed.

Iron City was so quiet before dawn. Streets normally choked with traffic were empty, as if the entire population had suddenly vanished, spirited away unknowing and unaware by some incredibly powerful but silent force to a distant realm. Maybe those who woke up before they were returned could stay in that better place. But none of them ever did.

And Hugo was the only one left out. The powerful force never took him, because he always woke before dawn.

Lack of sleep was starting to make him weird, Hugo thought as he rode past Ido's clinic. The sign saying it was closed except for emergencies was still up. But he wasn't riding past to check on that; he was just taking the long way round to CAFÉ café.

And he certainly wasn't thinking about going back later to try talking to that nurse again. She had already told him that the doc had had an accident; he'd broken his ankle but he would be all right, and that was all she could tell him. Anything else he wanted to know he could ask Ido when the clinic re-opened.

Hugo didn't tell her he needed to know if the doc's "accident" had anything to do with Vector. She'd probably want to know why he would think something like that, and he had no good lie to tell. So he had to wait and talk to Ido.

When he finally did, though, what would he say? Ask him if Vector's men had beaten him up? Confess he'd told Vector about the chip? Then what? Would Ido get really mad, say he never wanted to see Hugo again? Or would the doc forgive him? Hugo had no idea. Everything seemed equally likely and equally absurd.

But then he couldn't imagine really confessing to Ido what he'd done. He was no angel—he'd messed up plenty, let people down, done the wrong thing or failed to do the right one. But this was a betrayal he didn't want to admit to; he didn't want to admit this was something he was capable of.

Except he was, and even if no one ever found out he'd carry it with him.

Hugo fetched up at CAFÉ café, bought a coffee and sat at the counter running along the side window. This counter was shorter and it faced away from the city, towards the towers of broken causeway. Today the way they held their fragments of road aloft seemed oddly defiant, as if they didn't care that the time of highways was over. They stood because they had been built to stand, and they would continue standing until time itself was over.

Lack of sleep was *definitely* making him weird—super-weird, even. He had never made up crazy stories about the old crap left over from days no one remembered. The only thing he'd ever really wondered about, still wondered about, was Zalem.

This wasn't the best angle to look at the flying city. He should have got his coffee to go and taken it to the cathedral. It was a bit tricky climbing up to the spire platform with a cup of coffee but he'd done it before. He should have been climbing up there every morning. If he had to be awake at sunrise, he could have been watching the daylight come up on Zalem, the most beautiful place in the world.

One million credits: that was the price of a one-way ticket out of Iron City to the only place he'd ever wanted to be. One million credits: that was the price of a future where he would no longer be looking up at the underside of a better world. Instead, he would look up and see—well, whatever wonders danced across the skies above Zalem.

What *did* the sky look like from a place so much closer to heaven? A million times better than it looked like at ground level, for sure, but the price of that view was one million credits and no matter what, the price was the price. Whether he had to jack a cyborg in an access tunnel above a sewer; whether a member of his crew got her arm broken in the process; whether he worked for a bad man, or betrayed a good one, or couldn't sleep—the price was the price: one million credits. Vector had said so.

Vector might not be a good man like Ido, but he was the man in charge. Hugo was certain that Vector couldn't have got to where he was unless he were a man of his word.

He was also certain that he wasn't going to get any sleep until he knew whether Ido's "accident" had been courtesy of Vector. Not that it would change anything. The price would still be the price, and the price was one million credits.

Hugo's phone vibrated, making him jump; he'd dozed off with his chin cupped in his hand. Tanji was texting about a crate of servos that had fallen off the back of a truck. Hugo texted back, telling him to stash them in their own truck at the loading dock.

Lets not sell 2 Doc cut-rate, OK? Tanji replied.

Never thot it, Hugo lied. *Going bak 2 bed.*

"I didn't know they had beds in here."

Hugo turned to see Tanji by the front door.

"Is there really a crate of servos?" Hugo asked wearily.

"Yeah, and I already put them in the truck." Tanji took the seat beside him. "We can take them to the stadium for the next game. It's all brand new; the pit crews'll go nuts."

"Fine," Hugo said. "I don't think the doc's buying right now anyway. The clinic's still closed."

"Shoulda known," Tanji said. "Otherwise you'da already sold them to him."

"The doc's a good guy," Hugo said.

"The doc doesn't pay enough," Tanji said. "I'm getting a coffee. You want another?"

"Yeah. Extra-large."

"How do you want it?" Tanji asked.

"Just throw it in my face."

"Don't tempt me." Tanji chuckled and went off to order. Hugo turned back to look up at Zalem. Unbidden, the sign on the door of Ido's clinic blossomed in his mind's eye. One million credits and the price was the price.

I'm sorry, Doc, Hugo said silently.

But now the image in his head was of Nana, his brother's wife. *I had to—it was him or us, life or death*, Hugo imagined her saying. *What's your excuse?*

He didn't have an excuse—he had a million of them. Because the price was the price, no matter who paid.

EPILOGUE

Time did what time always does: it passed, and, even in Hell, it healed all wounds in one way or another.

A week after the unfortunate incident in the ruined cathedral, Dyson Ido reopened the clinic for business as usual. His patients were startled by the sight of him hobbling around with an orthopaedic boot, but the boot drew attention from the bruises on his face and around his neck, and masked the stiffness of his movements. Most people accepted his vague explanation of a traffic accident. Only certain patients knew about his night-time life as a Hunter-Warrior, and they didn't show up during regular office hours.

Maybe none of his patients in more mundane jobs would ever imagine that bounty hunting was how he kept the clinic open; they did have their own problems, after all. When something good came along, especially something like medical care costing next to nothing, you just went with it and hoped it would last.

It was more likely that a number of patients knew how he was financing the clinic now that he was out of Motorball—this wasn't the first time he looked like he'd been worked over. But pretty much everybody in Iron City had something they didn't talk about.

Ido used the time he was incapacitated to upgrade the Rocket Hammer. That it had been the weapon that had saved his life wasn't lost on him. He seriously considered adding an extra pocket to the case for a chunk of rock with a length of iron rebar sticking out of it, but there really wasn't room. Perhaps he should rework the blunt side of the Hammer to pop out a six-inch iron bar? But that would interfere with the propulsion elements.

In the end he decided to stick with his original design—it worked and it was deadly. He replaced a few worn components and improved the propulsion, tripling the force of the swing. Tests he conducted in the cellar yielded good results. Unless he was fighting a giant of unprecedented proportions, anything he hit with the Rocket Hammer would go down and stay down.

The quiet period also gave him time to reflect. He'd had a remarkable stretch of good luck, he realised. Since he'd started hunting, this was the first time he had come away with more than a hairline fracture or two. But thanks to Gerhad, his ankle was going to heal with no problems.

There were so many bones broken in his ankle that Ido had insisted on using the scanner to guide her through the setting process. Gerhad seemed to have a real talent for this sort of thing. She got everything right on the first try while causing him a minimal amount of pain. He wished he found her a lot sooner. Maybe if he'd hired her right after the clinic had opened, things would have turned out differently.

Or maybe the addict who'd broken in would have killed Gerhad too, and he'd have her death on his conscience. Or maybe it would have been her instead of—

Ido made himself stop. Second-guessing regrets was hardly constructive. All the more reason to get back to seeing patients as soon as he was well. They needed him, and he needed the structure and discipline as well as the human contact. Without it, he might disappear into himself and never come out again. Exile was bad, but solitary confinement was much, much worse.

There were all kinds of prisons, of course. He'd made the Total Replacement cyborg body to free his daughter from the prison of incapacity and poor health. He'd wanted to be the hero who had freed her—he could admit that now, that he'd done it as much for himself as for her. But wanting to be a hero to his daughter wasn't such a bad motive. There were people who only did things for material rewards. Maybe that felt like freedom to them.

Ido doubted what Chiren had now was freedom, except from him. But perhaps that was all the freedom she needed. Without him, she had nothing left to lose.

Gerhad couldn't get over how quickly Ido's ankle healed. The orthopaedic boot came off a full month earlier than was usual in Iron City. Granted, as an ER nurse she seldom followed up with any of her patients. They would come in, she would do her best to keep them alive, then on to the next case.

Not everything in the Emergency Room was life or death, of course. She'd seen her share of broken bones and assisted with casts and braces and orthopaedic boots. Eight to twelve weeks was the usual for anything worse than a hairline fracture. The diet of the average Iron City resident wasn't ideal for building strong, healthy bones, which was why so many of them decided to swap a broken limb for something sturdier.

Ido's boot came off after only four weeks. Gerhad had tried to argue for one more week just to be on the safe side, but the scanner showed it wasn't necessary. The day after, Ido went back to a programme of physical training in the cellar. It was practically supernatural, as though he was a superhero—which was just plain silly. Superheroes didn't need to call someone to scrape them up off the street or the stone floor of a ruined cathedral, and they didn't need pain relief.

Gerhad insisted on making up a medical chart for him. Ido had balked, but she told him she didn't want to start from scratch every time a cyborg kicked his ass so hard it turned him inside out. It gave her an opportunity to run a lot of tests that told her what she already knew: Ido wasn't from around here, or anywhere else she knew of. Wherever he was from, the people there enjoyed good nutrition as a matter of course, in an environment lacking most of the pollution and contaminants that were normal in Iron City.

As curious as she was, Gerhad didn't pry or investigate any further on her own. Whatever Ido's story was, his ever-after was in Iron City, and that said it all.

When Ido's clinic reopened, Hugo's first thought was to ask Ido what had happened to him. Not immediately, of course—he'd hang around like before and eventually, in the course of some lecture about a chemical or something, Ido would talk about the funny plastic boot he was clumping around in.

But the clinic was immediately deluged with patients. Some had actually been camping on the sidewalk outside, unable to work because a cyber-limb had malfunctioned so badly it had shut down altogether. There were other cyber-surgeons in Iron City but none that would treat a patient *before* asking how they were going to pay. And none of them were willing to accept, say, home-made mole poblano or a bag of oranges in lieu of credits—not even if the oranges had been smuggled out of a grove that morning.

Hugo tried to make it an opportunity to show Ido how useful he was. Now that Ido had a nurse, however, Hugo discovered he was more in the way than at their service. Gerhad was nice enough—she didn't take a swing at him anyway—but she had rearranged everything in the cabinets and on the shelves. Nothing was where it had been, and, for some reason, Ido didn't seem to mind, even though he'd always complained if Hugo put something down half an inch to the right of where it had been when he'd picked it up.

Even stranger, when Hugo asked him if he needed any particular parts, Ido had told him to ask Gerhad. Except in the case of servos—they *always* needed more servos, in all sizes.

All of that made it impossible for Hugo to tell whether Ido blamed him for the theft of the chip. Maybe not; he hadn't banished Hugo from the clinic. But Ido didn't get talkative the way he had before. Of course, playing catch-up meant he was a lot busier than before. Hugo would comfort himself with thinking that was all it was. But then Ido would look through him and ask Gerhad for something.

He was just going to have to ask Ido, Hugo realised. But how?

Hey, Ido, did Vector beat you up because you stole your chip back? Did my name come up?

Or he could just keep it simple: *Ido, will you ever forgive me?*

Yeah, because crews who jacked TR cyborgs always worried about shit like that. He should have kept it all business with Ido, no matter how much he liked him. Once you started caring about people, everything got complicated and screwed up. He didn't need that. He had his dream, and everything he did was to make it come true. Nothing else mattered, nothing and nobody—

Abruptly he saw Koyomi in his mind's eye, coming out of the emergency room in blue paper scrubs with her hot-pink cast. Koyomi's face when he put his mother's bracelet on her wrist, looking surprised and touched, as if no one else had ever done anything like this. And most likely, no one had, not for her.

So he'd done a good thing because he cared. And because he cared, it would have been wrong not to.

But did that make any difference to his dream?

Maybe not... But it made a whole lot of difference to Koyomi.

It was time for a change, the Watcher thought, and he had a nice big one waiting in the wings—or, more precisely, the sewer. It wasn't brand new, but he hadn't really explored Grewishka's full potential yet. And, frankly, he was just as glad not to have to break in a completely new person. Originally he'd planned to team Grewishka up with the cyborg with all the fancy extras. The cyborg had only just started trying to talk Grewishka into coming back up to street level. If only he'd got Grewishka to follow him—that would have given the jackers in the access tunnel a night they'd never forget, no matter how hard they tried.

But no, Grewishka had curled up in the muck like the great big failure he was. He was going to have to figure out some other way to get the great big failure out of the sewer and up to the street, make him remember what it was like to walk upright, reignite the spark of bitterness in him till it was a raging inferno of hate. Now *that* would be *entertainment*!

And while he was at it, the Watcher thought, he should check the Factory-installed chip at the base of Vector's skull. Vector seemed to believe he was calling the shots. It was time to remind him who was really in charge.

Ido was immersed in the trash pile, literally and figuratively. In the month he'd been away from it, the refuse and rubbish had shifted quite a lot. Much of what he came across now was new, brought to the surface by a combination of different forces—the steady traffic of scavengers, the addition of new trash at various times throughout the day and night, and occasionally thunderstorms with winds strong enough to send some of the northland rubbish all the way to south-town.

But none of the new things were novel. And all of it was unequivocally trash.

Still, Ido felt his spirits lift. Getting back to scavenging was a return to normal, like seeing an old friend.

Speaking of which; Hugo had been following him for almost ten minutes. If the kid didn't work up the nerve to approach soon, Ido would have to put him out of his misery.

The kid. Ido chuckled inwardly. How old was Hugo anyway—seventeen, eighteen? He probably didn't see himself as a kid. Kids grew up fast in Iron City, everyone said so, especially the kids themselves. Only it wasn't true. Kids ended up in situations that were definitely not for children and they reacted like kids, handled themselves like kids, and when they came out the other side, they were kids with scars.

Kids didn't grow up too fast here; they got scarred too soon. Some of them got so many scars, it stunted their growth, and instead of growing up, they only grew old.

Ido didn't want to think Hugo would end up that way. Hugo was bright, intelligent, lively. He wanted to believe something in Hugo made him better than that; that something could blossom or light up or wake up just in time for Hugo to save himself.

Of course, for that to happen, someone had to care about him.

Ido stopped and turned around. "Are you going to say hello or just stalk me all night?"

The doc seemed friendly enough, but Hugo was still nervous. After the nurse had told him Ido was out here, Hugo had figured it was now or never. But when he spotted the doc, he'd hung back like a kid afraid that Daddy was going to spank him. He should have known he couldn't sneak up on the doc. At least Ido hadn't sounded like he was mad. But he didn't sound normal either. Hugo hoped it was just because he was still recovering.

As they walked together, Ido told him what had happened—how the cyborg had beaten him up twice within a few days and how Ido had been forced to kill him in self-defence. He even talked about Gerhad giving him hell when she'd come to retrieve him from the ruined cathedral and then threatened to quit.

"I'm glad you're going to be okay," Hugo said when Ido finished. No mention of Vector; Hugo was so relieved he was practically lightheaded.

Ido didn't reply. The silence between them began to stretch. Hugo tried to think of something to say, something that would be normal and natural and not even a little weird, but his mind was fresh out, weird or not.

"I know it was you, Hugo," Ido said quietly. "I know you were the one who told Vector about the chip."

Hugo's heart tried to leap out of his chest. He had to swallow before he could speak and his mouth was still dry. "I didn't—it was—it just happened. I didn't know. I was in a tight spot and I needed something I could—" He knew he was babbling but he couldn't stop. "These guys in south-town beat me up and, and I was late delivering and I didn't know. I didn't, I just—"

"It's okay," Ido said, talking over him. "I don't blame you for anything."

Hugo felt his jaw drop. "But it was *my fault*—"

"It's your fault Vector's a scum-bag?" Ido said. "Or that my ex-wife would go along with him out of a desperate need for—" He gave a short, humourless laugh. "All the things she needs so desperately."

"I was in a tight spot," Hugo said, forcing himself to speak slowly. "I was late delivering and Vector was really pissed off. That was my fault—"

"It's *not* your fault some people are so greedy they don't care who they hurt," Ido told him firmly. "When you talk about something—just have a conversation—do you worry about what the person you are talking to might do about it later?"

"If it's Vector, definitely," Hugo said.

Ido alarmed him by bursting into hearty laughter. "But at the time you had no way of knowing he'd send someone to break into the clinic and steal the chip."

"Uh…" Hugo tried hard not to squirm. It hadn't exactly been a surprise either. "When I heard the cyborg got killed and someone stole the chip, I knew it had to be you. But then the clinic closed and your nurse said you had an accident—I thought Vector had—well, you know."

"He wouldn't dare," Ido said. "Chiren doesn't like him *that* much, and he can't afford to lose her."

"Uh," Hugo said again, baffled.

"Never mind, Hugo. The more complicated matters of the heart are still some years ahead of you."

Abruptly they heard the unmistakable sound of more trash falling from Zalem. Fortunately they were at a safe distance. It looked to Hugo like there were more large bulky items than usual. His gaze travelled up from the ground to the chute. Someday he'd never have to see this again. But the price for that was one million credits, as set by Vector, and the price was the price. Ido was a good man, but Vector was the only one who could make Hugo's dream come true.

"I gotta go," he told Ido. "See you later, Doc."

Ido stared after Hugo as he made his way across the trash pile. It looked like he was heading towards the ruined cathedral. Did Hugo live near there?

He remembered what he'd been thinking only a few minutes earlier, about how Hugo was so lively and intelligent, and all it would take for him to have a brighter future was for Ido to care about him. Now it seemed like a silly wish-fulfilment fantasy, concocted by someone without a child of his own who was still trying to be a parent. Or maybe thought you could have a child without any of the real-life mess.

Like there was any real way to avoid the mess. Children didn't just drop out of the sky. Trash dropped out of the sky, but never children.

And yet, Ido still felt hopeful—optimistic even. What the hell, he thought, why not? Why not be prepared for something good to happen? As every scientist knew, chance favoured the prepared mind. Something good might not happen tomorrow or next week or next month. But when it did, he'd be ready for it.

ACKNOWLEDGEMENTS

My thanks to: my editor Ella Chappell, who made this experience so enjoyable; my son Rob Fenner, who introduced me to manga and anime, including Alita, back in the day, and his lovely and talented girlfriend, Justyna Burzynska, for being highly wonderful; all my friends, near and far, who have kept my spirits up for years; and the doctors and nurses at the Macmillan Cancer Centre in London, especially my oncologist, Dr McCormack. And while I'm at it, I *love* the NHS.

ABOUT THE AUTHOR

Pat Cadigan is a science fiction, fantasy and horror writer, three-time winner of the Locus Award, twice-winner of the Arthur C. Clarke Award and one-time winner of the Hugo Award. She wrote *Lost in Space: Promised Land*, novelisations of two episodes of *The Twilight Zone*, the *Cellular* novelisation, and the novelisation and sequel to *Jason X*. In addition to being the author of *Alita: Battle Angel – Iron City*, Pat is also author of the official movie novelisation.